THE MAZE CUTTER

ALSO BY JAMES DASHNER

The Maze Runner Books

The Maze Runner

The Scorch Trials

The Death Cure

The Kill Order

The Fever Code

Crank Palace

The 13th Reality Books

The Journal of Curious Letters

The Hunt for Dark Infinity

The Blade of Shattered Hope

The Void of Mist and Thunder

The Mortality Doctrine Books

The Eye of Minds

The Rule of Thoughts

The Game of Lives

Adult Books

The House of Tongues

#1 *NEW YORK TIMES* BESTSELLING AUTHOR

JAMES DASHNER

THE MAZE CUTTER

AKASHIC
MEDIA ENTERPRISES

 Published in the United States by Akashic Media Enterprises, also doing business as AME Projects. Visit us on the web at AkashicMediaEnterprises.com. Printed in China by We Think Ink. Interior formatting by Hannah Linder Designs.

Publisher's Cataloging-In-Publication Data
(Prepared by The Donohue Group, Inc.)

Names: Dashner, James, 1972- author.
Title: The maze cutter / James Dashner.
Description: First edition. | [Red Bank, New Jersey] : Akashic Media Enterprises, [2022] | Series: The Maze cutter ; [1] | Interest age level: 012-018. | Summary: "73 years after THE MAZE RUNNER series, the descendants of dystopia have thrived on the island but must leave everything they know behind when a ship comes from the old world with news about how they are needed to save civilization"-- Provided by publisher.
Identifiers: ISBN 9798985955200 (paperback) | ISBN 9798985955217 (ebook)
Subjects: LCSH: Islands--Juvenile fiction. | Survival--Juvenile fiction. | Dystopias--Juvenile fiction. | CYAC: Islands--Fiction. | Survival--Fiction. | Dystopias--Fiction. | LCGFT: Dystopian fiction. | Action and adventure fiction. | Science fiction. | Apocalyptic fiction. | BISAC: YOUNG ADULT FICTION / Dystopian. | YOUNG ADULT FICTION / Action & Adventure / Survival Stories. | YOUNG ADULT FICTION / Science Fiction / Apocalyptic & Post-Apocalyptic.
Classification: LCC PZ7.D2587 Ma 2022 (print) | LCC PZ&.D2587 (ebook) | DDC [Fic]--dc23

ISBN 979-8-9859552-0-0 (trade pbk.)

First Edition

Akashic Media Enterprises supports the
First Amendment and celebrates the right to read.

This book is dedicated to Marisa Corvisiero.

Agent, friend, and life-saver.

EPIGRAPH

Even as the darkness whispers across my mind, beckoning with smoky tendrils of blackness and rot, even as I breathe in the stench of a dying world, even as the blood within my veins turns purple and hot, I feel the peace of a certain knowledge. I have had friends, and they have had me.

And that is the thing.

That is the only thing.

—*The Book of Newt*

PROLOGUE

Voices from the Dust

Thomas found the journal three weeks after the world ended. It still baffled him. How? When? When and how? When had his friend written all those pages and how had it gotten inside one of several boxes sent through the Flat Trans before Thomas and his friends made the trip themselves? Ava Paige had done it, of course, as she had done everything. But again. How? When? Those words occupied his mind like two guests refusing to leave, well after the party has wrapped.

He sat upon his favorite ledge on his favorite cliff, looking out at the vastness, the *forever*, the endless void of the ocean. The air was clean and fresh, bitten with the tang of fish and the sweetness of decomposing life. Small wisps of spray tickled his skin, cool against the heat of the sun directly overhead. He closed his eyes, blanking out the horizons that daunted him, made him feel as if he'd been stranded on the moon. Mars. Another galaxy. Heaven. Hell. What did it matter? He shifted on the jutting edge of rock to get more comfortable, his legs dangling over the roar and splash of depthless water, black-blue, as far away from the world as he could fathom.

Of course, that was a good thing. Right? Yes, it was. But escaping disease, madness, and death did nothing to replace the sadness at what had been lost. Which brought him back to the journal.

He opened his eyes and picked up the warped, tattered, muddied book from where he'd set it earlier, atop a single shelf of sandstone that appeared as if it had been sculpted by time's chisel to house a sacred artifact. Sacred. Artifact. That sounded about right.

He opened the book in his lap, casually but with care, and flipped through its many pages, every last one of them filled top to bottom with the scrawling penmanship of a child. The slant of the words, the urgency of the ink—pressed and dark with increasingly thicker strokes—the size of the letters . . . Each passing page visually represented what the actual content revealed in heartbreaking starkness—his best friend descending into utter, complete, savage madness. The journal ended with about thirty empty pages. The last one to contain writing had only one word, its letters filling the entire space, scrawled with violence: *PLEASE.*

Man, Newt, Thomas thought. *Wasn't it bad enough? Wasn't the end the peak of our awfulness? Why in the hell did you have to let this book exist, let it get into the hands of Ava Paige? Why?*

But even as those harsh considerations stomped across his mind, Thomas knew they were empty of meaning. He loved this journal. This book. These words of his friend's. Any pain they brought back only served to frame the bigger picture—the canvas upon which a piece of Newt's life had been painted, for them to have forever. For their kids to have. For posterity. A museum piece of memories, the good and the bad.

Thomas thumbed through the pages of the journal and chose one at random, though he cheated and erred toward the front, when Newt's symptoms had only begun to blossom. No one knew exactly when he'd started writing because there were no dates and not a lot of references to specific events. But the passage that Thomas read now had to be the day they'd left their friend behind, in the Berg, while they stole their way into the city of Denver.

Thomas breathed in each word, savored it, pondered it:

I feel like a dick saying this, but I gotta get out of here. Can't take it anymore. I love these people. I love them more than I could've possibly ever loved anyone. And I obviously say that because I can't remember my mum and dad. But I imagine it would be like this. Family. That's what they are. Thomas. Minho. Everyone. But I can't be with them one more day. It's killing me, and that ain't some bloody joke. I'm done. For them, I'm done. Gone. And that ain't a joke, either. I guess these words just come naturally. Killing. Gone. Gotta put this diary down, now. I have another note to write.

Thomas closed the book and placed it back on the shelf above his head. Then he lay down on his side, legs curled up to his body, head on forearm. And he stared at the wet fields of ocean that stretched to every limit of thought and sight. Beneath that rough, wavy, sketched-icing surface, he knew that billions of creatures lived, oblivious to things like Cranks and deserts and mazes. They swam and they ate, their world probably hurt by the sun flares that had ravaged the lands above, but just as likely healing all the faster. Someday, surely, the order of things in the natural world would do just fine.

But what about us? he thought. What about the humans?

And then, despite his eyes being wide open, staring at the fathomless reach of the ocean, all he could see were images of people. Newt. Teresa. Alby. Chuck. So many lives, lost.

Man, you're depressing, he chided himself. Somehow—for today, at least—he had to stop thinking about all this crap. He got up, grabbed Newt's journal, and headed down the path that wound its way along the cliff and through the sandy grasses, finally leading to the new Glade. It wasn't much as of yet, but someday it might be. Give the humans a chance, right?

"Hey!" someone shouted from up ahead. Frypan. "I figured out a new way to cook these damn fish!"

Thomas could already smell it.

PART ONE

73 Years Later

It's a funny thing, losing what you love. When able, I think often about loss. If I could go back in time, to my earliest youth, and some godly, magical being had shown me the future and given me a choice, what would I have chosen? If this god had revealed to me the two major losses of my life, and allowed me to prevent only one, which would I have selected?

Newt, this heavenly creature might have said. *Your mind, or your friends?*

I now know my answer:

What's the difference?

—*The Book of Newt*

CHAPTER ONE

Trinity of Terror

I
ALEXANDRA

In a place called Alaska, Alexandra Romanov stood on the balcony of her home and gazed upon the city, shrouded in darkness, sprinkled with the bright yellow winks of gas flames in windows and on street corners. Not a cloud blotted the stars in the sky, which shone down with perfect clarity, each one an almost perfect spear tip of light. The clean air hugged her like invisible fog, warm and moist, dampening her hair, her clothes, her skin. She breathed in, deeply, relishing this bird's-eye view of the quiet world below.

Her world. Alaska. There were others out there, other . . . *worlds*. The Remnant Nation, somewhere in the plains of Nebraska. There were the mad doctors down in California, doing things no sane people should. But they were far as things go and went. Alaska was hers.

Never mind that she shared it with two others. Nicholas. Mikhail. Nicholas and Mikhail. But she felt the ownership, felt the power, as if it were all her own. And someday, perhaps, it *would* be. Until that day, she'd refine her enhancements of the Evolution, perhaps sabotage the others bit by bit, while still letting the weight of their terrible purpose rest on them from time to time. Fight terror with terror. End tragedy with tragedy.

Didn't they say that all tragic things occurred in groups of three? Deaths, earthquakes, tornadoes. She'd only known one set of triplets in her life, but those kids had been hell on tiny feet, their piercing cries during the night of the Evolution still a memory that rattled her. She had not been the one to put an abrupt end to those cries, but it would be the greatest of untruths to say she hadn't been minutes away from finishing them off, herself. And, oh, what immense relief she breathed in at the sweet silence that followed.

Bad things come in threes. That was a philosophy as old as time. And *they* were three, the Godhead—Evolved; thoughts faster than a lifetime of words spoken at once; machine-like control of the senses, the physiology, the chemicals, the endorphins, all of it; the mental capacity of a universe to suck in all light and knowledge. They had Evolved, of that there could be no doubt. But she—yes, *she*—was beyond them, beyond the both of them combined. This, Alexandra knew. But for now, they were three.

Her mind flashed, memories upon memories, all in an instant. The Flare and its many variants, building minds to fix the unfixable. Maybe it had all served a purpose, millennia of terrifying trinities, preparing the human race for what had arisen, what had come into being to eradicate terror itself, by any means necessary.

The Godhead.

Hell, it worked for her.

"Goddess Romanov?"

Dammit. She'd hoped for more time, more time-wasting. She turned away from the beauties of her city and faced the man who'd spoken her name. A tall, gangly fellow, he always reminded her of a walking tree branch, the fact that his joints didn't crack and pop and splinter with every step a small shock to her subconscious.

"What's going on, Flint?" The man's name wasn't Flint, but she called him that for the sole reason that she wanted to. He seemed . . . lessened by it, and that was okay. Ideal, even.

"There's a kink in the rotation of pilgrims." His voice was like the spill of raw ore from a wheelbarrow. "I have the exact numbers here, but by morning we'll be off by at least eight percent in every part of the city. Everything will be thrown off."

Alexandra studied him, used the training she'd received in the Flaring discipline. Every tick of his muscles, every shift of his eyes, every movement, no matter how subtle, fed into the hyper-function of her thought processes. He was avoiding what he really came here to say.

"Spit it out, Flint. What the hell happened?"

He drooped a slow blink, let out a sigh of resignation, realizing how futile it was to hide his emotions behind what was—to her—a see-through mask. "Seven pilgrims were killed at the dye pools. It was done with . . . violence."

"Violence?"

"Immense violence." He'd been slowly raising his clipboard and charts, readying to share data. But now he dropped it to his side. "Four men. Two women. One child. A boy. They were—"

"Hollowed," she said. "They were hollowed, weren't they?"

His face had paled a bit. "Yes, Goddess. Done quite professionally, I might add. Cleaned out. The, uh, refuse was nowhere to be found. Only the ribs remained."

"Damn that man," she whispered, fury threatening to overcome her Flare sensibilities. She counted through the *digits*, that precise mathematical sequence she'd learned as an acolyte that brought peace, calmness, the brain having no choice but to release the appropriate chemicals. "Do you know where he is?"

Flint knew exactly who she was talking about—she read his eyes as easily as the charts and tables he carried with him at all times. As evident as sunlight, she knew he envisioned those poor victims in the dye pools, how they'd been sliced from aft to stern, their every essence of life removed with violent but precise efficiency. The blood, the stench, the horror of such a thing . . . only a certain type could do it and remain hinged. And the both of them standing there had already arrived at the correct conclusion.

"Uh, I believe that he's gone to the . . ." Flint cleared his throat, clearly uncomfortable sharing such personal information from one member of the Godhead to another.

Alexandra stepped close to him, controlled herself until she stood rigid as a corpse. Then she locked her eyes with his, utilizing the optic hypnosis techniques of her discipline. "Tell me where he is." The proper inflection in her voice sealed the deal.

Flint nodded in submission, then spoke, almost trance-like.

"Mikhail has gone to the Glade."

Alexandra tried to suppress her shock, but for the first time in an age, her training in the ways of the Flare completely abandoned her. A blinding flash of anger exploded within her mind, erasing the world around her for the briefest of moments. Why? Why did Mikhail do this now? She wanted to scream but snatched it back—literally snapping an arm out as if her voice were a physical thing. Her rage subsided; her vision returned. Flint had a red gash across his cheek, the skin sliced by her very own fingers, her painted nails. A petulant act; she needed better control.

She looked at the poor man, those eyes soaked with fear. "Bandage that, quickly. If Mikhail's in the Glade, we need to hurry."

2
ISAAC

Clank.

Clank.

Clank.

Isaac had been dreaming that sound for quite a while, now. Constant, incessant, annoying-as-hell *CLANK*s that found all kinds of ways to audibly haunt his nightmares. First it was a bird, a black, furry-looking thing, perched atop the wooden fence that surrounded Old

Man Frypan's acre on the northern side of the island. The creature's sharp beak hinged open and closed, open and closed, letting out that *CLANK* of a noise each time, like the bark of a mechanical dog.

Then it segued into a giant machine, a thing Isaac had been told about in the campfire stories of the old world, a thing he imagined now, as inaccurate as it may be. It was called a bulldozer, and for some inexplicable reason it was fruitlessly trying to plow over a mountain of metal trees, glistening silver and immovable. *Clank, clank, clank* it went, as the bulldozer rammed its way forward relentlessly, its giant scoop dinged and dented.

Then there was a man, standing in front of him, nothing but a dark sky as the backdrop, full of stars. The man had no hair and no eyes. He had half a nose. He had one ear. And although it was hard to tell for sure in the bare light, the man's skin glistened in rivulets that had to be blood, seeping from a dozen wounds. *That is one ugly son of a bitch*, Isaac thought.

The man tried to speak, but the only thing escaping his lips was that sound again.

Clank.

Clank.

Clank.

The apparition's throat bulged with each metallic utterance, as if he'd swallowed a plum and just wanted to cough it out. Isaac remembered more nightmares than he could count on every last finger and toe on the island, but this one chilled him to the core. He awoke with a startled yelp that wasn't far off from the *CLANK*s that had seeped into his dreams.

Worse, the sound still clanged around him.

Awareness coming back in leaps, he sheepishly got out of bed and zombied his way over to the window, peaking past the curtains sewn by his dad at least a decade ago. It was a gloomy day, the clouds a solid, soupy mass in the sky, the light gray and sad. No rain had fallen, but mist crept along the grass of the yard, gathered in big clumps along the fence, wafted through the air in random groups of thinly stretched cotton. And out beyond the houses on the east side of the island, down near the beach, someone was beating the hell out of hot iron with a very large hammer.

The Forge.

Isaac loved the Forge. It had been set by the beach so that the constant, stiff breeze could keep the fires stoked and hot. He didn't quite understand how they dug crap out of the craggy mountains and then turned it into red molten rock, and he didn't really care. It was that point in the process—and everything after—that consumed him. He loved the heat and the steam, the deep, glowing reds and the blinding, white-hot brilliance of the sparks. He loved the smell of ozone and burning cinders, the smoke, the constant clanging of metal against metal.

Yep. He wanted to be a blacksmith, and had been training under Captain Sparks for almost a month, now. No one else joined him in calling Rodrigo that ridiculous name yet, but Isaac had set a goal for the moniker to stick by winter. It was next-level genius and no one could convince him otherwise.

Today was Isaac's day off. He had plans. Miyoko, Dominic, Trish, Sadina, a few others—they'd been planning for two weeks to row the kayaks out to Stone Point and swim through the caves and jump off the cliffs. Chances were Dominic would strip naked and belly flop from the edge they called the Dead Man's Brow, and hilarity would ensue. Isaac couldn't miss out on such festivities and still feel like a respectable knucklehead. After all, Stone Point had been forbidden after the third drowning in five years, and he himself had never actually been that far. Which just made it all the more appealing. Kind of.

But none of these thoughts lessened his itch. Hearing the *clank-clank-clanks*, regular and rhythmic, like the beating of an iron heart, drew him as if a rope had been tied around his waist. He loved to watch Captain Sparks in action, and rowing, swimming, jumping for hours suddenly seemed like a lot of work.

Like an old sailor succumbing to the lustful call of the sirens—a story his grandpa had told him over the protestations of everyone else around the fire at the time—Isaac quickly got dressed and headed out the door of his yurt. Headed toward the flames and the molten metal.

His yurt. He still hadn't gotten used to that. He had his *own* yurt, the one-room dwelling in which most people of the island lived—except the ones crazy enough to have more than a couple of kids. Isaac had built and moved into his yurt just three months ago and still basked in the sense of accomplishment.

The day had suddenly popped open with a burst of sunshine, clearing the clouds and mist, the temperature perfect. People milled about everywhere he looked—on their way to the farms, the shops, the mill, the warehouse, the fishery—most of them too busy to take note of a young man on his day off, half-running toward the beach. But Mr. Jerry gave a wave, his giant eyebrows like combed wool, and a few yurts down Ms. Ariana gave a wink—harmless from a woman who was one of the first people born on the island, only a year after the Flat Trans. Her silvery hair and wrinkled eyes always made Isaac think of the grandma in the tale of Red Riding Hood.

"What's the rush, boy?" she called out, standing at the edge of her little lawn. She held in her hands the Daily Memo that his friend Sadina passed out every morning. "There a fire I don't know about?"

"Got some work to do at the Forge," Isaac responded, slowing down enough to give her a little smart-ass curtsy and a flourishing wave of the arm. "What're you up to today? Got another date with Old Man Frypan?"

She let out a hoot and a holler. "Don't he wish! That cheap bastard wouldn't know how to court a melon."

Isaac exaggerated a laugh and then revved up to a full jog, offering a last farewell wave.

"Run, boy!" she yelled. "Run like the wind!"

He loved that old woman.

3
MINHO

The Orphan stood straight and rigid behind the parapet of the fortress wall, his rifle resting upon his shoulder, its barrel aimed at the cloudy sky. As he had for the last eleven years, he stared at the endless fields that served as a waterless moat around his homeland. It was a dead land, all life and vegetation killed with poison so that nothing might obstruct the view of the Orphans. The waste lay dull and gray, like a cemetery without tombstones, as vast as the ocean.

The Orphan had no name.

Thirty feet away, to the north, stood another statue with no name, her shoulders square, her head shaved, her body sheathed in an artillery suit. A literal human missile. To the south, thirty feet away, there was another Orphan. This one didn't stand, however. This one sat upon a turret of metal, a machine of such firepower that it could destroy the entire wall upon which it rested. That Orphan had no name.

This was what they'd been told their whole lives, anyway. From the day they were born, taken from mothers who had the Flare. Although he obviously couldn't remember it, the Orphan knew that he'd been tested over and over, in every way imaginable, to make sure that he, too, was not infected. Even so, he'd been quarantined for five years, along with others like him, growing, learning, training. Then more tests. These, he remembered, although the day the results came in were a bit foggy. Not that it mattered. Those results had come in negative. Otherwise, he wouldn't exist. He'd have been thrown in the same pits as his mother, burned for one hundred days.

The Orphan's name was Minho, even though the Orphan had no name.

He couldn't tell anyone, of course. Not once in his lifetime had another person called him Minho. Even now, thinking of it, he felt a chill of fright that someone might know, that someone could read his mind, that the Grief Bearers would be informed that he'd blasphemed his calling in life by giving himself a name. The punishment was not in doubt, and it would be swift. There'd be no trial. So it had to remain a secret. No one could ever know. But his fingers gripped the rifle tightly and his lips pressed together and he breathed a little heavier, holding on to this one thing.

His name was Minho.

Despite the best efforts of the Remnant Nation, whispers abounded amongst the Orphans about the days when the Flare spread across the earth and devastated the human race. No one could possibly determine which stories were true and which were mere legends. Like all things, most of them probably lay somewhere in the middle. The tales of WICKED, tales of Cranks, tales of cures, tales of heroism and villainy. Tales about the Maze and those who escaped it. Most of it was a muddy blur on a window, impossible to decipher shapes that made sense. But there was one story that stood above the rest, and from that tale of undaunted bravery, Minho had chosen his secret name.

In his mind, he looked exactly like Minho of the mythical Gladers, thought like him, talked like him, dreamt like him. Fought like him. In his heart, he was worthy of the title.

Minho.

But, courage or not, it had to remain a secret until things changed.

A horn's deep, baritone growl sounded from the closest watchtower, sweeping away the silence and making Minho's jaw tremble from the brassy vibration rumbling through the air. His musings vanished, replaced with the alertness his training had mastered. He shifted his feet, bent his knees, knelt against the low wall of the parapet, his rifle locked into position on the top edge. Taking his breaths according to the litany of calm he'd been taught since the age of five, he peered into the distant, flat fields, waiting for what had prompted the warning from the watchtower.

Several minutes passed. Nothing but mud and dirt and rotted vegetation for miles.

Patience. No one had patience like the Orphans.

A figure appeared on the horizon. It approached rapidly, and it wasn't long before Minho could see enough to know. A person, on a horse, galloping closer and closer. A man, dressed in rags, unarmed, hair blowing all over the place like a mad pit of skinny snakes. The man rode the horse in a beeline, coming directly toward the spot beneath Minho's position. When the stranger came within a half kilometer, he slowed his animal to a trot, and then to a walk, and then stopped altogether, about eighty meters away. The man held his hands up, surely knowing the extreme weaponry that was aimed at him, and shouted.

"I'm not infected! I've been tested, quarantined myself for six months! No symptoms! Please! I swear it! I'll stay here until you can see that I'm not sick!"

Minho listened to the man's words, though they didn't matter. They didn't matter in the least. Like most everything else under the reign of the Remnant Nation, the outcome of this scenario had already been determined. The Flare was their devil, the Cure their God. He readied himself, knowing he didn't have the courage to disobey protocol, not yet, not for a long time to come.

"Please!" the man pleaded. "I'm as clean—"

A single shot rang out, its fierce jolt of sound echoing in all directions.

The stranger, a small wisp of smoke leaking from the new hole in his head, slumped off the horse and fell into the mud with a wet splat. Another shot, and the animal fell as well.

Minho breathed in the smell of gunpowder, feeling pride at the accuracy of his aim. Feeling regret that it had been needed.

The Orphan stood back up, came to attention, positioned the rifle on his shoulder, as he had done faithfully for eleven years.

The Orphan had no name.

CHAPTER TWO

Field Trip

I
ISAAC

"Oh no you don't."

Isaac was twenty meters from the fence that fronted the Forge when his friend, Sadina, seemingly popped out of nowhere and stepped directly in his path. She didn't do anything cutesy or pert, like putting her hands on her hips or wagging a finger in chastisement. She just wrinkled her forehead and did the rest with her eyes. Those dark orbs, lost in the largest whites of anyone's eyes he'd ever seen, had magical powers and no one could possibly disagree.

He came to a stop or they would've smacked foreheads.

"Hey," he said, already searching for an excuse in his occupied mind. The smells of ozone and woody smoke were almost enough to make him tear up, and not just from the cindery sting of it all. It was downright unnatural how much he loved this place of making things.

"There's no way in hell you're skipping out on us today," Sadina said, her voice as hard as the iron bars cooling in the water bins of the

Forge. "It's gonna get colder in the next month or so, and everyone will be too big of a wuss to go out to Stone Point. Today is the day, we're going today, it's your first time, and you're coming with us." She grinned to take away some of the bossiness, but that didn't mean she'd back down.

"I'm going to Stone Point?" he asked.

"You're going to Stone Point. Or die. Your choice."

Isaac gave an almost panicked glance over her shoulder, peeking at the Forge. It really was unnatural. He had a day off and he should enjoy it like a normal human being. But there were anxieties associated with water that surely the others . . . he swatted the thought away. The Forge had become his only escape from the family tragedy, and he needed another.

"I just wanted you to beg me to go," he finally said. "It's pathetic, really."

She barked a fake laugh. "You wish. I just need someone there who's even more chicken of the cliffs than I am. That way I don't look as bad."

"Thanks for coming to get me," he said, surprised at his own words. "I mean . . . you know. Thanks."

Although he expected an onslaught of sarcasm and eye-rolling, she surprised him right back. "Come on, man. There's no way we'd have nearly as much fun if you were stuck in the Forge all day. At least, I know I wouldn't."

Isaac went speechless for a moment, finally thinking of the things he'd been avoiding in his mind since the second he woke up to the *clanks*. His feelings, his swell of emotion had nothing to do with Sadina—she had a serious girlfriend for crying out loud. But her kindness triggered thoughts of the tragedies that had assaulted Isaac's life over the last few months, the real reason he was so desperate to lose himself in the hard work of the Forge. All that pounding of metal and heat and hissing and steam and sweat, all that hard work, protected his mind from where it wanted to go.

"You know we all love you," Sadina said. "We want you with us today. Screw everything else. We'll go and act stupid and if we wanna cry, we'll cry. If we wanna laugh, we'll laugh. But I swear on Old Man Frypan that we *will* have fun."

Isaac nodded, so full of gratitude that he still couldn't speak. Sadina pulled him into a hug, probably having decided that more words couldn't help at this point. She took him by the hand, gave him one of the sweetest smiles he'd ever seen, and then pulled him away from the Forge, its black pillar of smoke leaking all the way to the sky.

2

The hum of the ocean grew louder as they approached the north side of the island, where the waves hit heavier and higher, the beachhead packed with rocky cliffs. When those waves crashed against those cliffs, the roar of it filled the air, along with billions of spray droplets and sheets of white rain. Hundreds of tiny waterfalls appeared and disappeared on the black rock with each cycle, little pools scattered across the low places. The whole area was beautiful, and it never grew old, and Isaac's heart broke at the sight of it. This had been his mom's favorite spot on the whole island, or in the world for that matter.

He was still holding Sadina's hand when they reached the path that wound its way from the top of the cliff to the many places of adventure below. Their friend Trish had just reached the first switchback but when Sadina called her name, she turned and sprinted back up to them. The longtime couple embraced, kissed, but then immediately showered their attention on Isaac. He joined their hug, felt their kisses on his cheeks. Not a word was spoken for a full minute.

Finally, Dominic appeared, from which direction Isaac didn't know.

"What's with the lovefest?" he asked. "Should I avert my eyes?"

Dominic always said things that, in theory, would make him unlikable, but his delivery somehow softened the blow every time. It was a gift Isaac wished he could learn. Everyone loved Dominic, no matter how many insults he rained upon them.

"Oh, hello, Dom-a-prick," Trish said flatly. The nickname was terrible, and never came out of the mouth smoothly, but she used it every time the opportunity presented itself. Isaac figured it had about as much chance of sticking as his Captain Sparks moniker for the blacksmith.

As for Dominic, he'd chosen the wise route of pretending he never heard it. "Howdy, Trish. Howdy, Sadina. Isaac." He nodded with each name, but couldn't stop the glimpse of sobriety that flashed across his face when he came to Isaac. To his credit, he wiped it away quickly. The thing Isaac needed most in this world was for the pity parties to cease, forever.

"Always a pleasure to see you," Isaac said, who sucked at trying to match his friend's sarcasm.

"That it is, that it is." Dominic rolled his eyes with exaggeration, as if this had become the most awkward conversation ever. It kinda had.

"Who brought the kayaks?" Sadina asked.

Trish answered. "Miyoko just dragged them down the path. I was supposed to help her, so . . . I hope she didn't fall and break her neck."

"Yikes," Sadina replied. "Let's go."

They went.

3

Miyoko had made it about halfway down then given up. Five kayaks were lashed together with thick twine, and she'd been going downhill as she dragged them, but it still seemed a big job for one person to do alone.

"You guys were hoping I'd done all the work, huh." It came out as a statement, not a question.

"Dammit, yes," Trish replied. "We should've waited ten more minutes. Live and learn."

"Where's everyone else?" Miyoko asked. Sadina had told Isaac that Carson and a few others from the west side were supposed to meet them as well. Ten in all, two per kayak.

"They might be down there, already," Sadina answered. "Or late as usual. Who cares. Let's just get these boats moved. It's not gonna be daylight forever."

"Plus, I got a toothache," Dominic added.

"What does that have to do . . ." Trish was so perplexed that she couldn't even finish.

"And I have to pee."

To his credit, he was the first one to grab the lead twine and start pulling.

4

An hour passed. Isaac had recovered from the jolt of Sadina rescuing him from the Forge, when the truth of his running away had hit him hard and fast, along with all the memories that caused it. The work of getting the kayaks down to the ocean, untying them, getting them ready to launch, all the laughs and conversation—he felt as well as he had in weeks.

"Dude," Trish said, "I thought you had to pee." Dominic had positioned himself at the front of one of the kayaks, sitting like a schoolboy waiting for Teacher.

"Not anymore," he said with a wide grin.

"You do realize the ocean is not a toilet?"

"I'm pretty sure the fish love things like human urine. Adds flavor to stuff."

"Wow. I'd forgotten the high intellectual levels of the east-siders' conversations."

Carson said this, having arrived a few minutes earlier with several of their compatriots from the west side. He was a giant of a man, muscles bulging in places where Isaac didn't know muscles existed. Carson always looked a little out of proportion, as if he worked one part of his body too hard, and then had to spend some time evening things out with different exercises. When the day came that he got everything just right, all of it in perfect harmony, his skin would probably explode from the stress and he'd die in a bloody, meaty mess.

"We could've used those guns of yours"—Sadina pointed at his biceps—"as we dragged these suckers down the cliff."

"Yeah, sorry about that. Lacey, here, had a bit of a stomach issue and we decided to wait for her."

Lacey, her spirit about a thousand times larger than her diminutive size, punched Carson right in the stomach. He tried to hide it, but his sheath of muscles didn't entirely protect him.

"Am I lying?" he asked, half-groaning and half-laughing. His hand had found its way to the spot where she'd socked him.

"No, but you didn't have to tell the whole group. Gunk of klunk in a trunk."

The whole group snickered at that. Lacey was famous for her absolute refusal to use any of the traditional swear words because she thought it made people look very uneducated. But her grandpa had passed down some writing he'd made of his time with the Gladers of old, and he'd included a list of slang that had died out over the decades. Lacey was doing everything in her power to bring them back. No one had a clue as to why, but it did provide a lot of entertainment.

"That hurts, Lacey," Carson said solemnly, "even more than the right hook to my gut."

"Next time, I'll aim lower."

"Of that, I have no doubt."

Trish clapped her hands once. She had a double-oar in the crook of an elbow and looked ready to go. "Come on, guys. Not sure how it helps talking about Dominic's and Lacey's human waste procedures, but how about we get on these damn boats and row out to the Point?"

The group gave a hearty cheer in response, Isaac included. They had ten people—everyone who'd been invited had shown up. Himself, Sadina, Trish, Dominic, and Miyoko from the east side, Carson, Lacey, Boris, Jackie, and Shen from the west. Isaac didn't know the west-siders as well as he knew the others, but they all seemed cool enough. Boris was a quiet, deep-thinker type with a buzz cut and giant ears. Jackie had the darkest skin Isaac had ever seen, matched with the longest hair, always tied up into one thick braid. Shen was loud and brash and full of energy, even though he was as skinny as Carson was thick. With nine personalities like what Isaac saw before him, the day's adventures should never a dull moment find.

"You're with me," Sadina said to Isaac, gesturing toward one of the kayaks, in which she'd already thrown her backpack.

"You don't wanna go with Trish?" he asked, the words coming out a little sheepishly. He absolutely wanted to ride with Sadina—for one thing, she seemed the most seaworthy of the bunch.

Sadina scoffed. "You kidding me? We'll kill each other if we ride together."

Trish gave that comment a shrug but didn't argue the point.

"Alright, then," Dominic said. "Let's quit pussyfooting around and do this."

Isaac slipped into Sadina's designated kayak, sitting in the front because she'd thrown her stuff toward the back. Just enough water seeped through his shorts that his breath halted mid-throat, his skin burning from the icy cold. How was it that the ocean didn't warm up with the sun beating on it all day every day? Every last centimeter of him shivered.

Sadina plopped into her seat and pushed off with the oar. Then she dipped it into the water at her right. "You remember how this works?"

He wanted to reply that he wasn't an idiot, but he worried that his words might come out a little mousy. With a nod he dipped his own oar to the left. Then, following her cadence, they slipped out to sea. No one could keep up with them.

I'm not afraid of the water, he thought. *I'm not afraid of the water.*

5

Stone Point lay at the very tip of a long, craggy peninsula that stretched and curved out from the main body of the island, first heading north then bending toward the west in an arc. Isaac's and the four other boats had disembarked from the west side of that peninsula, now cutting across the open bay formed by the main island and the long spit of rock itself. Though at the greatest distance they were probably only a couple of kilometers from land, Isaac still felt a rush of danger and adrenaline. As if they'd soon be swallowed by the immensity of the ocean and had roughly a ten-point-three percent chance of dying a horrible death. Yes, he was practically as brave as the Gladers of old.

"There's an inlet right before you get to Stone Point," Sadina called up to him. "We need to bank and tie up the kayaks in there so they won't get pummeled by the waves. From there we can hike to the cliffs and the caves."

"Sounds good," Isaac replied, consciously keeping his voice steady. He suddenly knew, without the slightest of doubts, that he was the least brave person in this group of ten. Jump off cliffs? No cliff in sight looked like something a human should be jumping from. And there was no telling what the hell lived in those caves. Bats? Sharks? Alligators? He'd never felt so stupid in his life.

Soon enough they reached the inlet Sadina had spoken of, rough cliffs of black rock towering above them. They and the others ran their kayaks onto a low bank of pebbles and tied them to a massive tree that looked like it'd been dead since Napoleon roamed the earth. There wasn't another sign of vegetation in sight.

"Okay," Trish said once they'd gathered by the entrance to a cave that Isaac never would've spotted on his own. An overhang slanted from right to left, and the shadows it created hid a six-foot-tall opening into blackness. "Here's the plan. We'll squeeze through this tunnel that leads to the north side. If a wave comes rushing in, don't panic or you'll end up sucking down a gallon of salt water. Just brace yourself and wait it out."

No one laughed at this, least of all Isaac. Sadina had failed to share the little part about being inside a cave while a wall of water came crashing through.

Trish continued. "Once we get to the other side, there are a couple of cool cliffs we can jump off, and then a few more caves to explore. Some of those have awesome swimming holes inside. It'll be fun as long as no one freaks out."

Isaac was feeling more encouraged by the second.

Dominic spoke next. "Will anyone be offended if I swim in the buff?"

This was answered with a rousing and unanimous affirmative.

"I figured," he muttered. Isaac felt a little sorry for him. The guy's whole life floated or sank on his ability to make people laugh. He tried, bless his heart.

"I'll lead," Trish said, no more amused than the others. "Sadina will take up the rear so we don't lose anybody."

She looked around, eyebrows raised, expecting a question or two. When no one responded, she turned around, ducked her head slightly, and slipped into the darkness of the cave.

"Catch ya on the other side!" she yelled over her shoulder, the hollow echo of her words swallowed by the rocks.

6

Isaac couldn't remember the last time he'd been this cold. The tunnel that cut through the peninsula couldn't have been more than a hundred meters long, but it was grueling in the darkness. No one had bothered to bring a torch, and flashlights were a thing that only existed in the old world. How Trish knew her way through the turns and drops and inclines was beyond him. But they stayed close together, each of them doing exactly what the person in front of them did. Truth be told, once his eyes adjusted, just enough light seeped in from both ends of the tunnel to keep him from face-slamming into a rock every ten seconds.

But the water made Isaac miserable. Every step of the way, at the very least his shoes were completely immersed, and often the freezing liquid came all the way to his shorts. The splish-splash of their ten pairs of legs slogging through the narrow stream made Isaac think of Captain Sparks dunking lengths of hot iron into the cooling buckets. What he wouldn't give for some of the warmth from the Forge fires. Every centimeter of skin he owned shivered uncontrollably.

It wasn't really that much fun learning that he was this big of a wimp when it came to adventuring. *It's just the cold and the wet*, he thought. I can handle anything as long as it's warm. He'd hiked and climbed almost every square meter of this huge island, but usually with the comfort of the sun lighting the way.

"There's gotta be some dead bodies decomposing in here," Carson the giant said. He was two or three people behind Isaac. "Something don't smell right."

Isaac took a big sniff but didn't notice anything besides the usual strong scent of the sea, which pretty much anyone would agree smelled like rotting fish.

"Wasn't me," Dominic replied, to the surprise of no one.

Sadina spoke up from her position in the very back. "Over seventy years, I'm sure at least a few poor saps got lost in here. We're probably stepping on bones and body parts as we speak."

"Remind me never to go anywhere with east-siders again," someone said. Isaac thought it was the girl with the long, braided hair, Jackie.

"I don't remember inviting you," Sadina replied.

"Ouch," was her response.

As for Isaac, he was just glad for human voices, a reminder that he wasn't alone. On they went, trudging along, splish-splash, splish-splash, smart-ass comments in abundance.

Soon the darkness abated and the bright entrance to the north side presented itself, Trish a perfect silhouette within its frame. Relief filled Isaac, and he was already trying to think up an excuse to stay on the cliffs when everyone else explored the other caves. He'd heard stories of soldiers in past wars shooting themselves in the foot to get out of battle. Well, maybe he'd take an accidental tumble and sprain an ankle or two.

Trish hadn't moved since she'd reached the exit, and the others were grouping around her. All of them stared northward, toward the endless expanse of the ocean. It seemed a little odd that they weren't spreading out into the warmth of the sunlight. Isaac reached the crowd and felt a sudden desperation to push them out of the way and scramble to fresh air. But something had grabbed their attention, something he couldn't see yet. No one moved or spoke a word.

"What's going on?" Sadina asked, making him jump because she was only inches behind. "What're you guys looking at?"

Without responding, Trish finally exited the cave and stepped onto a wide ledge of rock, her movements slow and unsure, her eyes never leaving the distant spot at which she stared. Everyone else ambled along to follow her, and Isaac was finally able to leave the claustrophobic confines of that awful tunnel. But as he emerged, he finally caught sight of what the others had seen.

Drifting along the surface of the ocean, several hundred meters away, bobbing and dipping with the current and the waves, heading straight toward Isaac and his friends, was something that none of them had ever seen before. And yet they knew exactly what it was.

A boat. A manufactured boat from the old world.

A big boat. Bigger than any single building on the entire island.

A *ship*.

As soon as Isaac's brain registered that he was seeing what he thought he was seeing, the ship blasted its horn—the loudest, deepest, scariest sound he'd ever heard.

CHAPTER THREE

Old Names

I
ALEXANDRA

Mikhail had always told Alexandra that he had visions. She didn't like it. Mentions of a lost people sailing the seas, returning to the old, destroyed world. Mentions of orphan armies rising up against the Godhead and the Pilgrims of the Maze. Horrors, all. Gift or lunacy?

It was the part of their lives that scared her the most. Even after the greatest of her trials and experiments over the decades, the true nature of their disease still eluded her. How can one make a final judgment on a thing that is always changing, always evolving, always unpredictable? Even so, she'd been committed to the impossible since the day of the Evolution. Now, striding through the city with her Evolutionary Guard on all sides, marching, watching, alert for all enemies, she felt no regret. Not even a drop.

In her mind, everything had a purpose and a plan. All of it, leading to her *own* vision of the future. But not like Mikhail. When he mentioned visions, he sounded like a crazy person.

And that was the crux. The root of all her fears.

Madness.

Dawn had broken, the clouds above the city glowing from the faint light of the rising sun. That worried her, too, the timing of this. Fanatics of old often used the precise moment of the sun cresting the horizon as a centerpiece for their rituals and ceremonies. She wouldn't be surprised at all if Mikhail was doing just that. The idea of the Godhead had gone straight to the man's head, in all too literal a fashion. His lack of control threatened everything she'd worked for.

And now, this.

He'd gone to the Glade. At sunrise. A place where the sun had never shone.

The thought chilled her more than the cool air of Alaska ever could.

As usual, a crowd of pilgrims had gathered at the fortified entrance to the caverns below. An ominous crowd, to be sure. Some were naked, with slashes upon their backs, wounds they'd received of their own choosing. Others were dressed in the robes of their religion, its coarse wool the color of old mustard. A few even dressed in the false furs of the Grieving, their foreheads surgically adorned with two spikes on either side, slanted toward the sky like the horns of a beast.

A shudder ran through Alexandra's body. These people disgusted her, made her feel an illness that her very own disease could never match. And yet, by all accounts, they were free of lower virus strains that took away all rationality. Many, many tests had proven so. They followed their order with mostly normal brain functions, strived to walk the pathway of the Maze by their own free will and choice. She felt that the definition of insanity needed to be updated. Quite literally. She made a mental note to pursue the matter with whomever and wherever dictionaries were maintained. But one thing Alexandra knew for certain:

She was not insane.

The Maze pilgrims spotted the Evolutionary Guard well after the guards had spotted the pilgrims. It was always this way, which is why they'd been chosen as her protectors. The Godhead wasn't any safer from these fanatics than other people, perhaps even less so. By the time the wailing and the singing and the mad rush to touch a member of the Godhead erupted in a chaotic flurry, the guards were in perfect position. As always, their orders were to avoid seriously injuring the people unless no other alternative presented itself.

The filthy, sweaty, bloody bodies pressed in from all directions, their wild shouts and wails concussing the dawn air until it all blended into one nightmarish shriek. But no one got close. The guards maneuvered perfectly, utilizing their Launch Beams when necessary. The electric buzz of the Beams, the ozone smell, always served as a comfort to Alexandra. She was a member of the Godhead, and no one—friend, foe, or worshipper—could ever bring her harm.

A path had been cleared to the massive steel door that served as the only entrance to the stairs on the other side, the stairs that led into the depths of the earth. As she made her way between the packed barriers of bodies, many gave up the struggle to rush her and dropped to their knees, falling all over each other, screaming cries of adoration. It was necessary, being their deity, but that didn't ease the tightness in her belly, or the revulsion at seeing them, writhing, prostrate, causing some of the guards to stumble and step on their heads.

She reached the steel door, its gray face filthy from the countless hands of the worshippers who'd touched its surface. Only three people in the world could open this door. A technology recovered from the ruins of this sacred place, much like everything that had led to the establishment of the Godhead. There was power in technology, immense power. Others might call it magic. Miracle. Priesthood.

Alexandra knew the precise places to put her hands, palms flat, fingers outstretched. A thin layer of clouded glass covered the subtle fingerprint scanners so that it appeared more mystical than truth. A series of chirps sounded, a staccato, otherworldly sound to the people collapsed all around her. Then there was a loud *clunk*, the scream of straining metal, finally followed by the rumble of the giant door sliding to the right. The people oohed and aahed at the sight, even as they felt the thrumming vibration that rattled the ground. A faint glow of red shone from the yawning entrance, barely enough to illuminate the first couple of stairs that spiraled downward into darkness.

Members of the Guard had collapsed the perimeter into a semicircle around the opening, not a breath of air between them, facing outward. Their Launch Beams ignited in a brilliant blue lattice of bars, deterring even the craziest, bravest of pilgrims from charging. The hum was an awesome thing to hear, somehow overpowering even the clank of the door completing its slide into a hollow compartment of cement.

"I'll go alone," she commanded, and she sensed the guards' fierce unwillingness to let her do such a thing. But they were wise enough to keep their protests silent. The worshippers would of course be enraptured by her bravery, though needlessly so. She'd know if anyone besides Mikhail had passed through before her, and no one had. Also, she had a virtual armory of weapons hidden throughout the caverns. No, she must go alone. She couldn't risk a witness to those things about to occur.

Alexandra stepped across the threshold of the entrance, placing her foot on the tiny bump in the floor that triggered the closing of the door. Again came the rumbling, the vibration, the squeal of moving metal. Looking at the footprints Mikhail had left in the dust, she didn't move until the door closed with a hard thump.

After the last echoes of that thump bounced their way to oblivion, complete silence enveloped her. She closed her eyes and took several deep breaths. There was little doubt that Mikhail knew she had entered the stairwell to the caverns. There was *every* doubt that she knew how he'd react. No one had been to the Glade in over a year.

She began her descent, treading in the footsteps of a god.

2
MINHO

The Orphan had been standing guard upon the wall for over ten hours. His muscles were stiff; his joints ached; his lower back had begun to spasm, just a little. And he was hungry. *Damn*, he was hungry. If it were appropriate, he'd scale down the sheer cliff of his wall, march out to the man and horse he'd killed, and feast on their meat. Man or beast, he didn't care. Build a fire, cut some slices of flesh, roast it up.

Maybe the Orphan was going crazy up here on the wall.

Finally he heard the sound of a distant whistle, a sound that no Orphan could hear without wanting to sing, dance, or cry with relief. Maybe all three at once. He relaxed his muscles from head to toe, brought his rifle down to rest in the crook of his folded arms, and waited for a replacement. Another Orphan showed up within a minute of the whistle's shriek. No words were exchanged, no eyes meeting. Later, in the cramped quarters where they slept and ate and read and played, they could relax and pretend to be friends. But when on duty, they were nameless servants, focused only on the defense of the Remnant Nation. Orphans had no parents, no brothers, no sisters, no friends. Only enemies.

The Orphan walked to the closest tower, slipped past the scarred wooden door, and descended the stairs in a rhythmic pattern of skipping every other step. Down he went, seven levels, to the sub-basement. Only one level existed below the one in which he lived, and its name discouraged visits. It was called Hell. The Orphan had only been there once, to deliver an Orphan who'd decided to break the rules and allow sanctuary to a stranger from the north. But he'd revisited Hell often in his dreams, and hoped to never go back. Until the day he died, he would never forget the screams, the wails of anguish, the pleas for help, the sweat, the blood, the greasy hair, the buggy eyes, the filth, the mud, the stench. It was fascinating to him that he could remember a place so well, so vividly, having only descended the one time.

In his life, when someone told you to go to Hell, you made the sign of your favorite religion to ward off the foul curse. If you didn't adhere to such superstition, then you usually just punched them in the face or kicked them in the balls. Whatever got the job done.

The Orphan walked through the dank, carved hallways of his world, the black stone all around him looking as if it had been blasted and shaped a thousand years ago. For all he knew, it had been. The capital of the Remnant Nation had been moved to this fortress before he'd been born, and he had no knowledge of its history. Such things didn't matter to Orphans. But he'd defended the place long enough to know that many renovations and additions had been completed over the years. Those who lived within its walls would be safe for a long time.

He passed several sentries, sitting at desks with oil lamps casting their greasy glow on the walls and ceiling. The Orphans knew each other on sight, and no questions were asked. Others were also making their way back to quarters, and the halls grew more crowded the closer he got. Finally, his patience tested only a little, he made it to Barracks Number Seven and typed his code into the mechanical terminal at the entrance. This meant he was officially off duty.

The weight of protecting the most important nation in the world lifted from his shoulders, and, as often happened, he felt a giddiness that bordered on mania. An extreme burst of excited energy exploded inside of him, sourced from an impossible reserve that he did not understand, and he found himself unable to deal with it. He laughed, a sound that held no humor, and looked around, knowing he had to expend the energy that buzzed his every molecule. He ran to the closest wall, its surface black and mostly carved flat, and punched it with the bare knuckles of his left fist. He punched it with his right. Then again, both fists in turn. Again. Again. Left, right, left, right, left, right. He didn't stop until the skin of both hands was raw and bloody.

He stopped, chest heaving to catch his breath. Then he looked up.

Several Orphans stood nearby, staring at him. Not out of shock, but understanding. They nodded at him, and he nodded back.

"Glad I ain't that wall," one said, a skinny fella with a bent nose.

"Please," a woman with orange hair replied. "I'd be impressed if you'd at least cracked the damn thing."

They were both Orphans. Neither had a name. But he knew them. Skinny and Orange. Simple enough.

"Just wait until I get something to eat," he responded. "I'm starving. Put some steak and potatoes in my belly and I could bust a tunnel to Number Eight."

"I'm sure you could," Orange replied. "But you might have to get your hands replaced. Might hurt, too."

The Orphan shook his head. "Nothing hurts."

"We just got back, too," Skinny said. "Wanna head to the cafeteria?"

"That, I do." He swore they could hear the rumbles in his stomach clear down to the worst parts of Hell. "But I go first. There might not be any left for you guys."

Orange rolled her eyes and started walking in the direction they needed to go.

"We get it," she said. "You're hungry. Come on."

He and Skinny joined her, and it wasn't long before he smelled the wonderful scent of cooking meat. His mouth watered. He liked Orange and Skinny. He had some other friends, too. But he could never share his secrets with them. There were so many things hidden inside him.

But for now, all Minho wanted was food.

3
ISAAC

Isaac's friends reacted the same way to the approaching ship as he had. Quietly, somberly. Isaac sank to the rocky ledge and sat down, dangling his legs over the side of the cliff. Of course he had ideas of what a large seagoing vessel looked like—the aging and dying generations of the island had done a good job of passing down the ways and walks of life in the old world. But hearing the description of a shark and bumping into one while diving for clams were too vastly different experiences.

He felt a chilling fear, mostly of the unknown.

The boat was big, probably twenty meters long and half as much wide. Although originally painted white and filled with chrome railings, the thing looked as far from brand new as Old Man Frypan. The entire vessel was filthy, paint half gone to scratches and collisions, patches of rust everywhere. Most of the windows had been cracked or busted to shreds, teeth of glass clinging to their roots in some places. Altogether it looked like it had floated its way through several wars, hurricanes, and hailstorms.

Who was on that ship? Who had blown that ominous horn?

No one spoke for several minutes as it approached, ever so slowly, propelled by nothing but waves. Isaac had a feeling that the answers to both his questions were about to be answered. Finally, Trish broke the silence.

"There's something on the back deck. Lots of somethings." The pronouncement had a foreboding tone to it, as if she knew exactly what it was but didn't want to say.

"Yeah," Sadina added. "It looks like . . ."

One tiny word came out of Dominic's mouth, but it said more than the others.

"Oh."

Isaac had to stand up to see what they were talking about. He did, barely maintaining his balance with a little help from Jackie, who grabbed his upper arm.

"Not a good time to go jumping, big fella," she said. "Or falling."

"Thanks," Isaac replied absentmindedly, straining his eyes past the sunshine and sparkling glare from the water to see what the "somethings" were. It didn't take long to make out. At first he saw lumpy, oblong shapes, then noticed clothes, hair, hands. Bodies lay scattered across the deck, eight or nine of them. The ship was too far away to determine their condition.

"Maybe they're asleep," Dominic whispered.

The suggestion was so ludicrous yet full of innocent hope that Isaac almost hugged the guy. No one wanted that ship to bump into their island while full of dead people. It was a horrifying thought on a hundred levels. Not the least of which was remembering the old virus that had driven their grandparents here. Who knew if their descendants were also immune? They'd heard stories all their life, but most of them assumed the Flare was something they'd never have to worry about. Not for a few more generations, anyway.

"Someone blew that horn," Miyoko said. "They can't all be dead."

"Maybe it's on a timer," Trish suggested. "Or goes off automatically when it gets a certain distance from land."

No one responded and no one needed to. There was at least one living person on that boat, and they all knew it.

Sadina cleared her throat and then spoke, more rattled than Isaac had ever seen her. "I don't know which is worse. People dead or people alive."

"What do you mean?" Dominic asked.

She gave him a sharp look that Isaac didn't think he deserved.

"What do you think? A boat full of dead people can't possibly be a good thing. But if some of them are alive, who knows what they have that might hurt us? Weapons we've never even heard of, diseases we've never been exposed to . . . I don't know. But look at that thing. There's no way it's some kind of rescue ship—and even if it were, I don't think we *want* to be rescued!"

"What do we do?" Isaac asked. "It's definitely going to hit the cliff. Or twist sideways and float along the peninsula until it runs up on the beaches."

"I'll tell you what we do," Dominic replied. "We run our guts out getting back to town and we tell the Congress that we have some visitors. Some dead ones and maybe live ones."

It might've been the most reasonable thing he'd ever said.

Trish had come over to take Sadina's hand. "I hate to say it, but I agree with Dom-a—"

"Don't say it," Dominic interrupted. "Please don't call me that anymore." He seemed to have grown up ten years in the last five minutes. Isaac felt the same. It was like they'd spent their entire lives believing everything outside their little island was a fairy tale, especially the scary parts. But something about this ship, getting closer by the second, made the horror stories all too real.

"He's right," Sadina said. "We need to warn the others."

Isaac couldn't move. He didn't want to go back. A curiosity like he'd never known threatened to overwhelm him. The most exciting thing in his life was a Forge. Melting things then banging them into tools. An honorable life, sure. But seeing this boat had changed something deep and inexplicable inside of him. He wasn't leaving.

"I'll stay," he said quietly. They could agree or not agree, but he was staying put. "You guys go and tell the Congress, a constable, somebody. I'll keep a lookout and follow them, see what they do."

"Not sure that's a great idea," Dominic said. The others added various forms of agreement.

"What if they have a weapon?" Sadina asked. "What if . . ."

Isaac put as much confidence into his voice as possible. "Guys, come on. Go back and let everyone know. It makes total sense for someone to stay here and see what happens. We shouldn't let even one second go by without tracking every move they make. If they come out with guns and bombs, I promise I'll run into the caves and hide."

His friends looked at each other, kind of blankly. He'd never been known as the bravest wolf in the pack, and he'd shown that again as they'd made their way through the pitch-black tunnel. But he knew that *they* knew that what he'd said was a wise course, and not even that dangerous. The ship was here, and there could only be so many living people crammed inside of it. It wasn't like he planned to take a kayak out there and board the stupid thing.

"Go on!" he snapped. "The sooner you tell people the sooner they can get back here with real boats and weapons to figure things out."

"I'll stay with him," Miyoko said.

That did the trick, as if two people were perfectly safe compared to one. Or maybe they just trusted her to act more reasonably. Isaac didn't care, and he was glad not to be alone.

"Okay," Trish said. "Just . . . don't do anything stupid. Come on, guys."

"Got it," Miyoko replied, coming to stand next to Isaac. "Nothing stupid. Only smart things."

"Smart things, only," Isaac added.

With visible reluctance, the others finally left, disappearing back into the tunnel.

4

A constant breeze, full of the salty taste of the ocean, blew against Isaac and Miyoko as they walked along the narrow ledge of a trail, following the ship's course. So many sounds wafted through the air. The incessant cries of seagulls, waves smacking against rock, water lapping against the sides of the boat, the creaks and groans of the vessel itself as it bobbed up and down in the sea. But there hadn't been another howl of the horn, and still no sign of movement from inside.

As he'd predicted earlier, the natural movement of the current twisted the boat until it was parallel with the cliffs of the peninsula, its prow pointed eastward, then south-eastward, then southward as it continued to drift toward the more solid landmass of the island proper. As the gap between them and their visitors narrowed, details came into sharp focus, only adding to the ominous, but almost adventurous feel of it all.

"Can you tell what those letters make out?" Miyoko asked. A half hour or so had passed since the others left, and the two remaining islanders hadn't said a whole lot. But all four of their eyes stayed glued to the floating vessel. Miyoko pointed to the broad, dented, barnacle-infested side of the ship, where a ghostly image of three words ran along the front, just below the rusted railings. Holes in the right places indicated that plastic or metal letters had once been attached there, long since fallen off.

Isaac focused, squinting a little. "I think it says . . . *The* . . . something . . . *Cutter*."

"Maze," Miyoko said. "Holy crap in a handbasket. It says *The Maze Cutter*."

Isaac stared at the phrase on the side of the ship, its every letter now obvious. His mind had gone blank, unable to comprehend why this boat was called such a thing.

That word meant a lot on this island. It seemed a reference to their most famous resident, Thomas, who'd been dead for over twenty years. Countless stories existed about the man and the Maze from which he and his friends had escaped. The Gladers. WICKED. Ava Paige. The Flare. Many tales, impossible for all of them to be true. But after so many decades and after so many tellings, one thing had stayed consistent. More people referred to Thomas as the Maze Runner than they did his actual name.

And here, right in front of him, seemingly out of a dream, now only fifty or sixty meters away, was a large boat with starkly similar words etched in rust and grime along its side. He'd heard people claim they were speechless before. That's exactly what he was now, his brain a scorched valley.

Miyoko didn't have the same problem. "What in *the* hell? What's going on, here, Isaac? I'll tell you what's going on. This freaking boat came here *looking* for us. They know about Thomas and everyone that came here with him. After all these years, someone somewhere decided they weren't done with the brave little Gladers that escaped through their magic machine. Kids, grandkids, great-grandkids, doesn't matter. Thomas is some kind of god to them and they went on a pilgrimage. Or maybe they came to kill us. Or help us. Or tell us something."

Isaac finally tore his eyes away from those ghostly words, *The Maze Cutter*. He looked at Miyoko.

"What did you say?"

She gave him a grim smile, then frowned, then tried to smile again. "Nothing. I have no idea what to say." Her weight shifted from foot to foot.

"Me, neither," he replied. "But we've gotta get on that boat."

He expected her to say something like, let's not be hasty. But she surprised him.

"Should we swim out?"

This broke him a little; he started laughing. She joined in. They were losing it.

"I don't think we'll need to," he finally said. "Look. It's getting really close now."

The boat had continued drifting at a slow and steady pace, moving toward the cliff and the beaches to the south at roughly the same speed. Isaac and Miyoko had walked along with it, things moving so incrementally that it felt sudden when they realized the thing was only about twenty meters away, as if it had skipped a beat in time. And now they could *really* see all the details that had been fuzzy before. The bodies.

"There's . . . eight of them," Miyoko whispered, almost as if she worried she might wake those lying on the deck. But there wasn't much chance of that. Each one had a bullet hole in their head, the wounds crusted with dried blood. "What the . . . Who killed them?"

"Whoever blew that horn, I guess."

The lifeless people were dressed in warm clothing, most of it still sopping wet—the boat must've gone through a storm right before it reached the island. There was a mixture of gender, hair lengths, races, sizes. But they all appeared equally dead. Although the deck itself—made of warped, cracked wood—had no bloodstains he could see, that could be explained away by the storm. The murder spree couldn't have been too recent because the bodies looked . . . spent. Not fresh.

With every one of these passing thoughts, the boat drifted closer. In a matter of minutes, they could probably leap across the gap and onto the boat if they wanted to.

As if she'd read his mind, Miyoko said, "We promised the others we'd just watch and observe. Shouldn't we go and hide? If someone comes out of the cabin toting a gun, we're dead unless we jump into the water."

"We should definitely go and hide," Isaac agreed, but neither of them made a move. Instead, they just kept walking along, one slow step after another. Never in his life had he felt such a thrilling fear, like electric eels were swimming through his guts. Something. Something was about to happen.

5

The ship finally ground to a halt twenty minutes later.

Once its starboard side had edged so close to the cliff that it risked slamming into the rocks, an amazing thing happened. An engine underneath the boat rumbled to life, gurgling and bubbling water toward the peninsula as if a giant squid were about to rise from the depths of the sea. It only lasted a minute or so, but it kept the vessel from crashing. Then the engine shut off, and *The Maze Cutter* continued drifting southward.

Isaac and Miyoko had stopped on instinct, now looking at the squared-off back edge of the boat, where they had the best view of the dead bodies.

"Guess that answers our question," Miyoko said.

Isaac didn't bother responding. Someone was definitely alive on that boat, and maybe it wasn't such a good idea to stay close to it after all. But he wanted to. He *really* wanted to.

"Let's just keep a good distance," he said. "They're obviously heading for the beachhead down there. It's a gradual slope. Probably the best place on the island to wreck a ship if you gotta wreck a ship."

Miyoko agreed. "Yeah, whoever's on there must only have a drop or two of fuel left. Saving it for emergencies."

The boat drifted on, bobbing like a toy. Isaac and Miyoko followed, staying roughly thirty meters behind the vessel's back end. Drifting. Drifting. Walking. Walking. The air so full of tension that it buzzed in Isaac's ears.

Finally, they descended from the peninsula's black wall of rock and approached the sandy beaches on the north side of the island's main body, which formed a right angle to the cliff. Nobody was in sight—people didn't really come up here except for holidays in the summer. It was harvest season, and it wasn't easy running a civilization on an isolated chunk of land in the middle of nowhere. Everyone else was hard at work.

"I hope that thing doesn't flip over," Miyoko said.

Isaac understood her meaning. Once you crossed the threshold from the peninsula to the beaches, it was like a magical barrier. The deep, deep waters in front of the wall of rocks prevented huge waves from forming. But the geographic terrain from there to the beach changed at a tipping point where waves as tall as five meters rolled up like charging horses and crashed in a violent display of white, watery power. However, there was a small section within the transition from rock wall to sandy beaches that just might give the ship a chance to ground itself. Almost as if . . .

"They knew," he whispered. "She. He. They. Whoever. They knew."

"Knew what?" Miyoko asked.

"Enough about the island to land their boat. It's the perfect place as long as they—"

A sudden rev of engines cut him off. The ship was just passing the tipping point and it now turned sharply to the right, giant bubbles of water boiling from the back. With perhaps its last burst of energy, the boat sped toward the firmer, deeper sand nestled in the geological corner. The engines sputtered out but the ship had all the momentum it needed. With a grinding, hissing sound, it slammed into a bank of sand and stuck there, the current from the east and the dwindling waves from the north enough to keep it locked into position. Isaac didn't know much about the old world, but he knew his island like he knew his own face, and he was certain he'd just seen someone pull off a masterful job of landing that boat in dire circumstances.

He and Miyoko had stopped walking at some point, though he didn't remember doing so. Everything seemed so quiet now—after that short but powerful engine burst. A sound rarely heard in his little world.

"What do we do?" he whispered.

"Quick, over there!"

Miyoko ran toward a last remnant of the peninsula's rocky landscape, big enough to hide behind. Isaac followed her and they crouched close together to peek around the edge, maybe forty meters away from the sand-docked vessel. He knew the boat's occupants had already spotted them much earlier, but at least they had cover if someone came out with a horrible weapon intent on killing humans.

"This is so crazy," Miyoko whispered.

"Tell me about it." Isaac found it hard to breathe, every one of his bodily systems running at hyper speeds they weren't used to. He focused on pulling the moist and salty air into his lungs, letting it flow back out his nose.

Seconds passed. Minutes. Felt like months. Nothing moved on the boat. Water lapped in equal strengths against both sides, but the vessel didn't rock back and forth, not in the least. The forward-most tip of *The Maze Cutter* angled upward, looming three meters above the surface of the water and twice that much from the sand beneath it. The ship seemed firmly stuck into place.

A loud, metallic echo broke the lull and the silence. Isaac instinctively clutched on to Miyoko, and she did the same to him. They leaned farther out from the edge of their hiding spot, searching for any sign of movement.

There.

Something . . . some*one* was crawling along the walkway from the cabin to the back deck, where all those dead bodies lay. A woman. She was as frail as any person Isaac had ever seen, her body like a hastily assembled set of bones underneath ratty clothes. She moved with weary, slumping motions, barely able to pull and kick her way across the warped surface of the deck. Her skin was dark, her hair a disheveled mess. Her every movement seemed a monumental effort of sheer will, before she finally made it to the railing closest to where Isaac and Miyoko were hiding, watching.

"That lady needs some help," Miyoko said in an egregious understatement. "Pretty sure she isn't going to pull out a machete or gun. Come on."

"Wait!" Isaac snapped. "Just . . . are you sure?"

"Yes, I'm sure. I'm not gonna hide here behind a rock and let that lady die."

"But what if they have a disease?" Of all the things taught to them by their elders, it was to fear disease.

"They were shot in the head, Isaac. Getting shot in the head is not a virus I've heard of."

The woman was groaning, reaching haplessly for the first rung of the rusty railing.

"I get that, Miyoko, but maybe she *shot* them to put them out of their misery."

Miyoko was one of the smartest, most reasonable people Isaac knew, and she paused to consider what he'd said. Then she made a decision, a decision that Isaac knew he'd follow because he sucked at making decisions.

"No. All at the same time? They all reached the point of no return at the exact same time? And why didn't she off herself, in that case? No, there's something else going on. Come on, we'll be careful."

She stepped away from the safety of their hiding place and started walking down the slope of the beach. Isaac hurried to catch up, but he couldn't shake his concerns. "Okay, then, isn't that even worse? This evil lady shot and killed all of her shipmates?"

"Look at her," Miyoko said.

Isaac did. The lady was emaciated, her face skeletal, her eyes sunken into hollows. But somehow she managed to lift herself to the top rail, scrabbling to get her feet securely planted on the deck. She leaned heavily on the bar, oblivious to the rust cutting her skin.

Miyoko continued, walking at a steady gait with Isaac on her tail. "She might be the most vicious, evil woman in the world, but she couldn't step on an ant at this point. This is the first time in the history of our community we've had someone show up from the outside world. No chance in hell we're going to pass up the chance to learn something."

"You're right," Isaac said, and he meant it. That had really hit him in the gut. They needed this woman to survive, even if they had to quarantine her for a while. "Good thing we have food in our—"

He stopped short because the woman grunted an inhuman sound then swung her leg over the top railing, letting the momentum of her effort do the rest. She toppled off the boat and fell, splashing into the sea a moment later.

6

Isaac had the lady by one arm, Miyoko by the other, both of them gasping for breath as the cold water shocked their system. Isaac held her at the elbow and the armpit, trying his best not to hurt her any more than she already was. The stranger had used her last bit of strength to keep her head above the surface until they had gotten to her, and they now dragged her up the slope of slippery sand to the beach. As soon as they cleared the water, the three of them collapsed in a heap of exhaustion.

Isaac, catching his breath, finally sat up and put his arms on his knees, looking at the woman they'd just saved. She was on her side, spitting out water and gasping for air in short, hitched inhalations. She was so thin, so weak, it hurt his heart to see it. But if anything she seemed a little stronger than she'd appeared from a distance, and he knew she'd recover with food, water, and rest. The word *disease* pried its way back into his mind, then—they had to keep that on top of their stack of worries.

"Miyoko," he said. "Now that she's safe, we really need to keep our distance."

His friend nodded, not about to argue something so sensible. The two of them got up, walked about ten paces away, then sat back down. Miyoko reached into her backpack, pulled out some bread, cheese, and fruit wrapped in cloth and a metal container full of water, then chucked the food over to the stranger, where it plopped into the sand right in front of her face. A sprinkle of the gritty stuff dusted the woman's eyes and nose and mouth. She spat it out and blinked rapidly.

"Sorry!" Miyoko yelled. "We're just trying to be careful. You need to eat and drink."

"You need to work on your aim," Isaac whispered, feeling a little out of his mind.

"I don't think she has the strength to open that stuff."

Miyoko got to her feet and ran to where the food had landed, then quickly spread open the cloth and unscrewed the cap on the water.

Then she scrambled back and sat next to Isaac. All they could do now was wait.

The woman moved, but everything she did was in slow motion, almost agonizing to watch. First, she pushed her weight up to rest on one elbow, steadying herself. Next, she reached out with a shaky hand and grabbed the container of water. Appearing as if she might drop it at any second, she put it to her lips and took a long, steady drink, the muscles and tendons of her neck moving against the thin veneer of her skin with every swallow.

After she put the water back down, twisting the metal until it stood firmly in the sand, she reached over and picked up a piece of bread. Then, for the first time, she looked over at Isaac and Miyoko. Her dark, sunken eyes seemed to connect with Isaac's along two invisible threads sizzling with static electricity.

"Thank you," she said weakly, then took a bite of bread.

Isaac had a million questions. He was certain that Miyoko had a million more. But the stranger could barely chew, much less reveal where she'd come from, why those people had been shot, why she was here . . . endless questions.

The lady had taken three bites by now. It had to be a trick of the eyes, but it seemed as if she'd gotten a little bit of strength back. Then she spoke again.

"I'm not sick, you know." She finished off the piece of bread, stuffing the last, giant piece into her mouth. It took a few moments for her to swallow. "I swear it on the life of everyone I've ever known or ever will know."

"You know us, now," Miyoko countered. "Seems like a lame deal to be included."

The woman let out a tired sound that might've been a laugh. "Touché. I should've known the first people I came across would be smart-asses. Look. Do you have some way of testing for viruses? Bacteria? Do you have a medical center at all?" She held up an arm and gestured toward the crook of her elbow. "Stick me with as many needles as you want."

"You sure talk a lot for someone who seemed three-quarters dead a couple minutes ago." Miyoko wasn't backing down in this test of wills, and Isaac was more than happy to stay silent. "How could we possibly trust you, anyway? Where'd you come from? Why are all those people shot in the head? Why'd you bring that big ugly boat *here*?"

"Doesn't the name of it give you a clue?" the woman responded. "I know the letters fell off—ocean voyages are a pain in the ass, believe you me—but it's still plain as day what it says."

This time, Miyoko didn't answer. Neither did Isaac. It seemed best to let the lady talk and spill her secrets without giving away any of their own.

The stranger grabbed a few grapes, popped them in her mouth. Then she slowly, painfully sat up, the agony and weariness plain on her face. But she probably couldn't have done even that when they'd first dragged her out.

"Listen," she said. "I'm not sick. Those people on my boat weren't sick. It's complicated, and I'm happy to tell the whole story, but I'd rather talk to your . . . leaders. Older people, anyway. Some gray hair, couple wrinkles would be nice. No offense."

"Oh, don't worry," Miyoko chimed in. "They're coming. Lots of them. But you better tell us why you're here or we'll save them the trouble of getting rid of you. And don't bother lying. It'll just waste our time and yours."

It took every ounce of effort for Isaac not to react to that. She was being absurd, but had played the part pretty well.

The lady sighed, a sadness like the death of children melting her features. "We came because we know who you are. We came because the world has changed. A lot. We came because we're hoping to find descendants of two very important people from a long time ago. My partners, there?" She pointed at the boat and its deck full of dead people. "They wanted to quit, go back. They threatened me when I wouldn't let them at the fuel reserves that would ensure we could return if . . . *when* we found you. So I put them to sleep, then shot them. *That's* how important this mission is. You wanted honesty? Well, there ya go." She ate some fruit, drank some water.

Isaac had been silent, but was somehow stunned into being even *more* silent.

It took a moment for Miyoko to recover her resolve and speak, but she avoided the scarier parts of what the stranger had said. "Descendants of whom?" she asked. "What two people are you talking about?"

The woman finished off the container of water, tilting her head back to get every last drop. Then she looked at Isaac, those dark eyes boring into him, and then she looked at Miyoko.

"There're others who are . . . immune," she said. "I'm sure you realize they couldn't possibly have found all of them before sending you here. And we've spent our lives studying the children and grandchildren of those people, trying to figure out what makes them . . . makes *us* . . . immune. It's never been enough. Never enough. And now there are enough variants of the virus to make the thing infinitely more complicated."

The stranger paused, as if all that speaking had sapped the tiny bit of strength she'd regained. She took a few slow, shallow breaths, then continued.

"But we have samples that survived the collapse of WICKED. And there were two people that stood out from the rest. Like . . . like mountains compared to anthills. Something special in their cells and in their blood that we've found nowhere else. We need to find them or their descendants, or we might as well give up and quit."

"Who were they?" Miyoko asked. "Which two people are you talking about?"

The woman lay back down on the sand, looking up at the sky. The more she talked about all of this, the more pain it seemed to cause her. But after a minute or two, just when Isaac thought she'd given up on speaking, she finally answered the question.

"They were brother and sister." She paused, closed her eyes for a few seconds, then opened them again. "Their names were Newt and Sonya."

CHAPTER FOUR

The Keeper of Ruin

I
ALEXANDRA

She stood amongst ruins.

Alexandra, Godhead, Second to One, Second to None.

A full hour had passed before Alexandra reached the bottom-most level of the caverns, a journey more threatened by boredom than any visceral fear. Her mind had taken on many new delights since the full-scale Evolution of thirty-one years ago, the day that changed the world forever. One of those new delights was the ability to find joy in the most unlikely of places, thanks to the Flaring discipline. As she tap-tap-tapped her way down the endless stairs leading from level to level to ever-lower levels, a minor compartment in her mind took pleasure in counting each footstep and calculating angles, distances, pace.

By the time she'd reached the bottom—with additional jaunts through corridors, hallways, secured doors, even a random chance to go *up* stairs instead of down—she'd been able to calculate several items of interest that kept her entertained if nothing else. Number of steps;

overall pace as well as current pace of speed; total distance, both descended and traversed; the precise angle from Point A at the steel door to Point B, where she stood now. Another compartment of her mind noted the various temperature readings as she traveled deeper into the earth, translating every tiny sense and feeling and perception—every wick of moisture—on her skin, on her body's many parts, into a reading. It fascinated her as to why the temperature dropped at such uneven rates, no consistency whatsoever. She stored the information away, determined to calculate a pattern at a later time.

But, for now, greater challenges awaited as she stood within the awesome sight of total ruin.

This had once been a mighty place. A place of power and potential. She looked at the huge expanse of it all, feeling the wonder and awe of how it must have appeared in its day. Before the great walls crumbled and toppled, and crashed onto the ground. She imagined the immense storm of dust swirling through this vast cavern on the day it happened. Presently, she observed the countless heaps of broken cement and metal, the jutting arms of stone that reached from the rubble toward the reinforced ceiling far above, like monuments to those who'd suffered here, died here. Pointing to the heavens, as if in hope for their souls.

This is hallowed ground, you know, she thought to herself. The Maze. Where *he* lived. And where *she* lived. And oh, where old what's-her-bucket lived and where old what's-his-hatchet died a gruesome death. And the whole thing collapsed in a magnanimous display of bravery and sacrifice and honor and some other bullpucky, as her grammy would've said.

Alexandra let out a snort of derision, hopefully echoing to every curved corner of the gigantic cavern. She could only maintain her reverence for so long, and the expectation to perpetuate the charade around the other members of the Godhead pissed her off to no end. She loved—absolutely cherished—her Evolutionary ascension and role in this movement, and totally agreed with the direction they'd taken over the decades. She just wished people would lighten the hell up every now and then. She was no Athena. Mikhail was no Hercules. And . . . and . . . *He* was sure as shit no damned Zeus.

Well, she thought, *I should've just stayed home. I'm not in the mood for this.*

But then, she smiled. If she'd sat this one out—something she never *would* have done and she very well knew it—she'd be back in her rooms thinking about all the exciting things she might miss.

So, here she was, looking at a vast field of ruins, over seven decades old. There was a distinct path through all that twisted metal and cracked stone and broken cement and strewn machinery that somehow still sparked now and then. She knew the path. Two others knew the path. One had walked its holy treads sometime during the night.

And *that* pissed Alexandra off the most.

She started walking, passing underneath an archway of cement splintered with steel rebar, poking in every which way like metal spears that felled a great antediluvian beast.

She headed toward the Glade.

2
MINHO

The Orphan lay curled in bed, the blanket pulled tightly over his head despite being drenched with sweat. He didn't want others to see his agony. His guilt. His shame.

He'd slipped again in the cafeteria—had thought of himself as Minho, as worthy of having a name. It was a blasphemy that would crush the hearts of those who'd come before him. Those who had trained him. Those who had died, giving him the opportunity to become an Orphan in the first place. He was a wretched embarrassment to his Orphan siblings, asleep in their bunks. All around him, in dozens of beds, lined up like tanks waiting to take off for war, were people who'd, at best, spit on him if they knew, kill him at worst. Nah. Definitely kill him.

He'd been born for this. Raised for this. Trained for this. He *was* an Orphan.

An Orphan has no name. An Orphan *needs* no name.

He couldn't do this. He couldn't lie here under his hot-as-hell blanket and sweat to death letting the weight of the entire universe weigh him down in misery. After peeking over the edge of the blanket for watchers, he swiped the scratchy wool off of his body and sat up, resting his bare feet on the cool stone floor. Elbows on knees, face resting on hands. He rubbed his eyes and forehead. What could he do? He couldn't stand one more minute in this bed or in this barracks. He had to get *out*. Now.

A pox on this.

The Orphan stood up, grabbed some clothes out of the small trunk at the foot of his bed, and quickly dressed, trying to stay as quiet as possible. If anyone asked, he had to take a dump. Not many people would wanna tag along for that adventure.

He made his way to the door, passing eight or nine beds on the way; a few tossers and turners gave him a look but didn't say anything. Outside the door, a sentry simply nodded his head, half asleep as he tried to read a dusty old book. The Orphan didn't understand why he was nervous—for one thing, he hadn't set out to do anything against the rules. For another, what *could* he do? Run around naked and scare people? Their weapons were locked away when off duty, and if he so much as carried a knife he'd be banned for life or executed as an example. Nah. Definitely executed.

And so, he relaxed. He just needed air. A break. Reset his mind and rededicate his life to the cause to which he'd been born and donated. This nonsense of calling himself Minho had to end before it got so big in his mind that he'd never be able to hide it. And not only from himself.

The Shaftfall. Yes. That's where he'd go. Perfect.

Walking through the corridors of the barracks in that direction, he passed quite a few people, surprising him. The job of protecting an entire nation had no reprieve, he reckoned. It only helped to dampen his worries that others might be alarmed at his insomnia. He moseyed, he puttered, he kept to himself, enjoying the exercise, the stone, the flames of torches, the almost-friendly faces. The smell of body odor, not so much, but he'd gotten used to that years ago. He reached his destination.

The Shaftfall was the only place in the entire sub-basement where you could look directly at the sky—albeit through a vertical tunnel of rock that measured at least two hundred meters in height. It was part of a vast ventilation system that ensured people like the Orphan could breathe in and breathe out. At the moment, water fell from far above, a steady sprinkle that splashed in tiny explosions across the glistening black rock of the floor. The Orphan went to the far side, loving the sweet chill of the rain against his skin, and sat down with his back against the curved wall of the shaft. The fresh air, the drizzle, the walk —all of it had invigorated him, helped him recover from the crushing doldrums he'd felt just a half hour earlier.

No one questioned him. No one bothered him. He closed his eyes.

Time passed.

3

A soft cry woke him from a half sleep in which he'd just begun to fade from the world. At first he thought it was the inkling of a dream, but after rubbing his eyes and letting out a brisk yawn, he heard it again. More than a cry, now. A scream of pain. A frantic shout for help. Shrieks of terror that suddenly cut off, far too abrupt to be voluntary. Then a steady, miserable sobbing.

The Orphan's instincts had ignited like a struck match on kerosene.

He'd already reached a small access tunnel to his right, one of a million such openings throughout the fortress. He had to duck but that didn't slow him down. Running at almost full speed, his ears guiding every step, turning left, turning right, going straight, whatever brought him closer to that pathetic cry for help.

He burst through an entrance to another vertical shaft, much narrower than the one in which he'd been resting. Whimpers came from a small tunnel above his head, one level up. Without hesitating, he leaped and grabbed the bottom edge with both hands, hauled himself into the dark hole in one swift motion. A man knelt there in a pool of filth, a small, pitiful child lying prone next to him, in the worst shape the Orphan had ever seen another human so tiny. Bloody. Bruised. Beaten to the point his own mother couldn't possibly have recognized him. And the pustule of a man had his arm raised to strike another blow.

Anger exploded within the Orphan, a thousand fiery pounds of dynamite rage.

He grabbed the man by his tattered shirt, lifted him off the ground, slammed him against the wall. With the ceiling low, the stranger's head cracked against the jagged stone, a sound the Orphan knew would haunt his dreams, a sound that made his nerves sizzle. And made him happy. Holding the man's neck with his left hand, the Orphan punched him in the face with his right. He pulled back and hit him again, with all the weight of his muscles and a hard, clenched fist. Again, then once more. Things creaked, and things crackled, and things shattered. The Orphan let go and the man collapsed in a broken heap onto the floor.

Heaving with each and every breath, he looked down at the horrible man's victim. The poor kid was badly beaten, but alive. Thank the Cure, alive. Their eyes met.

The Orphan knelt in the cold, squishy refuse, readying to lift the small body. "It'll be okay," he said. "He'll never hurt you again. What's your name?" He didn't really expect an answer—the boy was barely conscious. But the kid surprised him.

"Kuh . . . Kuh . . . Kit." The boy sputtered, mere grunts through the pain. "What's . . . yours?"

"My . . . ?" The Orphan went from surprise to shock. Downright gobsmacked. This was not something you asked an Orphan. He found it hard to speak. He couldn't quite catch up with what his lungs demanded.

"What's . . . your . . . name?" the boy repeated. He was a fragile, terrible thing to look upon.

"My . . ." *Run*, he thought. For some reason, he wanted to run. Away from this. From all of it.

"Please . . ." The boy's eyes had closed, his breathing gone shallow. "Name . . ."

Why! Why did he want to know so badly? Why would this shattered child use his last remaining strength to ask the question that tormented his life!

The boy coughed, cracked open his eyes. Pleading. "Name . . ."

The Orphan looked down at him, ashamed of the spite that filled his chest, bulging up in his throat like a cancerous lump. But he finally answered the wretched kid to shut him up.

"I don't have one."

4
ALEXANDRA

As she walked through the ruins, it was hard to envision what had once been.

Stone, everywhere. Cement, everywhere. Broken steel, everywhere. All of it covered in the dust of decades. As is so often the case, life had figured out a way to survive—vines of ivy wormed their way through the countless holes and crevices and cracks. The only reason she could actually *see* any of this—instead of the eternal darkness of most caverns—was due to the Godhead's decision to reignite the fake sun that had once shone upon the Maze. That had been a monumental task, achieved only by the greatest of efforts, a task worthy of beings who had the hubris to call themselves Gods. How ironic that the actual power came from resurrected solar panels, fed by the *real* sun—the first deity humans had ever worshipped.

Still, she had mostly walked in shadows, the ruins of the Maze like a toppled forest of stone and steel, towering above her.

The Maze.

What a wonder of architecture and technology it had been. So many devices to deceive the eye. So many corners to turn, so many paths to the unknown. Much had changed, and much had not.

She came upon the final stretch of immense rubble that marked the entrance to the Glade. Great, moving walls had once stood here, now reduced to broken blocks of ruin. Just beyond it, a vast expanse of emptiness waited for her. She stopped in the darkest shadow she could find, in sight of the Glade, and looked for Mikhail. It didn't take long to spot him because he was exactly in the spot she'd feared.

Kneeling, head lowered, hands clasped. Kneeling at the edge of what had once been known as the Box, for obvious reasons. Flat metal doors, even with the ground, could be slid open to reveal a large steel cube beneath the surface. It had once been a lift of sorts, but had frozen forever in place from rust and grime and warping of parts. The horizontal doors still functioned, albeit by manual labor, due to many repairs and a lot of grease. Those doors were—at least for the moment—closed. There were things in that Box that should not be . . . unleashed. There were secrets that should not be shared. Alexandra had hoped—and planned—on living the rest of her life without those doors ever being opened again. She would've been perfectly happy never *seeing* them again.

And yet here she was. Here, Mikhail was. Kneeling in reverence.

The fear she'd felt earlier struck her again, right in the heart, like a hammer on hot flesh.

She steadied herself. This wasn't like her. She was a member of the Godhead, second only to one being in their known world. She'd completely mastered the Flaring discipline, and it shamed her that she'd let herself get in such a state. Quickly going through the mathematical *digits* and the breathing exercises, she calmed every part of her body and mind. Mikhail was *beneath* her in the hierarchy.

Alexandra became herself again.

She left the shadows of the rubble and walked briskly into the openness of the Glade, heading in a straight and confident line toward Mikhail and the Box. The weak light of the false sun lit the way.

"Mikhail!" she shouted, manipulating her voice with command even though it would have no effect on her counterpart. "What could possibly be going through your head? Coming here? Without even *telling* me? Stop acting like a damn nun and get off your knees!" She didn't slow down as she spoke, marching as if into battle.

Mikhail didn't move in the slightest, his training too strong to react to her provocation.

She finally reached him, came to a stop just a few feet away from his prone body.

"Mikhail," she said, on the brink of striking the man, hard. "You need to tell me what's going on. Please tell me you didn't have another vision. Please tell me you're not here to open that Box and start a process we have no need to start. Something we won't be able to stop."

Mikhail still didn't respond—didn't show the smallest sign he'd heard her. He was a tall man, bulky with muscle despite his age. His gray hair was slicked back, mostly full, but she could see the beginnings of a bald spot right at the crown. He had a smell that she couldn't explain, and even now it assaulted her senses. If the decaying of a soul had a scent, Mikhail exuded it in spades. She'd never been able to put her finger on it exactly, but she just really didn't like this man.

"Mikhail," she said. "Mikhail!"

"Alexandra." He spoke so softly, with so much control. "I'm glad that you came. Please. Join me in prayer. Things are about to happen. I've had another vision of the ship, floating upon the ocean, heading here. It brings change and death."

She couldn't take her eyes off of his sprouting bald spot. "Mikhail, it's just me. There's no one else here. Stop the charade. I'm here and willing to talk. Willing to listen. Visions, prayers, gods and demons, whatever you want. But we need to step away from the Box. We need to be many, many steps away from the Box. Deal?"

He let out a sigh, the most condescending of sounds she could imagine. Then he relaxed his hands from their clasp of prayer, let them fall to his side. His head rose to stare straight ahead. Finally, testing her patience—a patience developed by decades of painful practice—he slowly turned toward her and let his gaze find hers.

"We can talk," he said. "But I want to promise you something."

"And what is that, exactly?"

He got to his feet, so that now she had to look up at him. Up at his face, an angular stack of brows and cheekbones and jaws, his skull far more prominent than seemed natural.

She let out her own sigh. "What, Mikhail? Seriously. What's going on?"

"This is my promise," he replied. "After we talk, and I tell you what I've learned, you'll agree with me that we need to open the Box."

"Mikhail, enough riddles. Just tell me what the hell is going on."

He pointed at the sky. At the Heavens.

"He's back." A pause. "And others are coming."

CHAPTER FIVE

Theater of Slumber

I
ISAAC

Four days had passed since the boat's arrival. The longest four days of his life. He was there, had watched it creep to shore, had been the first to meet the woman named Kletter. And yet no one deemed him worthy of sharing the slightest bit of news. He was going insane with the absolute, desperate want of information. Anything.

Rumors upon rumors spread across their community like the spray of salty droplets after a massive wave crashes against the shore. She's crazy, she's evil, she's a witch, she's a nobody, she's the ancient Ava Paige herself. Not a thing he'd heard so far made an ounce of sense. But that didn't stop them, four days of frustrating blather.

He thought of himself as a pretty important human. Didn't everyone? But when it came to the island and the Congress and decisions that mattered, Isaac was a nobody. Barely twenty, and not even a very good blacksmith if he had to be honest. Improving, but kind of sucky.

But man, did he love it. He was busily beating a piece of hot iron with something approaching glee when Miyoko came to get his attention. She ended up throwing a bent, discarded nail at his back because apparently she'd called his name several times without a response.

"Hey, what's up?" He slid the hot piece of metal into a cooling bin —the work-in-progress was supposed to be a spoon but looked more like a paddle. "Did they decide yet?"

She made an impatient twirling gesture for him to finish up already and come outside the Forge.

"Captain Sparks was at the meeting!" he protested. "I'm supposed to run the place until he gets back."

"Isaac, get your ass out here. They called an island-wide conference to make an announcement. Just lock the place up and turn the fires off so it doesn't burn down."

He frowned. "Turn them off, huh?"

"Yes. Hurry."

He frowned even more frownier. "Do you know how fires work?"

2

Thirty minutes later they passed the secondary school then came upon the big pavilion that had been erected nearby—a huge awning with dozens of picnic tables. Isaac had managed to temper his fires and safety-inspect the Forge before leaving, and then he and Miyoko had sprinted the mile or so to town. It was customary to have a community meal after big deliberations by the Congress, something about healing wounds and creating solidarity after the leaders had spent hours or days on end yelling and swearing at each other. Isaac was anxious to hear what had been discussed and decided about the starving lady who'd shown up on a boat. But, as Dominic always said, a person should never, under any circumstances, turn down free food.

It was already crowded, so Isaac and Miyoko didn't bother finding their friends. Miyoko found an empty spot near the outer edge of the pavilion. The tables had stacks of food running down their centers—

several variations of bread and biscuits; whole fruits; blocks of cheese; baked potatoes and vegetables; a few platters of cooked lamb. That last one you had to eat sparingly or you'd get the evil eye from every old person on the island.

Isaac had worked up a mighty sweat and burnt lots of calories hammering away at the Forge. He practically shoved the food into his mouth—his teeth, tongue, and throat labored double-time to keep up. Miyoko gave him a look of utter disgust a couple of times, so he slowed down a bit. He was just tearing into a grilled lamb chop—which he'd saved for last—when Trish came up from behind and put a hand on his shoulder.

"That one's name was Tickles the Sheep, I think," she said. "I hope you feel guilty."

He looked back at her. "Hey! Heard anything?"

"Maybe don't talk with your mouth full." She leaned closer, her head right between Isaac and Miyoko. "Be sure and sit with us at the presentation—we'll try to save a spot. Something's going down, and you guys *have* to stick with us. No matter what. You didn't try to sneak any of the wine, did you?"

They had a strictly enforced rule on the island that you couldn't have alcohol until you were twenty-one. Of his friends, only Sadina and Dominic had reached that age. Because these types of gatherings were only meant for those who'd finished their schooling, Isaac and Miyoko were two of the few present who weren't allowed to partake of the island specialty. Isaac had stolen a few cups over the years, but it gave him the runs.

"Seems like a weird time to turn into our granny," Miyoko said. "No, we promise we didn't drink the wine."

Trish didn't smile at that. "Good. See you at the amphitheater. Don't be late." She held up a hand to cut off Miyoko's question. "No. Not here. Later. Just trust me and sit with us. Bye."

With that, she walked off.

Isaac looked at Miyoko, who looked back, four eyes full of questions.

"Let's go," Isaac said.

"Yep."

3

Galileo Auditorium was an outdoor theater that had been built against a natural stone cliff, backing a semicircular grouping of benches that faced a stage and one of the quieter beaches on the island. The cliff provided uncanny acoustics. Events were held at the auditorium quite often, like today's Congress report—which were usually snooze-fests, but today Isaac couldn't wait for it to get started. What could Trish possibly have meant, acting all clandestine and mysterious? *Something's going down*, she'd said. Really? That seemed a bit much.

The place was filling up quickly. On the wide, wooden stage at the front, the prominent members of the Congress had assembled, comparing notes, arranging chairs—most of them looked unhappy, and a few fumed with anger. Their friendly debate over the strange lady and her boat must've been quite the doozy. Isaac wasn't surprised. No one ever agreed on anything in the Congress.

"Sadina and Trish are toward the front," Miyoko said, pointing to the fourth row of benches. "We better squeeze in with them."

They maneuvered their way down, and although there wasn't an empty spot in sight, somehow Isaac and Miyoko managed to wiggle into the sliver of air between their friends. A lady at the end of the bench yelled, "Hey, I'm barely hanging on by one cheek down here!" and everyone in range of hearing gave it a good laugh. Isaac wasn't so sure these people understood exactly what it meant that a boat from the old world had arrived on their shores. Or maybe he was just spooked by Trish's ominous warning.

"Hey," Sadina whispered into his ear. She was to his right, Miyoko to his left.

"Hey, what's going on?" he asked back. He doubted she could hear him over the buzz of the place, hundreds of people jawing and speculating. They smiled at each other, then shrugged, mutually deciding that conversation had no chance over the din.

Isaac thought about the lady from the boat. A rescue team had arrived from town shortly after she'd revealed her purpose in making the voyage to the island—to find descendants of the old Gladers, Newt and Sonya. Isaac didn't know if they'd actually been brother and sister—he'd never read that in the histories of these very famous people. But the lady was adamant. Medjacks had taken her to the infirmary and he hadn't seen her since, now four days gone by. But those two names had flashed in his mind over and over, like the blinking of the sun between fast-scuttling clouds.

Newt. Sonya.

Everyone learned the story of Newt in primary school. They had his journal, required reading as soon as kids were able to put letters together. He was almost a mythical figure—and if he had any descendants, that'd be news to every person on the island. Sonya was less mysterious but almost as legendary. She'd been one of the survivors, arriving on the island with Thomas and everyone else over seventy years ago. She'd died a few years back, but had left behind several children and grandchildren.

A woman stepped up to the podium placed at the front edge of the stage. It was Sadina's mom, Ms. Cowan. As First Chairperson of the Congress, the job fell on her to add stability to the wild rumors that blanketed their island.

Ms. Cowan held her hands up. Waited for people to notice, then quiet down. It didn't take long.

"Thank you," the stately woman said. She was like a shorter, older, wrinkly version of Sadina. Everyone respected her, even when she pissed them off. That was the kind of bearing she had. "Thank you for coming. It's been an interesting few days."

Sadina leaned into Isaac. Very quietly, she said, "You know Sonya only had one kid, right?"

Isaac pulled back his head, frowned in confusion. "Huh? She had three or four didn't she?"

"Nope. Just one. Now be quiet and listen."

Sadina was always pulling crap like that, and curiosity over the whole damn thing was just about enough to drive him crazy. He'd missed the first item or two that Ms. Cowan had announced from the podium. The woman's voice bounced off the cliff walls and seemed to come from every direction.

"—a little disconcerting to all of us. But after several extensive interviews with our guest, we believe that what she's told us is the truth. However, the fact still remains that this is a person who, by her own admission, drugged, shot, and killed her shipmates. That's not a thing that we as a Congress can take lightly."

She paused, and murmurs rumbled across the crowd. She held several papers with notes in front of her, and stared at them now, her face betraying that she was extremely unsettled. Placing the papers down on the podium, she looked up and scanned the audience.

"I can't say what they told me to say. I'm sorry, but I can't. This is absurd. This is absolutely absurd."

"Cowan!" a man shouted from behind her. It was the Vice-Chairperson, Wilhelm. He stood up and walked briskly to stand right behind his immediate boss. He leaned forward and whispered fiercely into her ear. Although the acoustics picked up a series of sharp S and P sounds, no words were discernible.

Ms. Cowan swept the papers off the podium and they floated toward the stage like autumn leaves. Another member of the Congress whom Isaac did not know rushed forward to gather them up before a member of the crowd could grab them.

"I don't care!" Ms. Cowan shouted, having spun around to face Wilhelm. "I don't care about the rest of the world—I care about this one!"

She brushed past her second-in-command and had to step around the man scooping up her papers. Then she hurried down the steps descending from the stage.

The crowd was hushed. Wilhelm stood stock-still, his face as pale as the crest of a wave. Isaac looked at Sadina, who seemed way too calm for the situation. Ms. Cowan was her mom, after all.

"Sadina?" Isaac questioned, "What . . ."

She looked at him. "It's me, Isaac. They want to send me back to the old world."

4

Sadina had gotten up right after her explosive pronouncement and squeezed past the others on their bench, then taken off in a run after her mom. Miyoko had also heard what she'd said, and followed right on Isaac's heels when he followed Sadina. He had no clue what had just transpired, with so many layers to unravel. But instinct took over and he swore to himself that he wouldn't let Sadina out of his sight. Behind him, as he ran on to the beach, the temporary state of shock had worn off the crowd and now they were in an uproar, shouting so many things that he couldn't make out a single word.

"Mom!" Sadina shouted.

"Sadina!" Isaac shouted.

"Isaac!"

He looked over his shoulder. Dominic. Trish was right by his side, everyone chasing someone.

Ms. Cowan finally stopped, a good half kilometer from the amphitheater. She hunched over, hands on knees, catching her breath. Sadina reached her, then Isaac and Miyoko, then Trish and Dominic. They all stared at each other while heaving air into their lungs, waiting for someone to explain.

Ms. Cowan surprised him with her first words.

"Isaac, go back. Go back right now. You're not a part of this."

"What . . . what's . . . not a part of what?" He floundered like the idiot he felt like.

"Mom," Sadina said. "We want him to be part of it. If *he* wants to, of course."

The truth dawned on Isaac. Everyone in this little group knew what was going on. Everyone except him. He could tell by the looks on their faces. Even Miyoko, who had a sheepish, guilty expression that she couldn't hide.

He made an obnoxious, exaggerated shrug, holding it in place for a few seconds. "So. Who's gonna let me in on the big secret?"

The others exchanged a few glances, but eventually they turned their undivided attention to Ms. Cowan. Not only was she much older, she was literally the leader of the entire island. Well-spoken, smartest person ever, quick to anger and quick to smile. She'd always intimidated the hell out of Isaac—when he was little, he'd begged Sadina to come to his house instead of the other way around.

The woman had focused her eyes on him. "I always liked you, Isaac. You're a good person and you've gone through a lot of tragedy. I just . . . I don't want you to—"

Sadina interrupted her. "Mom, that's exactly why he needs to go with us. He's one of the few that doesn't have any family to leave behind. We're his family. Trish and I love him like a brother no matter how many times he bugs the shit out of us. We . . . I can't go without him."

Her words were too much to take in all at once. All that came out of his mouth was, "Go? Go where?" For a few seconds, the shallow waves washing up on the sandy beach were his only answer. But then Ms. Cowan stepped closer to him. Although she was a few inches shorter, he stepped back a little. Why did this little lady scare him so much?

"Okay, listen to me," she said. "We had a massive disagreement in the Congress. It was split almost down the middle, but let's just say my side lost. I honestly don't get it. At all." She closed her eyes and sighed, flushed with frustration. Then she looked at him again. "The woman. From the boat. Her name is Kletter. I spent hours with her—more than anyone else. I would bet the life of my own daughter—"

"Nice!" Sadina yelped.

"—that Kletter is telling the truth. I've lived a lot of years and been around a lot of people. I've swum through enough bullshit—pardon my language—that I'll never get the stink out. And this woman, from that boat, is telling us the truth. And, frankly, I want to do something about it."

"But the things you said on the podium . . ." Isaac trailed off.

"It was an act. Look, I don't want to sound like I'm trying to be some super-sleuth from the old books, but this has all been a setup. Between me, those who agreed with me in the Congress, my daughter and Trish, the friends they insisted on. I wanted to spare you, Isaac, with what . . . you know, your family, the tragedy . . ."

Isaac teared up but offset it by vigorously shaking his head. "I'll be okay. I can go. I *need* to go."

Cowan nodded, draped with a sad look. "Then I've been overruled. Are you sure you're okay with that?"

Isaac glanced over at Sadina, who gave him an encouraging nod.

"Yes, but I don't really know what I'm agreeing to. But . . . I . . . agree?"

Sadina and Trish laughed, and even old Ms. Cowan cracked a smile.

"It's simple, Isaac," she said. "We're getting on that boat, with our new friend and a few others, and we're setting sail for the old world. How's that for a quick recap?" She patted him on the shoulder and started walking back toward the amphitheater.

"Wait, really?" he asked, turning in a circle as the others moved to follow Ms. Cowan. "What is happening? She was just faking all that?"

Sadina pulled him into a hug, squeezing tightly. Then she whispered in his ear.

"Yep. And oh, by the way, they spiked the wine. But don't worry, it only puts them to sleep."

5

Isaac had never felt like this, not once in his entire life. He'd lost his mom, he'd lost his dad. He'd lost a sister, something that broke him to a point that he had to suppress it, hide it away, train himself to stop thinking about it. To stop feeling. But through all the pain and all the anguish, he'd never felt like *this*.

Groundless. Without foundation. Without gravity, as if nothing tethered him to the earth and never would again. Every step back to the Galileo Auditorium seemed temporary—like someone had slipped magic boots on his feet so that he could walk, for now. His mind was fuzzy. His feelings were fuzzy. He had that intangible sense of waking from a dream, the most realistic dream you've ever slipped into, that feeling that everything you know and want to keep knowing is about to fade away forever.

When they came upon the amphitheater, he stopped, almost unable to bear what he saw. But Sadina took his arm, made sure he understood.

"They're just sleeping," she said. Sprawled about on the benches, on the ground, many lying on top of each other, arms and legs flailed about in every direction, hundreds of them. Seemingly dead to the world. "That Kletter lady got the drug from her boat, gave it to my mom, the same stuff she used on her dead buddies. She said she didn't want to actually kill them but ended up finishing them off with a gun, anyway."

"And we're supposed to trust this lady?"

"I trust my mom. That's all that matters right now. And once we have time to talk about *why* we want to go back with Kletter, I think you'll be on board, too. No pun intended."

Isaac gestured to the heaps and piles of sleeping bodies. "And these people?"

"She said they'll wake up in about ten hours."

Not everyone had taken the drug—a few members of the Congress were already speaking with Ms. Cowan, and there were a scattered few who'd decided not to have the customary wine. They looked somewhere between dazed and righteously pissed off.

"*She said?*" Isaac repeated. "Some starving, murderous crazy lady who we've known for four days? Nice."

Sadina gave him a reproachful, disappointed look. "We outnumber her for one thing, and she doesn't seem the least bit crazy. Plus, my mom took the drug last night. Said it was the best night of sleep she ever had."

They stared at each other for a moment. Isaac laughed first, then

Sadina joined in, the two of them eventually reaching the giddy giggle of people who're losing it. But it did make Isaac feel better.

When it finally fizzled to a stop, he said, "So . . . what? You want me to get on that rickety piece-of-crap boat and bon voyage to the land of Cranks and the Flare? Sounds like a brilliant plan."

"Just wait till you hear what Kletter says. There's no way Trish and I are leaving without you. You gotta trust us. And my mom and others have it all figured out—they're going to make it look like Kletter herself broke out and did all this—" she pointed at the mass slumber party "—and took some of us hostage, left on the boat. That way when we come back, which we *will* come back, Isaac, we can say it was all her fault. Now come on."

She took him by the hand and dragged him toward her mom, who was barking orders like a cranky fitness coach. Isaac was glad for the connection to Sadina, to something solid like her fingers clasped around his, glad to be clutched by someone who wasn't about to dissipate and fade from the world he'd always—and only—known.

6

Kletter looked like she had gained twenty pounds as she marched behind the group. Isaac couldn't help but take a peek back at her every minute or so. Her dark skin shone, her eyes no longer hidden inside pits of hollow despair. Hair washed, newly clothed, well-fed, she seemed an entirely different person from the weak, feeble creature Isaac and Miyoko had pulled out of the ocean. She reminded Isaac of Ms. Cowan, as if two twins of might and strength had been reunited at last. It didn't hurt that Kletter held a large weapon that shone staticky blue in places, something never seen before on their little island. Holding it, she seemed about an even match with Sadina's mom.

Isaac and about a dozen others—including Carson, Jackie, and Lacey from the west side—each person holding at least two canvas bags of supplies, were walking at a steady pace toward the beach where Kletter's ship, *The Maze Cutter*, had been moored. As quickly as this rug had been pulled out from under him, as quickly as his entire future had been altered by these people, Isaac felt no panic. Just that odd, uneasy, untethered feeling, too numb to process the anxiety and fear that should be pumping through his nerves.

"Why are we letting her hold that weapon?" Isaac asked Trish since Sadina was busy getting instructions from her mom. Dominic and Miyoko were right behind Isaac. "First we let her drug our friends and now we let her walk around with some big-ass killing machine? That thing looks like it came from Mars."

"You know why," Trish replied.

"So it looks like she kidnapped us." He said it deadpan, showing just how stupid he thought the idea was.

"Yes, Isaac. So it looks like that. Not everyone is asleep, remember?"

"I just think we're trusting her too much."

"Amen." That came from Miyoko.

Trish offered a nonchalant shrug. "All I can tell you is that I'm convinced after talking to Sadina and her mom. Plus it sounds exciting as hell to go on a boat to places I've never been before. You wanna stay here, stay here. But you really need to hear them out first."

"Well, I'm waiting for that."

"I'm with Trish on this one," Dominic chimed in. "I don't care if that lady eats puppies for lunch, I can't stay stuck on this scrap of land when I know there's a chance to get off."

Isaac turned and walked backward for a few steps to address him. "And you're just fine with your dad waking up in a few hours, thinking he'll probably never see you again?"

"We're coming back, man. They'll be fine. It's not like we're going to the moon."

Trish grabbed Isaac's arm, pulling him close to her. "Kletter said there's a real possibility that Sadina has something in her blood, DNA, whatever, that might create a cure for a new version of the Flare. So it's an adventure, yes, but mainly it's a good cause!"

Miyoko scoffed. "Seems to me like some of us are forgetting the histories. Wasn't that the whole point of our ancestors being used and abused and having to escape in the first place? Because they thought they could find a cure?"

Isaac was glad someone else had joined him in using logic.

"This is totally different," countered Trish. "We're going voluntarily, and Kletter is immune just like we are. Supposedly are, anyway. She said it's just some medical tests they want to run, that it's totally different from the brain studies the Gladers had to go through. She used the word physiological, I know that. As opposed to psychological, maybe. Ugh, just wait until the damn woman explains it herself."

"Good idea," said Dominic. "You really suck at explaining it."

"Wah-wah," Trish replied. No one really knew what it meant when she made that noise.

Isaac breathed a little easier. Trish's point about it being an adventure had really struck him. It terrified him, yes, but it was also exhilarating to think that they could see the world—something he never thought in a million years would happen. It had been over seven decades since the Gladers had escaped what seemed like the apocalypse. Surely things back in the old world had been figured out, made safer. But his mind wouldn't let him off so easily. Kletter, starving, had arrived in a boat, its deck littered with corpses, all shot in the head. By her.

Isaac tried to out-walk his thoughts, wishing he could flip a switch and turn his stupid brain off.

7

They gathered at the stern of the boat, on the big deck that a few days earlier had been covered in lifeless bodies. Someone—Isaac had no idea who—had gotten rid of the dead and cleaned the place up. He had a ridiculous image in his head of pirates with mops and wooden buckets, slopping and scrubbing with soapy water, singing as they worked. From a story once told by the old folks.

"I know how to run this thing," the woman named Kletter announced to the people who'd been chosen for the voyage. Isaac had no idea *how* they'd been selected, but he was glad to have some of his friends aboard. Kletter had put her monstrous weapon inside a locked chest, hopefully to show them that she wasn't a threat. "But I'm going to need lots of help, and you'll just have to learn along the way. We have barely enough fuel for the return trip, you guys stocked us with plenty of food, and hopefully this heap of junk won't die on us before we get to where we're going."

"Where *are* we going?' a man named Alvarez asked. He was a tall, thin man, dark hair, always sporting a goofy smile. Isaac didn't know him very well, but he was a member of Congress who'd made the decision to support Ms. Cowan.

"We're heading for Los Angeles," she replied. Isaac had heard of it but that didn't mean a whole lot. "That's where we've set up our medical clinics, just far enough away from the Godhead in Alaska and the Remnant Nation in the northern plains." She obviously noted the blank looks on their faces. "Don't worry, we'll have plenty of time to talk about that stuff before we get there."

The Godhead? Isaac thought. *Remnant Nation?* He didn't know if that sounded promising or completely ominous. What were they getting themselves into?

"People might start waking up soon," Ms. Cowan said. "We made our decision, so let's get going. Pull up the plank, Wilhelm."

"Wait!" someone shouted from the beach, just as Ms. Cowan's second-in-command made a move for the long wooden walkway they'd used to climb on board *The Maze Cutter*. "One of you young whippersnappers come help me walk up this shuck thing."

Isaac looked. Everyone else looked. Everyone stared. Ms. Cowan stepped forward, her mouth open but as shocked silent as the others. An elderly man, his skin as dark as his hair was white, superbly healthy for his advanced age, put one foot on the edge of the plank where it stuck into the wet sand.

"Now don't bother arguing," he said. "I'm coming, and that's that. If I die along the way, then glory glory hallelujah amen." He gave them a loud hoot at that, and then, without waiting for help—a good thing because no one had moved a muscle—he hopped up the bouncy walkway like he'd shed forty years just at the thought of an ocean voyage. An adventure.

"Well, I'll be damned," Dominic whispered, more words than Isaac could find.

Old Man Frypan was coming with them.

PART TWO

Water and Earth

I'm left to wonder about the future, and all I can see is the past. A past emptied of wonder, a future I'll never see. That doesn't make a lick of bloody sense, but it sounds brilliant, don't you think?

—*The Book of Newt*

CHAPTER SIX

Below and Above

I
ALEXANDRA

She sat in the cold, wet air of the . . . *underneath*. Underneath all that hung above, beyond the stone and cement and steel, beyond the barrier of what was and what would be. Somewhere, even higher, unseen at the moment, the real sky loomed like a dome, droopy and drenched, gray clouds billowing angrily. As if prepping for the torrent that brought both life and misery to the inhabitants below.

It had been a week since she'd encountered Mikhail here, at the Box. A week since his revelations and pronouncements—terrible utterances of opening the Box and using its contents to erase everything they had built, or contrarily trying to increase the Evolution to such extremes that all may be erased regardless. In a word, danger. Too much danger to take these leaps now. Especially with the return of Nicholas Romanov, Glory in the Highest, God of All Who Tread, the One Above Two, He Who Sees, the Tip of the Spear . . . and so on.

More like the butt of the donkey, she thought. Ass of the Ass. Oh, she longed for the day she'd finally say that to the man's face. That day was coming. Soon. The buffoon had gotten far too big for his britches, what with these plans to utilize the contents of the Box, for good or external ill. The time had simply not come yet for those decisions. But she had to tread carefully. He still held the cards, if not the whole deck, and she had to play things right, keep to his rules. The day was coming.

Her day.

Alexandra shivered. The Box had been opened, its priceless artifact removed, all in the blue swift of night. Unless Mikhail had conspired with Nicholas—and he might have, she had no illusions about that—they were at a very serious crossroads. Decades of work, decades of planning, decades of protecting the Box and what it held within, decades of hunting down those who dared speak aloud hints of what they dreamed in their restless sleep. Words dribbling from their crooked mouths like saliva, spraying out through the snores and grunts and moans of those exhilarated by their traitorous dreams.

All citizens, no matter their pedigree, no matter their accomplishments or education or proofs of loyalty . . . all had been treated the same. The Godhead loved their people, but they loved the ultimate survival of their people even more. Perhaps it was irony, but for the Godhead to survive, with subjects on whom they could bestow their love and grace and beauty, others—and this couldn't be said with more clarity—others had to die. Those who dissented. Those who resented. Those who rebelled. Namely, the ones who simply did not understand the majestic leap of humanity the Godhead had planned. Planned for decades.

Having come full circle with her thoughts, Alexandra shifted on her cool stone chair and stared with dry eyes at the black pane of the open Box, the doors slid into their side compartments. Darkness shone from beneath that open space, as if the negative of light itself, beaming into the air with thick, oily blackness that could destroy all brightness in its path.

Alexandra stood up and walked to the squared edge of empty air, its depth impossible to discern in such darkness. But her servants had been down there, scoured its every inch, found nothing. She tried to clear her throat but a rough saw of ice had seemingly lodged itself there, making every breath painful. She needed to leave. Immediately. The sacred demeanor of the Godhead mattered most, even above her own desires, for now. She couldn't show the slightest weakness. Digits, breathing techniques, whatever it took. Sometimes she laid her hands softly in her lap, as if a princess resting in peace, all the while digging sharp and deep into her own palm with a nail.

Mikhail had promised her. *Promised* her. He swore not to open the Box until he, Nicholas, and Alexandra met together and made plans, set a path. She didn't feel they were ready, and she had the raw confidence in herself to convince Nicholas of that, if not the ever-growing fanatic, Mikhail. Besides that, every decision made by the Godhead was supposed to be unanimous. Unanimous or nothing. That had been their creed and should always be their creed. So regardless of Mikhail's unstable promises, the Box should *not* have been opened. Period. Not only had she not agreed to it, she hadn't even been *asked*—at least not by Nicholas, their leader.

They were cutting her out.

A terrible thought. A wringing, horrible thought. But it hovered there, in her mind, almost a tangible, touchable thing. She could almost see it, floating in her vision, and it looked a lot like Mikhail. What had she done? Where had she gone wrong? Why was Nicholas hiding from her, making excuses not to see her? The glorious vision of her world seemed to be collapsing, the pieces falling, the pieces getting larger.

She heard a cough.

Her servant, Flint, and several members of the Evolutionary Guard, waited nearby. They packed together about a hundred meters away, cowering beneath an ancient tree that had been dead for many years. She didn't have to look to know that each one of them had strained necks from gawking at the massive surroundings of the Maze cavern. None of them had ever been here— Alexandra had broken a sacred rule bringing them down, not to mention the risk involved. As she gazed at the vacant doors, so long closed, now open, she thought that other sacred rules might be broken soon. Very soon.

Much of her life, she had acted a part, played a role. She returned to that now.

Standing up, she summoned an odd mixture of rage and confusion, pulling in what she needed from the Flaring discipline. She marched toward her entourage with an inspired, terrifying gait, and enjoyed—not a little—the fear that sparked in their eyes. With a booming voice that belied her diminutive stature, she spewed an onslaught of words at them, high-minded nonsense purposefully designed to mean nothing while also geared to scare the living hell out of people.

They jumped into position, surrounding her, matching her speed, wisely keeping silent.

Nicholas was watching, of this she had no doubt.

With less control, she might've smiled. But she didn't smile.

She raged. She needed to be alone.

"Flint, after we get back, you have the night off. Everyone has the night off."

On they went, leaving the Maze behind.

2
ISAAC

Land, as foreign as the planets.

Isaac clung to the rusty flakes of the railing as salty spray blossomed in the air with each bump of the ship's prow upon the shallowing waters. Droplets licked his face in icy patches, a thrill that almost matched the awe of seeing a world he'd only ever known from the lips of old men and women. From stories told around a flickering fire in the night, shadows alive with the possibilities of the past. Of horrors and fears, replacing the joys of once was.

You sound like a grandpa, he thought.

A long line of sandy beach awaited them, the slow creep of the ocean eroding the flat coast with endless patience. Beyond that yellow-white beach, Isaac might've expected what he'd seen all his life, rising swells of green forest and jutting rock, eclipsing the horizon with jagged peaks of volcanic stone. But instead he saw a vista of human-built invasions of nature, endless blocks and pillars of civilization, buildings competing with each other to be the tallest or the ugliest. He'd heard of cities his whole life, had even seen pictures in the few ancient books they possessed on the island he'd left behind, but never could any of that have prepared him for what lay before his eyes.

A city. A real city, all broken glass and cement and wood and metal, each element dully reflecting the sunshine with a tired and lifeless lethargy. Although Isaac had never seen such a place alive and bustling, he could tell that it was dead all the same. Where once humans had roamed and ruled, nature was conquering its way back in. The closer they got to shore, the more trees and plants and vines he saw in places where they didn't seem to belong.

"Home sweet home!" someone shouted from behind, a voice lost in the roar of waves and splash. Isaac didn't bother to look, determined to be the first one of their haggard crew to sight a . . .

Crank.

The word came up like a demon from the depths of his mind, from the darkest parts. He'd not meant it when the thought formed, he'd just been eager to see another living human being, a sign of movement, any sign of life.

But *Crank* had formed in his mind, a word he associated with all the ills of the world, as clearly as if someone had carved it in the stone of his thoughts. It was an awful word, letters of the boogeyman, a sound that conjured images of bloodshot eyes and broken teeth and severed limbs—things that had been described to him but never seen. Still, he saw them. Somehow. In those dark parts of his mind from where the hideous word sprung.

Against all logic, he'd hoped to never come across such a creature in this new world. This new world to which he'd been taken by Kletter and her depressing boat. He was in less than a chipper mood, despite the obvious excitement of finally completing the vomit-fest of a voyage. He'd puked up enough half-digested food to feed a village of fish along the way, unhappily spewing it over the side railings once or twice a day. Of course, some of it had *been* fish.

He was cracking up. He needed to get off the damn boat, even if a welcome committee of hungry Cranks greeted them on the beach.

"Can you believe this?" Sadina said right in his ear, and for a half second he thought he'd leaped out of his own skin. "What if I'd told you a month ago that we'd be here? Back in the world."

Isaac tried to relax, uncomfortable with the fact that he was so jumpy. Like a premonition that nothing good would happen once they landed. Sadina plopped down next to him and squeezed her legs under the lowest railing, letting them dangle over the spray.

"You'll get wet," he deadpanned, as he was soaked from head to toe. "Might catch cold."

"Or the Flare," she said. "I hear that's a problem in these parts."

Isaac hadn't fully realized his uber-sour mood until that moment. He just felt like total crap, all the excitement of reaching their destination having drained into the passing water. So many dangers. Not only Cranks, but the stupid virus that *turned* them into Cranks! Who knew if they were immune. Kletter surely didn't. As smart as that lady acted and spoke, she seemed to have a hundred questions for every answer she dredged up. It didn't help matters that she was still having a hard time with her recovery.

"Come on, Isaac," Sadina said. "We're gonna land in a half hour or so and you're acting like it's the end of the world."

That got her a glare, and both of them knew she deserved it.

"Bad choice of words," she muttered, trying to hold back a smile. What the hell was she so happy about?

"Just nervous," he said. "Just anxious."

"Me, too. But excited. And scared. I wish we knew more."

They'd talked things to death over the two-week journey across the choppy sea, deciphering every bit of information from Kletter they could. But, mostly, their conversations consisted of guesses on top of more guesses. How many people were on the planet? How many of them were sick? Had the Flare mostly burned itself out? Were there any Cranks left, the walking nightmares of Isaac's childhood campfire stories? They couldn't blame Kletter too much for the lack of answers—she had lived a pretty isolated life, herself. That was the very definition of current human civilization, according to her. Life, isolated.

Isaac started to say something, hesitated, then spit it out. "I keep thinking about Cranks."

She didn't respond right away. The beach was only a kilometer or so in the distance now, the city behind it rising like the ugly teeth of a planet-sized god. The air smelled of salt and garbage and rot.

"I don't think we're going to find Cranks," she finally said. "Not like they were when our grandpappies and grandmammies barely escaped. I mean, it's not like those crazy people fell in love and had a bunch of babies. Not the ones . . . past the Gone or whatever. What's left are probably descendants of the few survivors or something different. Something in-between, I guess."

Isaac shivered with cold, and it wasn't just the water splashing upon the wind.

"Hell's bells," he whispered, having no idea what he meant.

But it seemed to fit the mood just right.

3

Kletter had been a crappy boat captain when they'd set sail, and she was a crappy boat captain when they "docked" at a long cement pier. The starboard side of the ship slammed into the pier then scraped along until sheer friction slowed them to a stop. Carson and Dominic had barely pulled their feet back before getting shortened for life, then recovered their wits and jumped onto the pier to tie them down. The whole escapade had put the fear of god in Isaac enough that he forgot about Cranks and viruses for a solid minute or two.

But then a silence like covered earth settled upon them, broken only by the soft lapping of the waves. A stillness, as well. For the first time in Isaac's life, and for most of the others, they were connected to the land of the "real" world. The one they'd been hearing about all their lives. The one that had been flushed down the latrine of apocalypse.

No one spoke. Kletter, a few pounds heavier than when she'd first arrived on the island, but still gaunt and pale and ill-looking, came out of the boat's cabin, a place she'd hardly left during the voyage. Without a word she walked to the edge of the craft and jumped the half-foot gap to the cement pier, which was laden with cracks, pitted like some beast with iron teeth had taken a chomping to it. She was shivering, and stood there on the pier for a minute or two, her head bowed, cupping her elbows in both hands as if to warm them. Isaac and his friends watched her, this strange new world become a church, waiting for her to start some ancient ceremony.

Old Man Frypan broke the reverence. "What're we waiting on, people? I gotta take my hourly piss and I'd like to use an actual tree on actual dirt."

Someone snickered, and to Isaac's shock he realized it had been Kletter herself.

She turned to them and said, "Come on, then. Trust me, not a soul on that boat is happier than I am to be back in North America. I'm gonna take a bath for three days and eat about seven cans of chili. And take a break from you people."

With that less-than-religious benediction, she started walking down the pier toward the land of their new life. Old Man Frypan was the first one to follow.

Then everybody, all at once.

4

"This was Los Angeles," Kletter said. "I mean, still is, I guess. City of Dead Angels."

They stood on a trash-strewn road, as cracked and worn as the pier. Abandoned chunks of metal and glass with four wheels—sometimes more, sometimes less—lay scattered like thrown toys wherever you looked. Cars. Trucks. Motorcycles. Bicycles. Isaac's parents and grandparents had described the old world to him ad nauseam, but that didn't lessen the impact of seeing it for *real*. Spectacular.

Buildings spiked the area, growing bigger and broader and taller the farther away from the beach they stood. All of them bore marks of abandonment, destruction, erosion, decay—countless broken windows, charred remains of fire, vegetation growing in places it had no business growing. In the distance, towered a majestic cluster of the main part of the city, impossible structures loomed over the land, their tips almost touching the . . .

"Skyscrapers," Isaac said. "Those are skyscrapers." It must've sounded dumb, but awe filled him top to bottom.

Ms. Cowan, Old Man Frypan, even Wilhelm and Alvarez—the two members of Congress who'd been convinced to come—were just as taken aback as the youngsters, mouths open but speechless.

Isaac glanced at his friends, enjoyed seeing their wonder.

Sadina and Trish, arm in arm, rotated in a slow circle, taking in the sights. Miyoko stared at one building in particular—a massive thing that looked like the arm of a god—as if she were determined to analyze each and every structure, one by one. Dominic stood inches from her, his eyes darting to all kinds of places, perhaps worried he might miss something grand. The west-siders who'd joined them, and become honorary east-siders in Isaac's opinion—Carson, Jackie, and Lacey—were no different in their awe. Carson in particular, giant of a man that he was, seemed to shrink into a wide-eyed child, given a room-full of toys. Jackie, absently running a hand down the length of her long braid of hair, also turned in a circle, trying to take in everything at once. Lacey, the shortest one of the bunch, had her arms folded in defiance, as if she refused to believe the city around them was actually real.

"This is insane," Trish whispered. "I can't believe my own eyeballs."

Dominic replied, "I can't believe your own eyeballs, either. Wow."

"How did a place like this even function?" Jackie asked. "All the people . . . I mean, I can't even imagine the logistics of . . ." Her voice trailed off.

Miyoko held her arms up to the sky then let them flop back down.

"Our grandparents held back on us. This is way cooler than I ever imagined."

Old Man Frypan perked up at that. "It's not like we were livin' the good life. The world had already gone to Hell in a bucket when we were kids. It wasn't like we wanted to sit around the fire and talk about the good ole days. The good ole days shat the bed long before I shat my first diaper."

Kletter let out a motherly sigh as if Dominic had made a fart joke. "I think we'd *all* be blown away if we could've seen it before the Flare. Imagine all those places filled with light, the air with music and car horns, people walking shoulder to shoulder, eating and laughing. I'd give my left foot for time travel."

Her conjuring of the past just made the present that much quieter and more empty. Besides the birds, besides the distant susurration of the ocean, besides the rustle of wind in the tree leaves, the city was a tomb.

"Are there any . . . people here?" Miyoko asked.

Cranks, Isaac thought. *She meant Cranks.*

Kletter sighed again; maybe that was just how the woman breathed. "We don't really know what happened here. A lot of flood damage, a lot of bones, a lot of nothing. But no people. They all died or left, I guess, decades ago. It's why my people set up camp on top of a mountain nearby. Seemed like we had the whole place to ourselves. Although it's not much of a place. You go to some cities, they actually have things like grocery stores and hospitals up and running. At least that's what we hear. That's not for us."

"What *is* for you?" Alvarez asked, a quiet fellow who hardly ever spoke.

Kletter cut him a glare that made Isaac think the man had said something wrong. "Sadina. *All* of you. Why in Earth's name do you think I just went through hell and back to get you people here? And . . ." She cut off abruptly and looked away. They all knew what she didn't have to say. She'd killed her own friends, associates, whomever they'd been, to accomplish the task of getting here with residents of the island in tow.

"Never mind," she finally said. "You all came by your own choice. You'll understand a lot more once we get to the Villa. It's about two days' hike from here."

Isaac and his friends spent a moment exchanging glances. No one said a word, but eyes attempted to communicate things, although Isaac wasn't quite sure *what*. The air had taken on an ominous, heavy feel, as if they'd been so preoccupied with getting off the ocean that the prospect of what awaited them had only just now occurred. That was, of course, far from the truth. Isaac had spent many sleepless nights wondering about the old world and the many terrors that resided there. And now, *there* was *here*.

Ms. Cowan spoke up. "We've spent our whole lives hearing about what happens to people who caught the Flare. Cranks, whatever you wanna call them. Do we have to worry about people like that leaping out of these dark buildings? Coming out of the sewers? Jumping out of trees?"

Those questions gave Isaac a shiver that started at his feet and shimmied itself all the way up to his shoulders. But he was glad someone finally put a voice to his fears. He wasn't the only one who looked at Old Man Frypan, his face a mask of mystery. What must *he* be thinking, the only one in their company who'd had the pleasure of hanging out with Cranks?

Kletter wearily shook her head. "You all think I'm a wealth of knowledge, don't you? I know maybe ten percent more about the world than you do, if that. But as far as I *do* know, in this city at least, Cranks are a thing of the past. I've never seen one. Not a single one."

"So we're safe," Dominic declared.

That made Kletter bark a laugh that echoed off the decayed walls of the closest buildings, and she went on laughing for a solid five seconds. Then the smile swept right off her face like she'd wiped it with a rag.

"You're not safe, boy," she said. "You're never gonna be safe again. Now let's get walking."

5

It was a long walk, through streets filled with trash and weeds; past buildings broken and crooked; under a sky that slowly darkened toward dusk. To Isaac, the rusted skeletons of old vehicles remained the starkest reminder that this place had once been inhabited by humans. Despite the rotted wheels and the broken glass and the faded paint, their purpose remained obvious—a carriage for people who no longer existed. Like hands and feet without a body to move them. The buildings took on a tableau of nature, as if they were mountains and hills and ridges of stone, their surfaces riddled with countless caves into the mysteries of the deep earth.

As they trudged their way along the filthy roads toward a rise of foothills scabbed with bushes and scrub oak, Isaac noticed pockets of odor that brought back the nausea of their sea voyage. Although he tried to deny it, he knew they were the smells of rotting bodies, the wet decay of flesh.

Animals, he thought, convincing himself. *Just animals. It's been too long for it to be . . . people.*

Cranks! his mind screamed at him.

This spurred him to ask a question, make people talk. He addressed the distinguished members of Congress, all of whom looked like three days of rough road, as his grandpa used to say.

"What made you guys do this?"

Ms. Cowan looked at him, a little dazed from daydreaming. "Do what?"

Isaac couldn't help his chastising expression, no matter her age. "*This*." He gestured at his friends, at the city. "Go against the other Congress folks and bring us on this trip."

Sadina's mom shrugged. "It was the right thing to do. Sonya, famous Sonya, was Sadina's paternal grandma. And Kletter says that means something important."

"We know that, Mom," Sadina piped in, "but there had to be something else. For all three of you."

Wilhelm was the oldest and crankiest of the three, the one who seemed most likely to have dreamed as a child about taking over the island and becoming dictator someday. So his reply surprised Isaac.

"I was sick of that place," the older, bald, tired, wrinkled man said. "I'll be honest with you all. I didn't care much about Kletter's reasons. I just wanted off that island, a chance to see the world. It was a prison to me. Always was."

"Same," Alvarez agreed, he of few words. "Same." He of one word, for the moment.

"What about you, Mom?" Sadina asked.

Ms. Cowan shrugged. "Maybe there was a little of that. Or a lot, I don't know. But if there's even a small chance that a few samples of your blood or whatnot can change the world for the better, we have to take it. And I know you agree with me, sweetie. It's not like we haven't talked this to death already."

Sadina only nodded, then gave her mom a quick side-hug.

"You'll all feel better soon," Kletter said. "If it makes you happy, when we reach the Villa, you can have a knife to my throat and slit it the moment you think you've been betrayed. You won't be. You'll finally know we did the right thing in coming back.

The Villa. At some point she'd started referring to her mythical compound with this fancy moniker, as if they should know what it meant.

Lacey surprised them all when she was the one to respond. "I'll do it. I'll have the knife to her throat." She shrugged. "Just in case, ya know."

Kletter smiled, a curiosity more rare than Lacey speaking. "Sounds like a good plan to me."

That kind of shut everyone up for a while.

6

They reached the steeper incline of the foothills.

Businesses and shops transitioned to once-bright, dilapidated homes, their yards gone rogue with hideous, choking weeds that could survive with little water. Each and every house looked haunted to Isaac. No one said much as they made their way through the creepy neighborhoods. If the others were like him, it took every breath just to get air to their lungs—not enough left over for talk. Two weeks of doing absolutely nothing on a boat is not an ideal exercise regimen, and he was really feeling the effects of it. The quick, deep breaths racing through his mouth and throat dried them to a desert landscape.

"Anyone got water left?" he asked in a rasp, the first person to have uttered a word in at least an hour.

"Aren't you sick of water after floating on it for two weeks?" Miyoko retorted.

Isaac gave her a look.

She did something with her face that kind of resembled a smile. "Yeah, I could use a drink, too."

"Let's take a break," Kletter pronounced. "We'll have a hot meal and plenty of water once we reach the Villa."

The Villa. It still sounded silly to Isaac. But the word "break" had never sounded so good, and he figured she could call her place whatever she wanted.

Backpacks slipped off shoulders; bodies collapsed to the ground in exhausted heaps. Isaac wandered a piece—as his mom used to say—and found a thick palm tree, its bark worn from the passage of time. He sat, propped his back against it, closing his eyes. A few seconds later, someone nudged him with a foot and he looked up at Sadina.

"You can have my last sip." She held out her thermos.

"Really?" The word felt like air blowing across sand.

She unscrewed the cap and held it out again. Isaac gladly took it and drank the sweetest swallow of cold liquid in his life.

"Thanks," he said with an intake of breath. "I was five minutes from death by dehydration."

"You're a softie is what you are. Don't worry, I am, too. Our parents should've trained us better in case we ever returned to live in the apocalypse. Before this trip, when was the last time you were hungry?" She flumped to the ground next to him; he handed the thermos back to her. She tipped it toward the sky and finished it off.

Isaac thought about it. "Sometimes I'd skip breakfast because I was so excited to work at the Forge every morning."

Sadina didn't dignify that with a response. Isaac glanced over at Kletter, who sat alone in the middle of the road, legs crossed beneath her, staring at a spot in the distance with no life in her gaze. He'd assumed in the beginning that they'd get to know her inside and out by the time their voyage on the sea came to an end. But the reverse had happened. She was more of an enigma than ever—more than she'd been on the day they'd helped drag her out of the ocean.

"Hey."

Isaac's thoughts froze inside his mind. Someone had uttered the word in a harsh whisper from behind his tree. It definitely hadn't been Sadina. Though fear tiptoed its way into the crevices of his brain, his rational side assumed it was somebody in their group. Casually, he leaned over and peered around the trunk of the ancient palm. No one. A quick look around revealed that everyone was in the road or on the other side. Out of easy earshot, anyway. The small trace of fear suddenly scratched a heavier tune on his heart.

"Did you hear that?' he whispered to Sadina.

She furrowed her brow then shook her head. "Hear what?" She had the awareness to speak in a voice just as quiet as his.

"I swear I heard someone say—"

"*Hey.*"

No mistake this time. Isaac jumped to his feet and leaned into the palm tree, using it as a shield as he searched the area on the other side. Sadina scrambled behind him, pressing against his back. The house in front of them had been a two-story home once, but the roof and most of the upper floor were missing, replaced by the dark remains of a fire that appeared somewhat recent. With the sun sinking ever closer to the horizon, the ruins of the structure and the wilderness of the yard were a grand festival of shadows. Whoever had spoken could be hiding anywhere.

"It couldn't have been a ghost," Sadina whispered directly into his ear. "Ghosts don't say, 'Hey.'"

He closed his eyes and reopened them in a long blink. "You think this is a joke?"

"Tell your people you want to explore the house," a disembodied voice said from somewhere in the yard, just loud enough to decipher. "I'll meet you inside. You need to hear what I have to say." There was a rustle of movement in the weeds and the dart of a shadow. The measured flurry of words from the intruder, the avuncular sound of them, made Isaac think it was an older man.

He turned and looked at the others. No one had heard. No one but Sadina.

"There's no way we go in that house," she said.

Isaac couldn't have agreed more. "So much for what Kletter told us. That guy might not be a Crank, but he's definitely a human!"

"Your ability to figure things out always amazes me. Come on, let's tell the others."

He grabbed her arm before she could move away from him. "Wait. Just . . . wait."

"Wait? We have to tell them."

Isaac had a burrowing rat of suspicion in his gut, and the worst part was that he didn't know its source. Kletter was a weirdo, no doubt, but they'd all thrown their lot in with her and traveled across the ocean itself to show their trust. But . . .

"I don't know," he whispered. "Just . . . this person appears out of nowhere and wants to meet us secretly? Suddenly I'm doubting everything."

"You've lost your mind. Because of some dude in the weeds."

He knew she was right—knew it before she'd even responded to what he'd said. He wanted to get as far away from that house as poss—

A rock landed with a thud next to him, thrown from the direction of the overgrown yard. It was wrapped with a piece of paper, tied in place with a bit of twine. Letters had been scrawled across the paper with something like charcoal, and done in a hurry by the messy looks of it.

"*What* is going on?" Sadina asked. She glanced over her shoulder at the others as if they'd been creeping up on the secret whispers.

Isaac was too busy untying the string to bother with an answer. It slipped loose easily; he spread the paper flat on a large, flat root jutting from the old palm tree. The mystery man was a fellow of few words like Alvarez, but his message came through loud and clear.

MEET ME OR THEY ALL DIE

This had gone too far. Isaac straightened up, pulled his backpack onto his shoulders, then cinched the straps until the whole thing felt a part of his body. All the while, stuck with holding the tossed rock in her hands, Sadina stared at him as if he'd turned into a stranger that she failed to comprehend.

"What now?" she asked, said with a hint that she expected an absurd answer.

"Now?" Isaac repeated. "Now we tell the others because this creepy guy is threatening us."

Sadina bent over and picked up the paper, then casually flipped it to show another message scrawled on the opposite side, in the same charcoaled, messy handwriting.

TELL ANYONE, THEY DIE
TWO FOR THE PRICE OF ONE!
NO, SERIOUSLY, MEET ME

"This jackass has a sick sense of humor," Sadina said, terse enough to scare the man if he somehow heard. "Let's go kill him and be done with it." But then, her face fell, the true reality of the situation hitting both of them at the same time.

Indecision melted Isaac's insides, making it impossible to move. And the fear was no longer tiptoeing. It had moved in and made itself comfortable, bolting its furniture to the floor.

"Come on," he whispered, barely able to speak. "What do we do?"

She nodded slowly at him as if considering, and the terror that had replaced the fake mirth in her eyes made him incredibly sad. “We don’t know what we’re dealing with, Isaac. We grew up in a happy little bubble on a fairy island. We have no idea how the real world works. I think we need to tell . . . ugh, I don’t know.”

“He said we’d die if we tell them.” Isaac tried to look casual, glancing around at the others, all of whom seemed in no hurry to ramp up again, not even Kletter. She was in a trance of exhaustion, staring dully at nothing, eyes wide and unfocused. “He said we’d die.”

“I know what the note says, Isaac.”

“Then what do we do?” He didn’t bother keeping the frustration out of his voice.

Sadina grabbed his hand and pulled him toward the fire-wrecked, weed-infested house into which the shadow had disappeared a few minutes earlier. Isaac resisted for half a second but then gave in, surrendering himself to her whim, trusting her more than himself. They crossed the cracked sidewalk, entered the yard, all kinds of dry vegetation swishing and grabbing at their legs. The house loomed, holes of darkness dominating the facade.

Isaac reassured himself. Tried to. If this man wanted to hurt them or kill them, there were easier ways to do it than luring them into a house with a hastily written note tied to a rock. Or maybe that’s exactly what a psychopath would do. They didn’t teach this in primary or secondary school on the island. His parents had never told him bedtime stories of what to do when a creepy old man threatens to kill all your friends.

“Where are you guys going?” Trish yelled from behind them.

“We wanna check out this cool haunted house!” Sadina replied, somehow making her voice as light as a holiday morning. She didn’t break her stride, continued to pull Isaac along. “What’re you, my mom?” she added, then made a weird howling sound. Her real mom, Ms. Cowan, had been asleep in a patch of grass for twenty minutes.

They reached the porch, or what had once been a porch. Now it was merely a mound of greenery, traces of faded red brick peeking through, the bare remnants of a wooden railing hanging precariously over the edge. The house had no door, only an open maw of black space, the frame of the threshold resembling an oval more than a rectangle. If it had been up to Isaac, they'd have stopped at the foot of the broken heap of porch steps, but Sadina didn't hesitate, leaping up them like a frog scaling the mossy stones of a waterfall. He followed, and braced himself for what waited inside the house. They went through the vacant doorway.

The floor creaked beneath them, each crack of wood seeming to unleash the smells of an ancient, abandoned tomb. Rot and decay. Dampness, the kind that never had or never would have a chance to dry, its moisture a recipe for grotesquerie. The scant light from the front door stretched Isaac's and Sadina's shadows across a dusty minefield of warped floorboards, an obvious set of footprints the only disturbance. The deep impressions ended on the other side of the room, where a tall, bulky man faced them, his back against the wall, his face hidden in the darkness.

Just the sight of him sprinkled a shower of terror over Isaac's skin.

"What do you want?" Sadina snapped. In his entire life, Isaac had never seen such bravery on display, and he swore to become more like his friend.

"You need to listen to me," came the reply. Whereas before they'd heard only a harsh whisper emanate from the stranger in the shadows, now it was the no-nonsense growl of someone who's lived ten lifetimes in one. "That lady you're following out there, you can't believe a word she says. She's the devil, and you're nothing but demon guinea pigs to her."

Isaac, from somewhere—maybe inspired by Sadina's performance—grasped on to a spout of courage. "We're supposed to believe you? The guy who was just bragging he'd kill every last one of us if we didn't come in here?"

"I had to get you inside, somehow," the man replied, a little too jauntily for Isaac's liking. "Give me a break, boy. You know how many ways I could've killed you once you stepped through that door? The bare fact you're alive and speaking is all the trust in me you'll ever need."

Sadina wasn't having it. "We should leave. This conversation is getting stupider by the second."

It was the phrase "guinea pigs" that kept Isaac still. It seemed so . . . certain, such a specifically chosen term. And the stranger had a point —why lure them in here just to talk gruffly and act spooky?

"Just tell us what's going on," Isaac said. "Who is Kletter, and if she really is the devil then why're you bothering to warn us? Why do you care? Tell us why she killed those eight people on the boat."

He didn't respond.

Isaac turned to Sadina. "Just say it. Do *you* trust Kletter?"

"No. Yes. Well my mom trusts her and I trust my mom. So yes. Mostly."

Isaac sighed.

"You don't have a choice but to trust me," the man growled.

"Step into the light," Sadina added. "I'm sick of talking to a ghost."

The shadow walked forward, with all the confidence in the world that he had nothing to be afraid of by revealing himself. With each step creaking on the floorboards, wafting up dust, Isaac watched as the light slowly maneuvered itself up the man's body. Black boots, dirty denim pants, a rough-cut plaid shirt, then a face only a mother could love. He was a gigantic man, well over six feet tall, heavily built, and ugly as a mildewed stump. Scraggly beard; tilted nose; pockmarked skin, red and leathery; eyes that seemed hammered deep into his skull; long greasy hair that had gone beyond needing a wash, something only a sharp blade could defeat.

"That better?" the man asked. "Are you ready to listen?"

Isaac looked at Sadina but she didn't take her eyes off the newly revealed stranger.

"What's your name?" she asked.

The man folded his apelike arms, which made his muscles bulge all the more against the plaid-printed material of his shirt. "It's Timon. We don't have time for this get-to-know-you nonsense. Your friends aren't gonna last another five minutes before they come in here after you."

"Fine, then talk," Isaac said, not believing for a second that the man's name was actually Timon. Timon? Really? His name had to be Slayer. "What did you call us in here for?"

The man replied tersely. "Have you heard of the Godhead? Do you know anything about them? Has she . . . has Kletter talked about them?"

Isaac opened his mouth but no words came out. Godhead? He did remember her mentioning that word before, but that was it. Easy to forget amidst a life-changing sea voyage.

"Like in the Bible?" Sadina asked. "Never read it."

"No I'm not talking about the damn Bible," the man shot back. "What has Kletter . . ." He stopped, rubbed his bearded face, visibly shaken with uncertainty. "Listen. You need to come with me, right now. Out the back door, away from that woman. We can get help and we can save your friends later. If you don't even know what the Godhead is, then we're about twenty steps behind the mule."

"Isaac? What's going on?"

It was Kletter, her voice like a crack of thunder without lightning, right behind them. Isaac swung around, filled with a suspicion that had no justification, based only on a few words from a man they'd never met. But he felt a wash of terror at her sudden intrusion, with a stab of guilt. She stood silhouetted in the light of the doorway, appearing taller than she'd ever seemed before, thicker, a malign presence without a face.

He searched for words. "We . . . uh . . ."

Something slipped over his head, cloth, black, cutting off his vision. It cinched around his throat and then he was being jerked backward, toward the spot where Timon had been standing. A stifled yell escaped his lips, swallowed in the scratchy material that pulled against his mouth and nose, making it hard to breathe. Then the world tilted, darkness spiraling on darkness, and his back slammed against the floor with a thud that thrummed through his bones. He heard a muffled shriek from Sadina, a thump, and knew she'd met the same fate as he had.

"What—" he started to yell, but a hand as hard as iron clamped against his mouth, pressed against his teeth. He kicked out with his legs, tried to squirm away from that grip, but other hands had him by the arms, pushing down on his chest, others now squeezing him by the ankles, holding him in place as if he were about to have a limb amputated without numbing herbs. Where had all these people come from? It was as if the undead had risen through the floorboards, as if . . .

CRANKS! the terrified voice inside his mind screamed. But he knew, he *knew* that wasn't it. This was too measured, too . . . *planned* to be the nightmare crazies that had haunted his grandparents' people. Flooded with fear, he finally seized upon his own instincts and forced himself still, forced himself to wait for an opportunity to understand what was happening, an opportunity to resist. He lay under the pressure of those holding him, swathed in darkness and the cold ice of terror. The room had grown silent.

There were footsteps, the creaks of the floorboards coming closer to his head. A new voice, one he didn't recognize, a woman's, sounded from nearby. She said two words, as laced with dread as the drip-drip-drip of liquid from a corpse.

"She's gone."

Someone grabbed Isaac by the arms and started dragging him across the floor. It was a bumpy ride.

CHAPTER SEVEN

A Cold Cliff

I
MINHO

K*it.* The boy, Kit. The boy he'd saved from his savage father. (Uncle? Stranger? Didn't matter.) The boy was all the Orphan could think about, for days and weeks, even now as he'd marched into the middle of nowhere with priests and priestesses of the almighty Cure.

The group—old and young, all who deserved to see—stood in the midst of a snowstorm, although the snow more resembled sharp, pointy pellets of ice flying through the air like small bullets. The only reason the group as a whole hadn't been sliced and sheared by the flying pricks of ice-blades was because the wind howled incessantly, in both strength and direction. The frigid air with its accompanying bites of hard snow swam in great circles around them, shifting up and down and out and back, never gaining the fierce impetus needed to damage and cut.

The Orphan thanked the Cure for small favors, no matter how tiny and very unlike an actual favor they were. He had bands of leather fastened, tightly, around his upper arms, his wrists, his thighs, his ankles. Bound tightly enough to warp the natural contour of his muscles and nerves and tissue with great pain, burning like a microscopic flow of lava had leaked into the tiny spaces between his cells. Together with the harsh environment it inflicted a great, searing discomfort that would make him a better man, a better servant, a better participant in the troubles to come. Which suited him fine.

Kit.

Saving Kit had changed something deep inside Minho. No, not changed. *Completed.* He squirmed his arms and legs, seeking comfort against the bindings. Yes, completed.

Each band of leather was attached to a long wooden pole, themselves banded in iron every few inches along its length to make them strong, unbreakable. At the opposite ends of those iron-bound spears of wood, which poked away from him in all directions like the spikes of an injured porcupine, stood a Bearer of Grief, the Orphan's masters. These Grief Bearers were so named from the Grievers of old, the menacing monstrosities of machine and flesh that had terrorized the people of the Maze. It was symbolic . . . or some such absurdity. The only thing the Orphan knew for certain was that he'd been chosen to wander the wilderness at least three years ahead of schedule, and that he'd be the one bearing all the grief known to this pocket of the world for the foreseeable future. His life was about to become pain-defined, pain-manifested in all its many, dastardly, excruciating, demonic forms. Or maybe that was a bit dramatic.

Wandering. Pain. Hunger. Forty days and forty nights. That was expected of him, though he had different plans in mind.

Was he ready? Was he scared? Did he fear failure? Minho of old would have answered yes to all of these questions, and now he did, too. Yes. I am Minho, and I am ready, I am scared, and I fear failure. So let's kick some ass, shall we? I am the Orphan. I am the Orphan with no name, named Minho. That's who I am. Someday, perhaps, Kit would grow up to be proud of him.

"Wrap him tight, for Flare's sake," one of the Grief Bearers said in a harsh, spiteful voice that gave something away about the man's day so far. He'd been the Bearer of Grief to the Orphan for many a year, and Minho knew his moods and peculiarities, his eccentricities, his proclivities. Griever Glane had been denied his sweet delights the prior evening, spurned by those he didn't think capable of spurning him. He'd be a grouch of sadistic extremity this day. He was always a grouch, but in the hours ahead, he'd take it to new levels of hateful debauchery.

The Orphan was ready. Scared. He feared. Time to go.

Shadows approached, moving shadows mostly obscured by the heavy blizzard that swelled over their imaginary dome of life. Those shadows were acolytes—priests and priestesses to the Cure, cloaked in the sacred weaves of the rough and scraping vines that purportedly descended from the sanctified vines of the Maze itself. It was a cloth, of sort. That was the nicest way the Orphan could bring himself to describe the long, rough-hewn drapes of material in which they intended to wrap him. Wrap him up head to toe, leaving not a centimeter of his parts exposed to the harsh elements of the plains.

Once he became a caterpillar in its cocoon, hoping to someday break out and fly, the acolytes would use the iron-bound lengths of wood—still attached to the leather shackles on his arms and legs—to move him to his destined location. No one knew where that might be. Literally no one. Even the Great Master in the Golden Room of Grief did not know where the Orphan secretly named Minho would be sent. But he would be sent all the same, and when the acolytes found the spot, they would leave him there to wander for forty days and forty nights. To return as a Bearer of Grief, himself.

Also, no one knew how exactly one was supposed to survive such a nefarious task. Some didn't.

Minho honestly didn't give a Flare's barnacle, anymore. He just wanted this madness of a ceremony to be over with. He had a dark secret hidden within his soul and mind and psyche that no necromancer of the most devious dark art could ever compel Minho to reveal. Like a seed that takes a hundred years to sprout, needing little water, little sun, little care, but eventually grows into its purpose. This would be the Orphan, nameless, named Minho.

When his seed sprouted, it would grow to the ends of the earth, digging its roots to the deepest parts of bedrock, and raising its limbs sky-high to create a canopy of endless green, covering the four corners of the world. This was all a metaphor, of course. The real intention was simple and as plain as the sun being eclipsed by an enlarged moon.

The Orphan, Minho by name, had decided that destroying the Godhead—the very reason for the Remnant Nation's existence—was a terrible idea. Evolution was progress. It shouldn't be stopped. By definition, it *couldn't* be stopped.

No, his ultimate desire and purpose was not to destroy the Godhead.

It was to join them.

Minho didn't resist or complain as the priests and priestesses began draping the coarse cloth of the vine around his body and all its parts, cinching and pulling and tying along the way, pulling no punches—as Griever Glane would say—or showing the slightest regard for his discomfort.

The Orphan looked into the future like the ancient seers of old.

The farther he reached, the more unbearable the pain. But it would all be worth it. If nothing else, he couldn't wait to stop thinking in these ridiculous, sanctimonious metaphors. Thinking of Kit, the life he'd extended, brought him peace.

The acolytes completed their task. Rough, thorny threads now encased his entire body, woven into a tight tapestry that would both protect him from the worst of nature's weapons while also keeping him humble. The cocoon of cloth needled and bit and scratched and bothered. It sucked, one might say.

"Take him," Griever Glane said, his voice muffled by the holy canvas that covered the Orphan's ears. But did he detect a hint of sadness in the man's words? "Take him to the edge, and be gentle enough. I know this boy. He won't resist." The old man clapped the Orphan on the shoulder. "Next time I see you, son, we'll be peers. Be tough, and remember what you've been taught. If you come back with the Flare, you'll be executed. May the Cure watch over you."

It was almost comical. Almost. But it fed the Orphan's desire for a new destiny.

The strong hands that gripped the other ends of the guiding poles began to force him forward. Pushing, pulling, swiping, his guides moved him away from the fortress he'd protected for so many years, across the empty plain where one met a death sentence if they approached from the opposite direction. When he and others like him returned, it was through a path known to only a few, a secret more guarded than the identity of the Great Master in the Golden Room of Grief. The Great Master, whom no one had ever seen.

Forward, forward they marched, the Orphan not resisting, moving as elegantly as he could along the trail his guides set. The wind whipped, the icy pellets of sleet bounced off of his rough, woven armor, making a sound like war drums. No words were spoken. The cloth pressed against his nose smelled of freshly dug earth, the deepest grave, still waiting for a body to call it home.

He marched forward, forward, the guiding poles chafing his skin.

Hours later, they reached the edge, the very edge, to which they guided him carefully. The Orphan could feel its stony threshold under the balls of his feet. The wind was stronger than ever here; he felt as if he could lean into it without fear of falling. They'd have to give him a really strong push. Even as he thought this—with something close to giddiness—the acolytes unfastened the poles from the leather belts that still were like vices around his arms and legs. Once those were freed, unleashing waves of pain as blood gushed within his veins, he sensed the priests and priestesses line up behind him. He continued to face the abyss.

"Any words before you depart?" one of them asked.

Beetles of fear scurried across his skin, as if they'd burrowed beneath the cloth that wrapped him so tightly. This was the moment that began his future, a future unlike the ones his Bearers of Grief envisioned. He quoted the litany of calm in his mind, a device that still worked despite his blasphemy.

"Eh?" a woman shrieked across the wind. "Want to say something, lad?"

The Orphan spoke as loudly as he was physically able.

"Yes! Long live the Cure, and may She bless my path! May I wander for forty days and forty nights and return a Bearer of Grief in Her service! May the Godhead die, and the Cure rule the earth for evermore!" *And may you all go to Hell*, he added in his mind. *I, the Orphan called Minho, will never return.*

Hard hands pushed him from behind, and he fell over the edge.

Thoughts of Kit gave him wings.

2
ALEXANDRA

She sat in the quiet dark of her room, drinking a strong tea, urging the panic that threaded through her veins to unweave, to leave her with some semblance of peace. This was a problem that could be dealt with, and she already had several plans of action lined up inside her mind. However, this very second, there was nothing she could literally do to make those happen any faster, and she tried, tried very hard, to allow herself some measure of respite.

But that peace refused to come, even after going through the digits. Images of the Coffin—the artifact taken from the Box by Mikhail—continued to flash across her vision, as if it floated in front of her, an inexplicable thing that stirred up her ancient terror of madness. A terror so deep-set that it often made her worry that she'd go mad from it. Oh, the circular logic, the irony.

She stood up and walked to the sink and poured out the remains of her bitter tea. It tasted like the bile of a starving, emaciated beast. Something stronger. That's what she needed. Something stronger that would scorch her throat, warm her stomach, deaden her brain.

There was a knock at her door.

"Flint?" she called out. In how many ways could she tell the man that she didn't want to be disturbed? Was it time to throw a little violence in? It had been a while . . .

The door opened—she heard the barest of creaks, the swish of the bottom rail against the thick carpet. Violence. Yes, violence. Her anger ignited, she marched out of the kitchen and entered the main hallway of her apartment, ready to unleash all the frustrations of her day on to poor Flint. But it wasn't Flint.

"Nicholas?" She barely recovered in time, barely dissolved her anger and rage and haste. Citing the digits within her mind, calmness spread through her like a quick shot of drugs. But if anyone could perceive . . .

"Why so agitated?" Nicholas asked.

Though most people probably imagined the First of the Godhead to be an enormous, imposing, powerful, frightening giant of a man, he was very average, in every way. Medium height, medium build, neither handsome nor ugly. He never smelled particularly good, but he didn't really stink, either. Some whispered that Nicholas had Evolved so far as to read the minds of others. She highly doubted such a thing, but she'd also watched her thoughts like straying servants lately when he was around.

"Why so silent?" Nicholas asked when she didn't respond. He always exuded so much patience that it made her want to punch a wall.

The truth, she thought. *For now, the truth.*

"Agitation and silence are the least of my worries," she said. "Don't come in here and insult my intelligence and ask your clever questions. Why did you do it?"

Nicholas pinched his lips together, forming an expression that almost implied admiration. "Good way to start. I didn't think we'd get here for at least a half hour."

"Why?"

"Because it's time. You know it's time. We have to take the next step or the worst thing that could possibly happen to us and our people and this world will happen. You know this and it's asinine to argue about it." He walked past her, brushing her shoulder, then entered the living room and flopped himself down on the couch. At the same time, it was both ungodly and the most condescending thing he could do to her. "Come and sit. Let's have the requisite argument before you finally admit that I'm right as usual and we move forward."

Alexandra closed her eyes, ran through the digits again, this time reciting them at a slower pace. She'd learned from experience with Nicholas to battle patience with patience, calm with calm, indifference with indifference—that was the way to gall him.

A minute or two passed in silence. Then Alexandra sauntered back into the kitchen, where she poured herself a glass of water. She didn't do the same for Nicholas. *Let him get his own damn drink if he's so all-powerful.* After heading into the living room with her glass, she sat on a chair as far away from her visitor as she could. She took a sip. Then another. She said nothing.

"Well?" he finally asked. "Aren't you going to say something?"

Victory.

"No. I'm just waiting for you to explain yourself. I'm ready when you are."

Nicholas straightened his posture a bit, crossed his legs. "It's been over thirty years since the Evolution, Alex. We've accomplished all that we possibly could accomplish, and we've set things up exactly how we planned. It's time to move on. It's time to Evolve the others. You can't possibly disagree with this. What else is the point of everything we've done?"

Alexandra took another sip. "Did you come here on your fancy Berg?"

"Why does that matter?" He sighed and took an extra-long blink. "Is that what this is? You're jealous because I have a Berg that actually works?"

"Can you utter even one sentence without condescension? That's always your first thought—that we're jealous or hiding in closets wishing we could be more like you. That's not the case, Nick old boy. I have what I need and I have what I want. When you have everything you want, you literally don't want anything. Does this concept make sense to you?"

His face flushed with anger, something he'd never allow to happen by accident. She was pushing her luck, and she relished it.

"The reason I asked about your Berg," she continued, "is because I want to know where you've been. It's been almost three months since Mikhail or I have seen you. *Where* have you been?"

"I've been away. I've been planning. I've been scouting. I've been spying. We have some pretty nasty enemies in case you've forgotten, but we also have many, many potential source communities. It's time. The next wave needs to Evolve, and the Godhead needs to take its proper place—you know, on top of the heap. I'd be happy to hear your arguments otherwise. Go."

He pointed at her and settled deeper into the couch, as if getting comfortable to hear a long dissertation that he already planned how to repudiate. His look of ultimate confidence had fully returned.

Alexandra stared at him, unmoving. She'd had such a great plan, devised over many years to take place over many years. This turn of events had surprised her, utterly. She hadn't the slightest notion that Nicholas was ready to remove the Coffin from the Box, much less do it without consulting one of his partners in the Godhead. Relying on every single element of the Flaring discipline she'd ever learned, she ran through calculation after calculation in her mind, reaching out to multiple futures and branchings of those futures, analyzing the possibilities and their respective probabilities. She could still do this. Despite the enormous disruption, she could still do this.

"I need an answer, Alex. We need to move on this."

As the arrogant bastard spoke the words, she continued to look at him without looking, her mind expanded to the very reaches of her ability. Her great, magnificent ability. And then, like a thousand gears of a giant machine rotating, grinding into action, it all fit together.

"Okay," she said.

After that, she went to her room without another word, shutting the door behind her. Eventually, he left.

3
JACKIE

She'd finally started feeling comfortable around Kletter and the other old people—most of them having made the leap from suspicious creepers to sketchy acquaintances—when all hell broke loose. She'd had a good rest. Her legs feeling like pounded meat from all that walking—*after* all that sitting on a boat—she'd been slouched next to Carson and Lacey for at least a half hour in complete silence. Carson was asleep, his head leaned back against a tree, mouth open, snoring just loud enough to be heard. Just loud enough to be annoying. Lacey sat with her legs crossed under her, picking at the sparse grass, lost in her thoughts as usual.

There'd been a little commotion. Isaac and Sadina went to explore an old house that looked as haunted as Peak's Graveyard back on the island, then Trish had yelled at them and been ignored. When Kletter herself jogged over to the dilapidated front porch and climbed up the rickety steps, through the tilted doorway, into the darkness, Jackie first wondered what in the world was going on. She didn't have long to ponder before several alarming sounds erupted from that twisted mouth of the house.

A shout; a scream; more shouts—muffled, this time—all words indecipherable.

Jackie leaped to her feet, smacking Carson's shoulder on the way up. He grunted, flinched, started to say something, but Jackie was already on the run, following Lacey, who'd somehow beat her to the punch. But in front of all of them was Trish, sprinting pell-mell as if an expanding sinkhole collapsed behind her every step. Others joined the rush toward the house—Miyoko, Dominic, Old Man Frypan, everyone—the air suddenly pulled taut like cloth, making it hard to breathe.

Carson yelled her name from behind. She ignored him, tried to catch up with Lacey. They were in the yard now, weeds grabbing at their ankles. Trish cleared the steps of the porch with one jump but then ground to a halt right before the yawning maw of the doorway.

Lacey stopped just short of the porch, Jackie right next to her. Ms. Cowan, Frypan, that old bald dude she didn't much care for—they all gathered there in seconds, watching Trish's back, which had gone rigid. Then someone stepped out of the house.

Kletter.

A soon-to-be-dead Kletter.

The woman's eyes were wide, the whites of them like full moons partially eclipsed by round shadows. Her skin was slick with sweat, her lips as pale as a pig's underbelly. And her neck . . . that was the bad part. The really bad part. It had been slashed with something sharp, from one side to the other like a necklace, and blood poured down the front of her body in gushes.

Trish had stepped back on instinct and now lost her balance, falling butt-first and crashing through the rotted bottom step. Above her, Kletter collapsed to her knees with a terrible double thump, then fell forward, the smack of her face against the wood one of the worse sounds Jackie had ever heard. She lay still and no one stirred for a horrible moment that stretched beyond any sense of rational time. Then everyone was moving at once.

Lacey grabbed Trish under the arms and helped her get back up. She'd barely gained her feet before shooting back up the porch again, jumping over Kletter's body like it was nothing more than a stray log. Sadina. Thoughts of her could be the only thing in Trish's world in that moment. Jackie was too stunned to process it all at first, but then recovered herself. Isaac and Sadina both had gone in there and now Kletter was dead.

"Trish!" she yelled, already in motion. "Trish get out of there!"

But it was too late. Lacey had already gone after her, then Ms. Cowan, shrieking with despair, then several others. Jackie followed them, avoiding a direct look at Kletter's grisly remains as she side-stepped the body. When she crossed the threshold and entered the dark gloom of the interior, it took a second for her eyes to adjust. But before she could see that the room was empty—no people, no furniture, nothing—she heard the cries of Trish shouting Sadina's name.

Over and over, *Sadina, Sadina, Sadina*, growing louder and softer as Trish ran through every inch of the house, coming and going, finally leaving out a back door, searching the swath of dusty hardpan and weeds in the small yard. Ms. Cowan trailed her, fraught but silent.

"Sadina!" Trish screamed. "Sadina!"

Dominic shouted Isaac's name through cupped hands. Miyoko and Carson were peeking over the run-down fences, searching for signs.

Jackie's mind had slowly been growing numb, unable to comprehend the horror that had descended upon them. She seemed unable to move.

"What's going on?" she whispered, knowing it was too soft to be heard over the commotion. Old Man Frypan stepped up to her, gently placed a hand on her shoulder, squeezing it as if he'd been her grandpa all along. She expected him to say something, but he didn't. There was no need for words.

Bad people had come. Bad people had killed Kletter. Bad people had taken their friends.

Sadina and Isaac were gone.

And the only person who knew how to sail The Maze Cutter back home—back *home*—was dead.

CHAPTER EIGHT

Story by Oil Lamp

I
ISAAC

He didn't understand.

He . . .

He didn't understand.

What had happened? He remembered the cloth on his face, on his ears, on his head, wrapped tightly and roughly around his neck with a cord. He remembered the bumps and thumps of being dragged, then the stomach-tilting whirl of being lifted from the ground, thrown across someone's shoulder. And then he'd felt it—a prick, a little stab of something sharp. Then the world had faded just as he felt his captor begin to run.

His eyes were still closed and he couldn't open them. But his thoughts lifted out of the haze.

How? How had they been taken so easily, taken before his friends could come to the rescue? Kletter had been there; surely the others had been right behind her. The man named Timon was by himself. Or . . .

there had been another . . . a woman . . . he'd heard her voice. And the ones who'd carried him away.

It was a blur. His head hurt. Why couldn't he open his eyes? Why did he feel nothing solid, as if he floated in the middle of a dark and warm ocean? What had happened? Who had taken them?

He didn't understand.

He slipped away from consciousness once again.

2

It was a light that brought him back, this time. A bright one, piercing his eyelids as if they were made of stretched wool. He blinked them open, squinting into the white brilliance. It disappeared, replaced by a man's face. An ugly, bearded, pockmarked face. Even though the light had messed with Isaac's vision, he could tell that much, at least.

"Bless me," the ugliness said. "It's like you people have never been given a drug in your life. Knocked you out cold."

Isaac groaned. He tried to say something but coughed instead.

The man jerked back and sat on his haunches. "Hooboy. Get this man a mint. He smells like Gilgamesh's vomit."

Isaac rolled on to his side, groaning again; it felt like he'd been asleep for three days, every inch of him drenched with weariness. And his head pounded, right behind the eyeballs. His mind swam through the weariness, trying to break the surface. He felt the alarm of being taken, felt the panic, but it was dull and distant, like a throb in his ankle. Until he remembered Sadina.

He sat up, a sweet explosion of pain rocking his head, followed by a spill of nausea.

"Where is she?" he sputtered. "Where is she!"

"I'm here, Isaac."

He looked to his right and saw her, sitting on a chair. They were inside, in a room of a house, although it was too dark to decipher any details. He breathed a deep sigh of relief.

"You two must be close." A woman's voice, spoken from a corner draped in shadow. Isaac thought he made out a folded set of arms, the rest of the body leaning against the wall. "At least you're together in this."

"Tell him what you told me," Sadina said. Her voice sounded awfully steady for someone who'd been kidnapped with a bag over her head. "I'd love to hear it again, myself."

The woman stepped forward, coming into the scant source of light, which Isaac now realized was a small oil lamp sitting next to the ugly giant of a man they'd met at the start of all this. His partner came closer and squatted next to Isaac.

"My name is Leticia." She had skin somewhere between dark and light, brown eyes, brown hair cinched up into a ponytail. Her long-sleeve shirt had a warped picture of the moon on it. "But Timon here calls me Letti. You can call me Letti, Isaac. That's how good of friends we're going to be. The others have gone on ahead of us, but you'll meet them later."

Timon. That was it.

"You drugged us," Isaac said. "Put a bag over my head and dragged me out of a house. Doesn't seem the best way to start a friendship."

"That's exactly what I said!" Sadina shouted. Then she laughed, and Isaac wondered if she was still drugged.

The woman named Letti eased herself into a sitting position then pulled a small, round container out of her front pocket. She snapped off the lid and pulled out a white pill, offering it to Isaac with a smile.

He raised his eyebrows. "Really? You like me better when I'm knocked out?"

"It's a mint. Timon said you needed a mint. I agree with his opinion. You need a mint."

Isaac glanced over at Sadina, who said, "I think you're fine. If they wanted to kill us we'd have been dead by now."

He took the white pill, sniffed it, smelled peppermint. "Sorry, lady, but where we come from we don't have fancy white pills for bad breath." He threw it into the darkest corner of the room. "Maybe just move back a few feet if you can't handle it."

She scooted back a full pace from him, her expression one of amusement.

"Am I dreaming?" he asked. "This is not the way I expected it to go the first time I was ever kidnapped by somebody. What the hell is going on?"

"We're not your enemies," Letti answered. "You have absolutely no reason to be scared of us. You'll notice you're not tied up or anything. And, like your friend said, it would've been a lot easier to kill you than bring you here. You'd still be in that house where you met Timon, in fact. Kind of like Kletter."

"Kletter? What'd you do to Kletter?" He had a vague memory of a woman saying, "She's gone" after the coarse bag had been slipped over his head.

Letti didn't answer right away, her eyes drifting toward the floor.

"They killed her," Sadina said. "Slit her throat judging by the gurgle sound I heard right next to me."

"Kletter is a very bad person." This came from Timon's rolling thunder of a voice, now sitting with his back against the wall near Sadina. "She's dedicated her life to bringing down the Godhead, and she'd use you up like a roll of toilet paper to get her way. The woman is vicious and doesn't know the meaning of the word *compromise*."

"Don't you mean *was*?" Isaac asked. "She *was* a very bad person?"

Timon didn't appear ashamed. "Yes, that's exactly what I meant. We weren't going to kill her, until she came barreling into that house. Listen . . ." The man leaned forward, focusing his intense gaze on Isaac. "We had to save you from her. We had to *stop* her. This wasn't a situation where we could do our best and see what happens. There was only one acceptable path, and she got in the way at the wrong time. I'm sorry she manipulated you, I'm sorry she killed those people on the boat, but I'm *not* sorry she's dead."

Sadina stood up, then sat back down, too frustrated to sit still but with nowhere to go. This eased Isaac a bit—they weren't restrained, and neither of their captors moved a muscle when Sadina got up from the chair. Maybe they had a chance to escape, or would have that chance soon.

"You really think you're doing the right thing, don't you?" Isaac said. "You think you're so right that Sadina and I are going to go along without being forced."

"That's exactly spot on," Letti said. "But don't you want to hear what the thing is?"

Isaac took a second to look at each person in the room. "Not really. At least one of you is a murderer and both of you are kidnappers. Can we go, now?"

Timon stood up. It seemed like he kept standing up and standing up for a full five minutes because he was so tall and bulky. He groaned a time or two like a grandpa getting out of bed. He walked over to where Isaac still sat on the ground, standing in front of the oil lamp like a solar eclipse, his face masked in shadow.

"Do we really have to get tough?" the man asked. "Do we really need to be the bad guys, here, and tie you up and keep drugging you and drag you all the way to Alaska? Is that what you want? Because we don't wanna, but we will. You understand me? We *will*." He folded his giant arms to emphasize the point.

"Alaska?" Sadina said. "You didn't say anything about Alaska. Isn't that kinda far from here?"

Letti answered with one word. "Very."

"Can someone just tell me what's going on?" Isaac asked. "Mr. Timon, sir, I don't really want you to beat me up or drag me in a sack again, but I'd at least like to know why you want to take me and my friend all the way to Alaska. I've looked at maps, before, you know."

Timon grumbled something under his breath and went back to his place by the wall. He seemed like someone who was tired of dealing with his own kids and had given up. When he plopped back to the floor the house shook as if struck by an earthquake.

"Listen to me," Letti said. Isaac returned his attention to her—she seemed nice and was a lot smaller than her partner. "Alaska is our home. It was one of the most stable places after the sun flares and near the south coast is a huge, functional, safe city. A lot of that we owe to the Godhead. They've saved us from the worst of the apocalypse this world went through, and we are sworn to our last drops of blood to serve them. And they need you. Well, more specifically, they need to keep you from Kletter's people." She sighed in frustration and rubbed her forehead with both hands. "It's a very long story."

"You're caught up," Sadina said. "I woke up a half hour before you and they talked the entire time and I still don't know anything."

Letti stood up and paced the room for a few seconds then stopped at a point where she could easily look at both Isaac and Sadina. "You're both smart alecks but I guess that's the way with young people, isn't it?"

She didn't sound angry at all, just defeated. The whole situation had taken on an air of absurdity to Isaac.

"Why don't you start from the beginning," he said. "That's what my . . . my dad used to say. We're not going to try anything with Timon the Gentle Giant sitting over there."

Timon grumbled under his breath again. Oddly enough, Isaac didn't feel threatened by the man despite his size. Maybe it was the drugs still coursing through his system.

"He's right," Sadina added. "Just tell us. *Tell* us. And if it sounds halfway promising we'll go find our friends and go with you to Alaska and this wonderful city full of gods without having to be dragged there."

Isaac perked up at that, not realizing that was a viable option at the moment. But he stayed quiet—he didn't want to impede the chance of hearing the story behind these two strange people.

Letti nodded her head a few times, as if considering Sadina's words. Then she started talking.

"The Evolution began thirty years ago . . ."

CHAPTER NINE

Crossing Paths

I
MINHO

The Orphan walked.

He didn't know a human could walk this much without his feet or legs falling off, or both. He didn't know a human could be so hot and so cold within the same day, or that a human could be hungry and thirsty enough that he considered devouring one of his own hands for the meat and blood. But he knew, now. Every inch of him wanted to go back to his people—to the monotony, the food, the schedule, the safety. He missed his shifts atop the wall, searching the horizon for intruders that rarely came. Even all the sanctimonious metaphors. He missed saving kids from savage beatings.

He wondered, often, about the boy. About Kit. It was very possible that Minho had made life worse for him, that maybe dying would've been the merciful route. But he avoided those lines of thought, imagining instead that Kit would grow up and do something great. Someday. Yes, definitely. Someday.

Sleet and rain had turned into sunshine and heat. He'd been across a vast plain, through a dusty canyon, up and down a mountain. He'd eaten berries, leaves, the remains of a recently deceased deer, joining the birds and the rats in their feast. It had been quite the task to keep it down, to keep it from coming back up—but then what a waste. After such a degrading, disgusting meal, he didn't want it to be for naught. He'd maintained, eaten more, accepted the nourishment.

Water had finally arrived, in the form of creeks and rivers that had been sparse the first couple of days. Whenever he quenched his thirst, slaked by the cool glory of natural streams or pools, it only served to remind him how hungry he was. There'd been only one dead deer in his week of wandering the wilderness. *Walking* the wilderness. However, contrary to the expectations of the Grief Bearers and acolytes back home, he walked in one direction without turning back.

West. To the ocean, to the shore. Then he'd head north, knowing there'd be no stray path from that point on. The sea to the left, land to the right, up and up until you run into the place called Alaska.

Home of the Godhead.

Being an Orphan had trained him to be patient and tough. The journey might take months for all he knew. Probably would, in fact. He didn't fear it. He feared nothing.

A building, up ahead.

This made him stop. Unsurprisingly, he'd come across few signs of civilization so far, and those obviously abandoned for years if not decades. Burnt-out vehicles, weed-infested farms, the hulk of slouching towers and rusted machinery, most of them a grand mystery as to their original purpose. The western part of the country was known for its vast open spaces, no area more than the one through which he'd been slogging. He'd yet to see another person, living or dead, not even so much as a skeleton.

And now, this building. A house. Lived in, current, no sign of decay or overgrown vegetation.

The door nearest him opened.

A woman came out.

This woman walked toward him, no weapon in her hands. He

didn't know what to do but felt no fear. He could kill her in the time it took her to sneeze if he had to. As she approached, he saw that she was middle-aged, average in every way except for the smile that brightened her face in a way he'd rarely seen back in the Remnant Nation.

She stopped. She spoke.

"Hungry?"

2
ALEXANDRA

She had a plan, now she needed help.

Her plan was crazy, so she needed crazy help. That's why, with hair pinned up, wig in place, yellow robes of the pilgrims pulled over her shoulders—big and frumpy, scratchy—face dirtied, eyes hidden with archaic glasses, she found herself walking the backways and alleys of the city. She wandered toward the docks and the dying pools, the warehouses and the mills. Where the people were. The most devout of them all.

It had been many years since she'd worn a disguise—why worry about safety when you have an entire squad of Evolutionary Guards constantly at your side, ready to inflict harm without so much as a sniff. And why not enjoy the prestige of being a God, especially after she'd worked so hard for so many years to gain such a divine status. All in all, she'd had a good run and always knew, deep down, that things would have to change someday. Haven't they always?

She would be the greatest of them all, a phrase from a book she'd once read.

And not just for herself.

She was ambitious, power-hungry, vicious when needed. But she also cared about the world and believed with utter certainty that her vision for the future was the best. Period. No matter how brutal a time it took to get there, it needed getting there. Evolution. It was all about

Evolution, no going backward. She'd use the contents of the Box in the *right* way.

Without guards, she should be afraid, and was. In some ways, her disguise could make things worse—a lone female wandering the dark streets at night. But her training in the Flaring discipline had prepared her well. It would have to be an entire mob if they wanted to take her down, and if all else failed, she'd reveal herself as the Goddess she was.

Gas lights flickered on the street corners, tilting and swaying with the wind, like music come to life. The salty air smelled of a thousand revolting things—rotting fish, chemicals, charred remnants of the waste fires, sewage and trash and mold and mud. But with all of it combined, it wasn't entirely unpleasant. It was the odor of thriving life.

"Spare some buttons, ma'am?"

She stopped and looked down at the man, huddled against the wall, swaddled in a pile of every possession he owned. The light scarce, she still saw that he was a filthy man, rags and bones as they say, but he had a kindness in his eyes, shining with yellow points of reflection from the nearest gas flame. The Godhead had done everything in their power to keep the people fed, busy, happy. Satisfied. And here was proof that even that couldn't last forever. *That* had been falling apart for years, now.

"Buttons, ma'am," the poor wretch repeated. "Just give me the one, mayhaps, gods bless you for it."

She gave him two.

He uttered thanks, as sincerely as she'd ever heard. She smiled but didn't speak in return, honestly not knowing what to say. Perhaps it would be better for this man if . . .

Hollowed.

The word sprang to her mind as if loosed from a trapdoor. It seemed the new way of dealing with people like this, the awful . . . *remnant* of the situation having its own purpose, something to do with the pilgrims, with the pathways of the Maze, some kind of sacrificial ritual. The thought made her shudder as she walked away from the beggar, but she also did nothing to prevent such a possible future for the man. In the end, if nothing else, Alexandra was a pragmatist. Means to an end and all that.

And so, she kept walking, through the dark and through the growing mist of fog, creeping in from the sea. Alleys and backways, lefts and rights, narrow straight-aheads. People passing by, people laughing, people crying, people begging.

She came to a door.

She knocked.

A man with horns opened it.

3
JACKIE

They'd banded together, then split into groups. Then banded together again.

No sign of Isaac. No sign of Sadina.

Jackie sat with Trish by a small campfire, a few others scattered around it in a circle, most of them asleep. The group had drifted away from the route that Kletter had been following, just enough to feel isolated in case someone came searching for them. No one could agree on what to do yet. Continue on, try to find the Villa that their guide had talked up so much? Keep searching for their friends? The only thing settled upon was to keep to themselves, avoid others until they knew more or discovered a clue, any clue.

And so, here they were. A secluded place sunk between four squat buildings and surrounded by trees. A park of some sort.

Trish was inconsolable.

Jackie had been paired up with her during the searches, and felt a connection, seeing the burden of sadness and panic consume the poor girl. Jackie had been through something just like this only a few years ago. Turns out an island cut off from the rest of the scary world can have bad people, too. She tried not to think about the night her life had fallen apart, and instead put all her efforts into comforting Trish.

"We're going to find them," she said, probably for the hundredth time.

"Stop. Saying. That." Trish hadn't spoken for at least an hour, so this was progress. Words instead of sobs and cries of hysteria.

Jackie reached out but then pulled her hand back. Trish didn't like being touched right now, either. Not by anyone. She seemed to hate the consoling as much as what she was being consoled *about*.

"Okay," Jackie whispered. "I'll shut up. As long as you shut up, too. We're all sick of your boo-hooing. Let's just get some sleep and start over tomorrow." *Maybe tough talk is more up her alley.*

Trish didn't respond. She didn't say anything. But her cries did grow silent. She lay herself down and curled into a ball, wet eyes focused on the dying flames of the fire.

Jackie did the same but rolled over to face the other direction. She'd tried her best, and would try again in the morning. Nearby, Ms. Cowan —who'd been under control but crying for hours—and the other old folks had huddled together to discuss things, keeping their voices low. Jackie wasn't having any of that—they were all east-siders and she was sick of them making the decisions.

They looked up at her when she approached, arms folded to keep herself firm.

"What's going on?" she asked.

Wilhelm, the gruff and grumpy one, and Alvarez, the gaunt and goofy one, both hardened their faces and appeared ready to tell her it was none of her high-falutin' business, but she was rescued by Old Man Frypan. He was a good soul, and had been kind to her on the voyage even though they'd never met before the trip.

"Come and have a sit-down with us," the aged, gray, wrinkled man said. She accepted his offer and took a seat right next to him on the cool dirt. "There ya go. I bet you're plenty worried about what we're yappin' about over here, huh?"

She didn't love the slight patronizing tone of his words, but she knew it came from a good place. When you're older than the Flare, someone like her must seem like a toddler.

"Curious, for sure," she replied. "Come up with anything yet?"

Old Man Frypan glanced at his compatriots, then back at her. "What do *you* think we should do?"

More than a little surprised, she didn't have an answer ready. But he waited, patient, his eyes—lit up by the fire—saying he truly wanted her opinion. She scrambled for something that didn't sound idiotic, but finally settled on the words that felt right.

"We have to go after them. Search for them. Find 'em, save 'em."

"Damn right, we do," Old Man Frypan said, any trace of a smile having vanished from his face. "That's the truth, the whole truth, and nothin' but the truth, amen."

Ms. Cowan spoke next.

"Then it's settled."

4
MINHO

The Orphan's stomach was so full of food and water that he felt certain—so certain that he considered forcing an upchuck—that he was about to explode from the inside-out like an artillery suit packed in nails. He sat on a couch, leaning to the side, his head on a soft pillow, groaning every few seconds from the terrible episode of overeating. The kindly woman named Roxy sat on an overstuffed chair nearby, hands in her lap, smiling gently at him as if proud she'd made a meal so fantastic that it was about to kill a man.

It had to be a fever dream. He'd never been in such a ridiculous situation in his life.

"You're as full as a tick on a bull," the lady said. "Maybe go a little easy on the cinnamon bread next time." She laughed at this then waved her hand in the air as if shooing at a fly. "And believe it or not, young man, we have full-flushing toilets in this here domicile. Looks like that's destined to be a major perk for you in the next hour or so." She blushed a little, then shrugged a shoulder as if she didn't actually care two spurts about such talk. "Just be sure and wash up and don't leave the place lookin' like a rat's nest. Air it out a bit, too, if you could be so kind—just open up a window, rain or shine, hot or cold. Gets a powerful stink up there even when I take care of business, and I can only imagine the levels of nose-burners you're gonna unleash."

"Thank you," the Orphan said, unsure of what exactly he was thanking her for.

It had been a surreal hour or two, that was for sure. Roxy brought him into her home, showed him to a room with a giant bed, carpet on the floor, paintings and mirrors on the walls, a large window that looked out on mountains. There was even a giant stuffed bear on the floor, a thing so outrageous that the Orphan stared at it for a full minute before glancing away. A bathroom was attached, equipped to the core with a sink, toilet, and tub. A framed craft of some sort hung on the wall with words stitched across a colorful depiction of flowers. It said: *No matter where you travel, no matter where you roam, the best part is coming home.*

Yep. Had to be a fever dream.

He'd washed up, put on fresh clothes provided by his host, then joined her for a single meal that could've fed every last person in his barracks room back at the fortress. Just him and her, her and him. She had to be at least fifty years old, though he had no real basis for the guess. She just seemed matronly, old-fashioned, like a . . .

Well, like a grandma. A grandma in a fever dream.

The Orphan had devoured the food—beef, potatoes, beans, corn, cinnamon bread—offering only grunts and nods or shakes of the head as she talked his ear off, barely touching her own food. She'd lived alone for years since her husband died, and before that they'd lived most of their adult lives alone, loving each other and tilling the land, hunting the forests for game. This only added to the fairy-tale nature of the whole thing, but the Orphan mostly concentrated on shoving more food down his throat.

And now, here they were. The Orphan, tilted over on the couch, too stuffed to move, and Roxy sitting all prim and proper on her chair. Not for the first time, he wondered why he'd trusted her so much, so quickly—especially in a world drenched with mistrust and sorrow. He didn't know for certain, but his heart told him that he'd had no choice. That he'd reached the end of his rope. *Kind of like a boy named Kit . . .*

"You ready to tell me your name yet?" she asked him.

He gave her a quizzical look.

"I've asked you several times since you arrived, and, well . . . Don't take this the wrong way—you seem like a very nice young man—but you make lots of sounds and most of them aren't words. Now, I don't expect you to do a whole lot of talkin' the way you stumbled into my yard barely alive and skinny as a toothpick, but I would at least like to know your name."

The Orphan forced himself to sit up straight on the couch, wincing a little as the movement squeezed his full stomach. "I have a long way to go. All the way to Alaska."

Roxy nodded approvingly. "Not quite what I asked, but thank you for finally telling me something about yourself." She paused, nodding to herself. "Alaska, huh? May I ask why?"

Trust only went so far, no matter how much food was offered. "I'm sorry, miss, but I can't do that. I just need to get up there. I know it's a long, long way."

"Roxy, please. You will only call me Roxy—none of this 'miss' business, ya hear me?"

The Orphan merely nodded.

After a weighty sigh, she continued. "Listen to me, carefully. I have been alone and sad and scared of the world for what seems like an entire lifetime since my husband died. He was a good man, a wonderful man, and I miss him so much my heart feels like a beating wound. You came here because you're supposed to come here. I know it like I know I have two feet and nine toes—don't ask. You need to go to Alaska? Well, son, I have a powerful, working truck and thirty gallons of fuel and plenty of things to carry food and water. There ain't no buses or trains so you're gonna have to do with this old lady as your partner. This old lady and her truck."

The Orphan blinked. The Orphan didn't know what to say. The Orphan knew that he would accept her offer but could only manage a nod.

"Splendid. But first you gotta tell me your name, son. We won't survive very long if I don't even know your damn name."

A few seconds passed, but only a few.

"My name is Minho."

"Now that's more like it!" She slapped her leg. "Now tell me something about your past life—I don't care what, just a tidbit—and then we'll think about what we need to do. Come on, now, don't be shy. Just one itsy-bitsy thing about the man named Minho."

This woman was strange and used a lot of words and he really liked her. "I . . . was trained to be a guard on a wall. I'd . . . kill people if they came too close. And once, I saved a boy from getting murdered."

Roxy blinked. "That's very interesting. Not quite what I expected, honestly. Which is all the better—man, are we gonna have some doozy conversations around the old campfire." She stood up. "Alright, Minho. Let's get packin' shall we? That truck is itchin' for a road trip."

5
ALEXANDRA

She sat in almost complete darkness, a sputtering candle the only relief. It stood upon a small wooden table, directly in front of her, its flame unmoving, a teardrop of fire pointing toward the low ceiling. On the other side of the table was a man with horns—two of them, each one curved and almost a foot long, sewn to his head but looking for all the world like he'd been born with the things. Different people had different ideas of devotion, she reckoned.

He was a clean-shaven man, though nothing else about him could be described as clean. He stank, and every inch of skin not covered by the robes of the pilgrims had been smeared with grime or grease or the chalky white lines of evaporated sweat. A lovely man, really.

"What you ask of us," he said, his voice surprisingly un-Viking-like, almost gentle. "It can only be answered with two words, and I hope you don't take offense."

When he didn't say more, she prodded him. "Okay. What are the two words, please?"

"Hell, no."

"Hell, no," she repeated. "As in, there's very little chance you can do it?"

"That's about the gist of it. Ain't possible."

She sighed for dramatic effect and folded her arms, crossed her legs. All three actions were frowned upon by pilgrims of the Maze. Too casual. The man with the horns grimaced but didn't say anything.

She made her next move. "What if I told you there's no choice in the matter? What if I told you that no matter how many 'hell, nos' you throw at me, you will do what I ask because I can make you realize *why* you have no choice?"

He leaned forward and put his elbows on the table. "Can we cut the BS, please? Can we both just agree to stop the charade? I ain't got no power with the pilgrims, and if you *are* a pilgrim I'll donate my body to a Hollowing at the next Maze Mass. Fess up."

She affected a quick flash of fear on her face then wiped it away with a forced smile that made her look like she was trying to hide . . . oh, bother. She did most of it without thinking, anyway. But every step and every word were calculated.

"How did you know?" she asked. "What gave it away?"

He leaned back in his chair, visibly proud of his detecting skills. "Oh, I don't know. Maybe the fact you don't smell like a bucket of shite? Maybe the fact that your face is clean and looks like it ain't been hit even once with the ugly stick? You say words in the right order and ain't fallin' on your knees every time the word 'Maze' is uttered? I could go on."

"Okay. Your point is well taken."

"So, spill it. Why're you here? Ain't you scared? Do you have any idea how many bad people roam these here parts?"

"Aren't most of them followers of the Maze?"

"Damn, lady!" he said as he slapped the table. "Them's the worst ones! Worst by a long shot!"

She bristled. "Aren't you one, yourself?" She very pointedly looked at the horns sewn upon his head.

His eyes wandered up then rolled back down. "Those? Yeah, those. Let's just say that weren't one of my better decisions. Sleepin' with these is a task, I tell ya. But I was young and drunk and there might've been a lady involved. She's dead now and I still got these damn horns."

"We can help each other," she said. With the Flaring discipline, she threw all the compassion and reason and certainty into the words that she could. Her proposal from earlier would now seem like the most assured thing in the world to him.

"Yeah, yeah, I hear what you're saying. I'm pickin' up what you're puttin' down. Forget that whole 'Hell, no' thing I said. I'm in. For you."

"We'll need more of your friends," she continued. "They all need to be pilgrims, just like you. But maybe a little more devoted. A lot more. But not *too* much. A fine balance, I know."

"Okay. Alright. And you'll keep all those promises you made when you first sat down? Every last one of 'em?"

"And more." She whispered it, making him lean forward. "You get me what I want, and you'll be able to move into the towers. And those horns can be removed by a professional."

He liked that last one. Oh, you could see it in his eyes.

"Alright, then," he said. "What's this thing look like, anyway?"

"The Coffin?" she asked. "Here, let me tell you."

6
JACKIE

She'd almost missed it. Almost.

"Here!" she yelled, frantic, needing someone else to see what she thought—*hoped*—she was seeing. It had only been a few seconds and already she worried that her eyes deceived her. "Over here! Hurry!"

Dominic was the first one to reach her. "Holy crap," he whispered.

Miyoko was right behind him. Then Trish. The four of them had been grouped together in their continued hunt for Isaac and Sadina. Although there'd been several signs of human passage leading away from the house from which their friends had been abducted—fresh footprints, the remains of a campfire, human waste—Jackie and the others couldn't know for sure who'd caused them.

Until now, she thought.

They were two or three miles from the house in question, the clues leading them in a direct course away from the ocean, toward the east. Jackie's group had been assigned a small neighborhood that seemed a perfect spot for someone who wanted to break into a house for a night's sleep or simply to hide. One of the houses, up on a hill at the very end of the main street, had a three-foot-high brick wall encircling the yard—which had long ago given up its fight against weeds and bushes.

Someone had used a rock to scrawl a surprisingly large message across the bricks, right beside the little gate at the front of the yard. There could be no doubt as to who had done it, especially because it looked so fresh:

ISAAC THE BLACKSMITH WAS HERE
ALSO, SADINA THE WISE

"Does that say what I think it says?" Jackie asked, just to make sure she hadn't lost her mind after hours of relentless searching. The day had been very hot and every inch of her clothes stuck to her skin.

"I think it says what you think it says," Miyoko responded, her voice full of glee.

No one had to put words to the reason for her joy. They were alive. They were *alive*.

"I'll get the others," Dominic said; he took off running down the hill.

That's when Jackie noticed Trish, who'd wandered a few feet away. She had her face covered with both hands, crying, shoulders shaking with each silent sob. Miyoko saw it as well and moved to embrace their friend. Trish allowed it, and Jackie joined in the hug.

After a good long cry, Trish pulled away and stared at the words sketched across the brick.

"I can't even describe the relief I felt seeing that," she said. "Even though I'm scared they're hurting her or whatever. But oh man, at least we know she and Isaac are alive. I mean . . . this obviously can't be a coincidence, right?"

Jackie saw that she was already losing her renewed confidence from the message.

"No way," Jackie said. "It was obviously done in the last few hours—look how fresh it is. And I think that's why Isaac included the ridiculous 'blacksmith' part, so there'd be no doubt if and when we saw it. Even I know about his obsession with your Forge."

Trish let out something that was close to a laugh. "Yeah, he's a little weird about it." She sniffed and visibly gathered her wits about her, standing straight and tall. "You're right. This was definitely from them and now we know we're on the right path. That's the best news we've had all day."

Shouts rang up from the distance. Dominic was leading a pack of their friends down the street. He was running, trying to keep up with Ms. Cowan, who had to be as screwed up with mixed emotions as Trish. They all looked pissed and ready for war.

We're on the right path.

Jackie agreed. As strongly as she'd ever uttered anything in her life, she spoke two words for her friends and all the world to hear.

"We're coming."

7
MINHO

Roxy handed him a metal bowl, hot to the touch, filled with a gorgeous stew that smelled so good it brought tears to his eyes. They sat next to a fire—she had insisted on calling it a "campfire," a word better suited to their fun adventure, she liked to say. He didn't care. He wouldn't have cared if they'd given the flames a stupid name, like Casey. Brent. Jeffrey. Whatever. It was warm, it cooked food, and the food was tasty.

"We're going to have a lot of time to get to know each other," Roxy said after a swallow of stew. "You know? So I'm *not* going to do that old lady thing and constantly ask you questions. No, sir, I won't do it. When you want to tell me about your life, then, why, you just go ahead and tell me about it."

She nodded stiffly—as if convincing herself, not him—then took another bite of dinner.

He thought he'd throw a surprise at her. "Well, what about your life? I wanna hear every little detail. Leave nothing out."

She stared hard at him, the stew on her spoon sliding back into the bowl.

"Minho, you're teasing me. That's not very nice. You shouldn't tease a cool, level-headed, middle-aged lady like yours truly. No, sir. Really gives you a bad look."

Minho made a sound that might be a chuckle in other civilizations. "I'm not teasing, Roxy. I haven't teased anyone since I was saved from the Flare pits as a baby. Tell me about stuff. I'll open up eventually, but you gotta set the example."

"Well, that'll work just fine, young man." She beamed, a face lit up with a sincerity and genuineness he'd rarely—if ever—seen back at the Remnant Nation.

"Let's hear it, then." He scraped the last bits of stew from the bowl, licked the spoon clean, then settled back and put his hands behind his head. "I apologize in advance if I fall asleep."

Despite that, she started.

"My earliest memories, as a child, are mostly made up of images. Grandparents, feeble, more from the harshness of the world than from their age, sitting on stumps. A dad who was a wrecked person, always distraught, unable to get over my mom, who'd died in some horrible way that was never explained to me, no matter how many times I asked. My dad carried a little wooden stool wherever he went. I can still see him sitting on that thing, staring at the ground." She paused, doing what her dad did. "He ignored me, mostly. It wasn't his fault, you know. He was just so . . . broken from whatever he'd been through. From what happened to my mom."

Minho sat up, leaning forward on his elbows. "Roxy . . . I'm sorry to hear that. That's really, really sad." That was it. That was the best he could do. Hating himself a little, he lay back and settled on his blanket.

"I know your life has been just as harsh," Roxy said quietly, the words barely slipping through the wispy flames of the campfire. "*More* harsh. I think it would mean a lot to me if we could end up talking about these things. These . . . horrible, crappy things."

Minho shifted so that he could look up at her face. "Roxy?"

She pinched her mouth as if expecting a rude comment. "Yes?"

"Thank you for telling me that."

She definitely seemed taken aback. "Well . . . you're welcome. Thanks for listening. So what . . . do you want to hear more? Or do you want to take a turn?"

Minho snored, loudly.

He had to fake it a bit, but not much. His eyes had closed and his breathing turned weighty. He needed sleep. And it would come, what with yet another small beginning having graced the path of his hardpan life.

"Typical," Roxy whispered, but there was no hurt in the word. She shuffled and shifted and settled for the night. "Goodnight, you interesting young man."

He faked another snore.

"Typical," she whispered again.

"Roxy?"

She didn't answer.

"Thank you for that stew. It was the best meal I've ever had, except maybe the one we had at your house. Thank you."

A few seconds passed, the dying spits of the fire and flame the only sound.

Roxy snored, loudly.

8
ISAAC

Timon the Gentle Giant wasn't being so gentle at the moment, but he was still very much doing the giant thing. He had his porky ham bone of an arm wrapped around Isaac's neck, holding Isaac's right wrist and elbow sharply against his back, bending in a way that seemed contrary to nature's intention. It hurt all around, but every time Timon took a step—he was evidently performing the very important task of escorting Isaac back to the woman named Letti—each jounce sent a bolt of pain up Isaac's arms and into his shoulders. It was a dreary ache, not helped by all the jostling.

"Could you just let me walk," Isaac said through gritted teeth, his face frozen in a perpetual, rigid wince. "Please. I'm not going to run away or . . . OW! Just let me go! I can walk!"

Sadina marched along next to them, tears of anger in her eyes, looking like a raged-up lion waiting for the right time to spring in for the kill. She could do it, too. Isaac knew her better than anyone except maybe Trish and Ms. Cowan. She was tough as an iron bucket full of iron tools, especially when she'd been done wrong.

"Why are you doing this?" Sadina asked, her teeth just as clenched as Isaac's. "I thought we'd come to an agreement, to hear you out, stay with you, keep things peaceful. Ya know, go along for now. Let him go!" She stepped closer but then seemed to think better of it. Maybe the Sadina versus the Gentle Giant boxing match needed a little more time to marinate.

"You know what you did," Timon grumbled through heavy breaths—apparently doing the walking for two people was about twice as hard as just doing it for yourself. "Told me you're going to take a dump, next thing I know you're scratching words on walls with a big chunky rock? That wasn't part of our sweet compromise, sorry."

Isaac wanted to respond but he couldn't get enough breath in his lungs to sputter out a single word. He just kinda squawked and groaned. So Sadina took over for him since she practically read his mind all the time, anyway.

"They're our *friends*, Timon," she said with an ocean-full of sincerity. "They're our only friends in the world right now. Hell, one of them is my own mom. Can you imagine what she's going through? We just wanted to reassure them that we're alive."

A new voice entered the fray from up ahead.

"Oh that's it, huh?" This sounded like a bark coming from the doorway of an old coffee shop or something, the door hanging off its hinges. Letti stepped out and onto the street. "Really? That's all you wanted to do? Send a nice little message of love? We're not as stupid as Timon looks. We know you're trying to leave them bread crumbs along the way so they can follow us."

Isaac, temporarily insane, tried to shout, "Hansel and Gretel" because that had been a favorite story when he was little; his mom would read it to him at bedtime. Scary as hell and warped his mind, but he loved it. All that came out of his mouth, though, was a repeat of the squawk and groan from earlier.

Maybe the unpleasant sounds spewing from his throat had finally been enough to convince Timon; he released Isaac from his kidnapper grip. Isaac bent over and put his hands on his knees, releasing a mixed order of coughing, spitting, sucking in breaths, letting them out, then coughing and spitting again.

Letti walked right in front of him and lifted his chin with a firm hand so he had to look up at her.

"What did you write on that wall?"

Timon opened his mouth to answer—he'd seen it, after all—but Letti cut him off with a sharp swipe of her hand. "I want to hear it from the boy who wrote it. What did it say?"

Isaac straightened up, continuing to catch his breath. He knew any chance of lying to get out of this mess had gone out the window. "It was just one of those stupid tags kids leave. Johnny so-and-so was here. Regina what's-her-name was here. People do it all the time. So . . . Isaac was here. Sadina was here. No big deal."

Timon stiffened a bit. "Isaac the Blacksmith? Sadina the Wise? What was *that* all about?"

"What do you mean, what was that all about? They're called nicknames. Nothing to worry about. Let's keep moving."

The woman rolled her eyes and shook her head. Timon made a noise that sounded like he needed to clear his sinuses. Sadina still trembled with frustration but was wise enough to keep it simmering on the inside. Isaac could finally breathe again. Everyone seemed content to consider the situation settled and move on.

"Okay," Letti said. "Come with me, I want to show you something."

She turned and started up the rough remnants of a path that led away from the street and up a hill, through a jungle of weeds and bushes and small trees. Timon faced the other two and gave a stern nod toward the path, his message clear. Without a word, Isaac followed, then Sadina, the Gentle Giant being kind enough to take up the rear.

The hill was steep, the hiking tough; Isaac's heart thumped so hard he could hear it faintly inside his head. Sadina took deep, audible breaths behind him. Several times, they needed to grab a hanging branch or a strong weed to pull themselves up a section. Letti, above, bounded along like she was going downhill instead of up.

By the time they crested the top of the hill, Isaac had released at least a quart of sweat through his skin and his chest heaved with each breath. But it felt good, exhilarating. It made him miss the sweaty, smoky, hardworking days at the Forge back home.

"Come on," Letti said, waving her arm as she continued walking along the top of the hill. The darkening sky loomed over them, vast and unbroken now, the very first hint of stars beginning to peek through the heavenly facade.

Isaac was lost for a moment in the sheer beauty of the view. The sun glimmering on the distant ocean as it sank toward the horizon, the expanse of buildings in every direction, some of the remaining windows glowing orange in reflection. On the other side of the hill, mountains rose in the distance, their color somewhere between red and purple in the fading light. A sudden and powerful sadness gripped his heart. How wonderful the world must've been once. Why did it all have to be ruined by apocalypse and disease? Could it ever make a comeback?

"Here," Letti said. She'd stopped and squatted on her haunches, pointing to a spot down in the sprawling neighborhoods of the city, lying beneath a blanket of shadow. "Come here and look."

Isaac knelt in the dirt next to the woman and followed the trajectory of her arm. It took a moment to focus, to see movement in a spot maybe two or three miles away. People. A group of people, maybe ten or fifteen of them.

"That's . . ." Sadina began but didn't need to finish.

Letti looked back at her and nodded. "Yes, that's them. We've left just enough clues to let them stay on our trail. Thanks for helping out with that."

Isaac wanted to respond but he was speechless.

"Did you really think we'd let you do something like scrawl a giant message across a brick wall before stopping you?" Letti exchanged a glance with Timon. "It worked out, didn't it? We got to teach you a lesson about how important it is to do what we say, and you left a big sign encouraging them to keep coming."

"But . . . why?" Sadina asked. "I don't get it. Are you going to let them catch up to us or not?"

Letti didn't answer the question. She stood and started back down the hill, away from their friends.

Isaac knew they could make a run for it. It's not like either of their captors would risk killing them—at the very least Sadina was important to someone, somewhere for reasons unknown. Even now, he could probably push Timon and the Gentle Giant would very ungently tumble down the small mountain. But . . .

Not yet, Isaac told himself. *Not yet.*

Like a puppy dog, he followed his masters.

PART THREE

One Month Later

I've noticed something about myself. I'm still a human being, the bloody Flare be damned. Especially with memories coming back, all mixed up with the spurts of madness. I don't feel so good, that's for sure. But I miss my mom, my dad, my sister. I barely remember them, but they're creeping their way back into my thoughts and heart. And I miss them. I don't like the prospect of going crazy, or losing what I've just started to gain. And this helps me realize that I'm a human being even as I begin to lose my humanity.

There's a lesson in that somewhere. I'll figure it out later.

—*The Book of Newt*

CHAPTER TEN

The River

I
JACKIE

She woke up before everyone else, dawn just kissing the eastern sky.

A lifetime had passed since they first stepped from that damn boat onto the sandy beaches of the old world. She didn't know the literal number of days, probably three or four weeks—Miyoko was keeping a calendar but Jackie had told her to stop with the constant updates. She didn't want to think about it. Regardless, it felt like years. A lifetime.

A lifetime of walking.

North through the city, north along the coast of the ocean and its countless, abandoned, lifeless seaside villages. North and north and north. Sometimes east and then north and then east again, eventually leaving the coastline in the distance. No one knew why this route had been set or where they were going exactly. Only one thing guided them: Clues. Signs. Messages. Staying on the trail. Although none of her friends would dare say it out loud, it almost seemed too easy. But

Isaac and Sadina were somewhere ahead of them, never more than a couple days' worth, and both of them were alive and well by the looks of it. Jackie and the others just couldn't quite catch up to them. Always a step behind. A good number of steps, actually.

"Hey, you," someone whispered.

Jackie just about jumped out of her clothes but hid it well. She rolled over to see Dominic sitting on the ground not three feet from her, next to the previous night's campfire, its smoldering, wispy remains like gray ghosts leaking toward the sky.

"What're you doing up so early?" she asked. Dominic was notorious for having to be dragged out of his sleeping bag each morning.

"Had to pee." Somehow that was his go-to answer for about twenty different questions. "Saw you stirring, thought I'd say hi."

"That's sweet of you, Dom. Can you go take a pee for me, too?"

"I don't think it works that way. I could get you a bucket?"

She sniggered at that. "We probably won't leave for another couple hours. Don't you think you should get some more sleep? You're kinda grumpy even when you do get a full night's rest."

"Grumpy? I'm not grumpy." He looked genuinely hurt.

"I'm just teasin' you." She paused, growing more serious. "What happens after we find them?"

He looked down at the ground. "I don't know."

"Think we'll ever make it back home?"

"I hope so. We have to. I want to. What about you?"

She nodded, trying to hold back a sudden and unwelcome push of tears. "Yeah, I think we're going to make it back home. That, I do." Then she had an idea. "How about we go make breakfast for the others? They'll think we're the best people who ever lived."

His face lit up. "Yeah, let's do it."

2

She tricked Dominic into doing most of the work, saying she needed to use the bathroom just as the hot and heavy business of frying the eggs and deer meat over the fire got going. A nearby copse of trees—a rare sight in the sparse, scrubby, hardpan desert they'd been traversing—seemed the perfect spot. When she was finished, she leaned against a tree to collect herself, figuring Dominic was able enough to wrap up breakfast.

Thoughts of the past month swarmed into her mind.

The relentless walking through heat in the day and cold in the night; the adaptation to life in the wild; hunting for food with traps and knives; the daily search for clues of Isaac and Sadina; the lifting and dashing of hopes; the sheer emptiness of the world, as if every other human had been zapped from existence. She didn't know what she'd do without the others and their friendship, their knack for survival, their senses of humor and willingness to share a cry. Something told her she couldn't judge the greater parts of earth based on the few hundred miles they'd crossed—who knew what was out there. Seven continents. Countless islands. Decades since the Flare. Who knew.

But she missed home. She missed home so badly.

Back at camp, most of the others had already roused themselves once the smells of frying food permeated the air. Surprisingly, Dominic hadn't burnt anything or spilled grease on the fire. She kinda liked that big goof. Even as she had the thought, he spotted her and waved, dropping half the food in the dirt. As he scrambled to salvage it, she laughed because she had no doubt it would still be eaten.

"Find any clues?"

Jackie started. Ms. Cowan had sneaked up on her. Sadina's mom asked the same question about forty times a day.

"No, sorry. Nothing."

The woman let out a weary morning sigh. "Oh, well, that's okay. I think we're really on their trail for now. Pretty soon we're gonna hit a river that Alvarez scouted last night. It's really wide so I can't fathom they tried to cross it. I bet we follow that thing north for a good long while. Come on, let's get some of that food before all the dirt-free stuff is gone."

Soon they were eating with the others in a big circle—the deer meat was charred after all, and Jackie tried to ignore the grains of dirt that kept grinding against her teeth—and she had more time to think. All of her life she'd heard about Cranks, the Flare, the devastated apocalypse of the sun. And yet for weeks now, once they'd gotten out of the city and its surroundings, they'd seen almost nothing but nature, beautiful nature. The planet seemed to be winning the battle. However, the eventual run-in with other humans was inevitable, and she'd be a fool not to know it.

"You know what my dad used to say?"

Miyoko had spoken, her empty canteen hanging from the hand she'd propped on her knee.

"What's that?" Jackie asked. She took her last bite of venison and was glad to be done.

"A penny for your thoughts. I've never seen a penny in my life, but if I had one I'd give it to you. Where's your mind at? I can tell you've started thinking again."

Jackie was famous in the group for . . . dwelling on things. She wished she could be more carefree but it was in her nature to worry, to ponder, to reminisce, to wonder what could have been and question what's coming.

"It's all just so weird. I mean, why are we here? The whole reason we got on that boat was because of Kletter and now she's dead. We're wandering the wilderness like freaking Moses from the Bible. Or was that Joseph? Paul? Who the hell knows. Mr. Baxby never could shut up with his town-square preaching."

"Mr. Baxby?" Miyoko repeated. "Guess I never met him."

"You east-siders kept to yourselves, that's for sure." She didn't mean it as rudely as it came out and she quickly moved on after a peace-offering smile. "Everything just feels . . . untethered right now. Make sense?"

Miyoko could say a lot with her eyes, and right then she showed she understood, very well. "I get it. But life doesn't ever go the way you think, does it? Maybe we'll go back and find Kletter's people eventually. But right now, only one thing matters." She nodded over at Trish.

Jackie felt instantly stupid and ashamed. "Oh, I know. I know, I shouldn't have said that. Finding Isaac and Sadina is our purpose right now. That's all—"

"Hey," Miyoko interrupted. "Stop. None of that self-guilt crap. My dad used to say something else that was cheesy as hell, too. It's all about the journey. He must've said that once a week. Just go with the flow, Jackie. We're all in the same boat."

Their eyes met at that, and then they both were laughing.

"Now that, I can be thankful for," Jackie said. "No more boats for at least another month or two. Then maybe we can go back home."

As quickly as that, the air grew somber again.

Luckily, Dominic, Trish, Carson, and Lacey scooted closer to shift the mood. Dom made some weird joke about Jackie leaving a stink trail in the trees; Trish told him to shut up, then complimented him on the breakfast; Carson complained that he'd slept directly on top of a jagged rock all night; Lacey asked in the most nonchalant voice ever why he didn't just scoot a few inches to the left. Then she called him a slinthead, a word Jackie had never heard before.

All was well. At least, all was okay. Things could be worse.

Ms. Cowan came over then, hands on hips like a tyrant schoolmaster.

"Good to see you guys laughing, this morning." She always tried to greet the younger people with a smile, but Jackie knew the truth—you could see it in the older woman's eyes. She was distraught, a strain that couldn't be relieved until they found her daughter. And Isaac, of course. "You all ready to pack up and go? Frypan thinks it could be a hot one today, and it should be a lot cooler next to the river."

"Ready to go," Dominic pronounced. He stood up, groaning out loud like an old man. Soon they were all up and about, breaking camp.

The river, Jackie thought as she stuffed the ratty old backpack she'd found in the city.

Things would get better once they got to the river.

3
MINHO

The Orphan didn't know much in the way of vehicles, as they were mostly a rare thing in the modern world. The Grief Bearers of the Remnant Nation had trucks and cars to use around the fortress, and there were the monstrous machines that drove on giant wheels and could crush anything in sight. Some of them were relics from the past carefully restored, and others were the twisted inventions of people with too much time on their hands. And some came from a mysterious outside source that the likes of him only whispered about.

But still, a vehicle was a pretty rare possession, and he'd certainly never had a go at one, himself. Despite all this, in the past few weeks he'd come to an indisputable conclusion.

Roxy was a crazy driver.

She'd never met a hill, snowbank, stream, or boulder that she didn't love to drive straight over or through. There was no speed too fast, no slope too steep. Often, when he gripped the dashboard and closed his eyes and accepted that death comes to all people, she'd let out a loud whooping cry and then laugh even as the truck bounced or swerved or tilted precariously. At least she had the decency to act embarrassed after such episodes.

"When are you going to let me have a turn?" he asked for the thousandth time. Although he'd grown to love their nightly fireside visits—sitting in peaceful silence or venting about the past—he'd yet to feel likewise about her time "behind the wheel," as she called it.

"Never, son. And stop asking. This is my truck."

He'd ask again tomorrow.

They were driving down a long road, cracked and full of holes, straight as the shaft of a rifle. But it was drivable, unlike a lot of the other roads they'd come across. This usually didn't matter to Roxy, who thought the answer to such things was to drive faster and hope for the best. The Orphan had considered himself one of the bravest people in the world after all the training he'd been through, but his companion on this west-bound journey tested his courage each and every day.

"Could we at least stop and take a piss?" His bladder was like a rain-catch about to burst from weight. "I might throw up, too, just for good measure. It's a miracle how you can swerve so much on a perfectly straight road."

"Alright, alright." She slammed on the brakes and the truck screeched to a stop. His bladder almost gave up but he held it back. He quickly opened the door, jumped out, and did his business only a few feet into the scrub brush, no time for proprieties. Then he took a moment to enjoy the scenery—miles and miles of sparse scrubland and hills and valleys, the faint outline of mountains in the distance, a jagged shadow of gray against the deep blue of the cloudless sky.

He had changed as they'd been driving across the country. As they stopped each night and ate a simple meal cooked on a simple fire. As they'd talked and talked—he more than her, perhaps the most shocking development of all. About the Remnant Nation's brutal policy of killing, burning any and all those infected. About being orphaned. About *being* an Orphan. About training, about working, about manning the fortress wall, about killing of his own. And he told her about Kit, the boy he'd saved. Perhaps that had been the actual moment the transformation had begun. Who the hell knew.

He'd changed in ways he didn't know a person *could* change. Sometimes he thought back to how terse and tightly wound of a human being he'd been before his escape from the Remnant Nation. In many ways he'd barely resembled a human being—at least compared to what he saw in Roxy. Where she was full of life and kindness and humor, he'd been like a dried-up turd in an old bucket. Something no one wanted, or wanted to be around. He *had* to be that way, he'd been raised and trained to be that way.

But no longer. He never wanted to lose his toughness, his hardness, his skills as a living weapon. However, Roxy had introduced him to an entirely new world, both literally and figuratively. As they crossed the wide-open spaces of mountains, deserts, and grasslands, he started to realize that it was okay, every once in a damn while, to feel some joy.

"Boo." A tap on his shoulder.

She always tried this, but it was one of the many ways in which he *hadn't* changed.

"Do you really think I didn't hear you sneaking up behind me?" he asked without turning around. "I'm better trained than that. Also, sometimes you're really creepy. I'm trying to have a private moment, here."

She stepped up beside him. "It really is a sight, isn't it? I'm sure glad you forced me to come on this trip." She always tried that, as well. Being funny. "It's been one of the best times of my life."

"Yeah . . ." He faltered a bit, the brightness of the day dimming. This happened, sometimes. A lot, actually. Just when he was thinking about how much he'd changed, the darkness rolled in and tried to correct him. He never knew what might trigger it, but he felt it, now. A harsh thumping in his head and heart. A brutal beat to his pulse. Anger. For the smallest of moments he had the urge to push Roxy to the ground and steal her truck, take back his true nature, stop trusting her, assume she was the enemy. He didn't want to laugh ever again.

"Minho?"

He looked at her. It took a mighty effort to keep his face still, his hands at his sides, his breathing steady. "Tell me about your husband again."

She answered with a genuine smile. "He was a hard worker. He was kind. He was hilarious. He taught me how to cook but never expected me to do it. He loved roaming the woods, teaching me about plants, mushrooms, animals. He loved learning from me, too. We built that house together, you know. Yes, of course you know. He was a wonderful man, and I miss him every day."

Minho nodded, breathed. "Someday I want to be like him."

"You're well on your way, almost there. But you'll never quite make it. Almost is good enough." She always threw in a little grandma sass, just the right amount. She paused. "Are you okay?"

"Yeah. Let's go." He turned from her and walked toward the truck. It was all he could manage right then, and although she couldn't possibly understand, this was a victory. It was another beginning.

The next day, they came upon a river.

4
ISAAC

It was rare for him to dream these days. Usually, after a long day of marching beside Sadina, the Gentle Giant, and Letti, he collapsed into the pathetic excuse for a sleeping bag inside the pathetic excuse for a tent and fell asleep within seconds. A deep sleep. A blissful sleep where nothing happened, nothing at all. The only drawback to that was often it seemed that Letti was waking him up as soon as his head hit the pathetic excuse for a pillow—an old blanket wrapped with twine.

But tonight, he dreamed.

Nothing fancy. Just glimpses of his life on the island, when things had been good and happy. When his parents and sister had been alive and well. When his biggest worries were completing his chores in their yurt and convincing Captain Sparks to give him time in the Forge in the days before Isaac became an official apprentice. He dreamed of his mom, fixing a leak in their roof and swearing no less than forty times. His dad, arguing with a neighbor about the recent shift in ocean currents and what that meant for the weather and upcoming harvest.

And then, the day. The accident. The world twisting inside-out.

It had been raining. Raining hard. Sheets of it. Luckily it was several days before the planting that year or else a lot of it would've been washed away. Rain, rain, and then more rain.

He could hear it in his dreams.

Gushes of water. Cascades of water. Thousands of quarts of water rushing over other thousands of quarts of water. His eyes opened. The dream was over. And yet the sounds were still there, a roar of water upon water upon water. The simple word itself couldn't explain the sheer magnificent volume of it.

The river.

He was only hearing the river.

He sat up, surprised that for once he'd awakened without Letti and her annoying, lilting voice singing "good morning" over and over, sounding like a pissed-off seagull. Weird that the same woman who did that had also told them about the "Evolution," about how the Flare had mutated into several variants, and that some had the potential to create a human race far more advanced. Or kill every last person on earth. Whatever she said, it usually ended in a ramble that made little sense to Isaac.

For all that, she tried her best to act like all was well in the world, like they were a happy family enjoying the trip of a lifetime. But it did no good. Despite all their pretending, Letti and Timon found plenty of times to remind him and Sadina of the deepening threat if they tried to run. What had been done to Kletter could be done to anyone—that was Timon's favorite thing to say, although Isaac often wondered if he actually meant it. Both of them were hard to read for certain.

But he and Sadina had decided to bide their time, despite the days turning into weeks, the march north and east relentless and hard. They knew their friends were still on the trail, just a few days behind. It made no sense, and was one of the most bizarre things Isaac had ever experienced. The whole situation was like a dark secret that everyone knew but refused to talk about. What game was Letti playing? Why couldn't they just let them catch up and keep moving, safety in numbers? But it had been made crystal clear: that wasn't an option.

Isaac crawled through the loose flap of the ancient, tattered tent that he shared with Sadina. Timon was nearby, building a fire to cook breakfast. The man seemed to never, ever sleep. He watched over his captives until they were asleep, and he was always waiting for them when they awoke in the mornings. Every once in a while, Isaac got up in the middle of the night to take a piss, only to come back and see Timon peeking out of his own tent with his ugly mug of a face. Watching. Always watching.

"All we've got is the last of the bacon that we hoofed in," the Gentle Giant said, practically shouting to be heard over the roar of the river. They'd camped less than thirty meters from its west bank. "We really need to catch some bigger game today. I'm sick of rabbits and squirrels, don't know about you. I've seen wild pigs out in these parts. You up for it?"

"Yeah, sure, whatever," Isaac replied. It was conversations like this that made their situation seem so absurd. Everything was normal, no tension to speak of, almost always. And yet that threat hung over them, like a mist you could barely sense, almost felt more than seen.

Sadina came out, bleary-eyed, quiet. Then Letti suddenly appeared from the direction of the river, holding a length of twine with at least six large trout strung up. Of course she'd been up before them. Of course she'd been fishing and managed to catch enough to feed them a huge breakfast.

What in the world is my life? Isaac thought. Stuck with a tyrant woman who fishes one second, talks about evolution and extinction the next. But he wouldn't be complaining. The prospect of fire-cooked trout made his mouth water. And made him think of home. Again.

Timon looked at his partner in awe. "Letti, you are a walking miracle."

She handed the haul—a couple of the poor creatures still flopping and bopping—over to Timon. "I catch, you cook. At least for today."

"I wouldn't trust you to do it, anyway. Give me a half hour."

Isaac didn't know if he could stand the wait.

5

Although the savory smell and sizzling flesh of the slowly grilled trout almost drove Isaac crazy with hunger, it was finally worth the wait when they all dug in. The skin and meat were fiery hot to the touch and it was a delicate dance indeed to devour the fish as quickly as your stomach begged for it without winning severe burns on your fingers, lips, and tongue. The wait *had* been worth it. The burns had been worth it. The inevitable upset stomach and unpleasant afterworks of such a thing . . . yes, worth it.

"I think I ate more than you," Sadina said, staring at him with puffy eyes, as if fish juice had somehow made it through her system and found itself all the way up there, filling her head.

"If you did," he replied, "you stole it from me. Letti dished it out fair and square."

"Sorry, kid. She likes me more and gave me more. It's fitting since I carry twice the stuff you do. A woman needs her strength."

"So does a man," he whimpered, really wishing he could have one extra piece of that succulent, salty, tangy little beast of the river.

Sadina sat up. "Oh?" She looked around the camp, searching left and right and up and down. "Have you seen a man somewhere? Let me know right away and I'll feed him myself."

"That's so funny I forgot to laugh."

She really *did* laugh. "Thank you for proving my point. I think my cousin said that phrase last time she was at our yurt for Winterfest. Oh, she's three, by the way."

Isaac wasn't really in the mood for the banter, and Sadina realized that as soon as he'd formed the thought. Using her uncanny ability to switch moods, she scooted over to sit close to him. She gently pressed a generous chunk of steaming fish through his lips. He chewed and the ecstasy of taste filled him up. Meanwhile, Sadina pulled him into a hug, holding him tightly against her.

She whispered into his ear. "I know you, Isaac. I know what's got you down."

"You do?" He asked it even though he knew the answer. She did.

"Did you dream about them? That day?"

He nodded.

After another hard squeeze of a hug, she pulled back and stood up, now looking down on him. "We need to do this, Isaac. We need to talk about it. You need to tell your story, out loud, to others. Right now. Tell it to me, tell it to Timon, tell it to Letti. We know they care about us even though they try to act all tough and rough sometimes. We're in this together and we all know it. So . . ." She reached down and grabbed his hand, then pulled him off the ground to stand close to her. Another hug, another whisper in his ear.

"Will you do this? Please? It's for you, I *promise* it's for you. But it's also for me. If my mom taught me anything, it's that we can't bottle stuff up. We have to talk about it, talk through it. Let others share your burden. Cheesy? Maybe. But not a debate. This has to happen."

Through all that extrapolating, he wasn't even sure at first what she meant. Talking? With her, with them, with everyone? Give a speech? About what for Flare's sake? But finally he thought he understood. Sadina had wanted him to do this for a long time and he'd always clammed up or run away. Both, usually.

But you know what, he thought. *Screw it. She's right and she knows she's right, the former as annoying as the latter.*

"Okay," he said. "Fine. I'm ready to talk about it. Even with Letti and her big bouncy ball of a giant. The fire's not dead, yet—let's gather 'round shall we?" Sadina rolled her eyes at his formal manner.

Throughout this long path to making a decision, Timon and Letti had stood back, kinda watching with interest, maybe curiosity. They couldn't know what Isaac and Sadina were talking about, but surely they wanted to.

"Come on, then," Isaac said.

A minute or so passed as everyone got settled, four people around a fire, everyone able to see everyone else. The fire spat and crackled, slowly dying by unleashing waves of heat from the coals and white-hot ash.

"It was my fault," Isaac began.

Sadina, as predictable as ever, as loving as ever, started to protest but he quieted her with a look.

"You want me to tell the story or you want me to lie? It's my fault. That's how I feel. Sometimes. The tiny rational part of my brain knows it's not true, but the big chunk of dummy brain can't stop torturing me with it. You're always preaching that it helps to say things out loud. Well, there ya go."

"What happened?" Letti asked. She seemed genuine enough.

"Back on the island, we'd get some hellbent rainstorms a few times a year. This one was even worse than usual. It was like some kind of water-magnet had picked up the entire ocean then dropped it on us. That's when I made the worst decision of my life. I thought it'd be fun to be on the beach, soaked by the storm, watching the giant waves come in. Dummy brain, big, all that."

His eyes met Timon's, who then quickly looked down at the smoldering ashes. *Something's not right about these people*, Isaac thought. *They care about us way more than they let on.*

"Then?" Sadina prodded.

He didn't know how long he'd been quiet. "Then . . . well . . . I got hit by the biggest wave I ever saw and it grabbed me by the damn ankles like it had hands and swept me out to sea. I don't know how my mom and dad knew. But they came running."

"They're your parents," Letti said, her voice a little haunted, as if by her own memories. "Parents know when their child is in danger."

"Yeah, well, my sister came with them," he mumbled. "What about her?"

It was a cruel thing to say, and she did bristle a little. Just enough to make him feel sorry.

He sighed, completely aware that he was deflecting the pain like usual. And was that a bad thing? He decided it wasn't.

"Look, I know I was supposed to tell this big story but there's not much to tell. You think I was taking notes out there? Getting beat to hell by waves twice as tall as Timon the Gentle Giant, here? I hardly remember anything. I was choking on salt water and spitting and trying to breathe. I was drowning. That's what I was doing. Drowning. And I remember hearing my dad's voice, screaming, absolutely screaming my name. I never heard my mom or sister, though."

That got him. That got him, good. His chest hitched with an unexpected sob and then the cries poured out of him like the rain that day. Sadina was there in a flash, pulling him close. He grabbed on to her, embarrassed but thankful she was there.

After a few minutes, he'd had enough. He gently released himself from Sadina and stood up. "The rest is easy enough to figure out."

He walked over to his tent and started breaking it down. "Come on, I need to get out of here." He'd never worked so furiously or gotten it done so quickly. He went to the next task, and then the next. They allowed him to do it, mostly by himself. Sadina looked sad, but Timon was even more distressed, as if he'd been the one to lose his family in one day. Maybe he had.

Twenty minutes later, the camp was cleaned up and ready to go. Isaac was absolutely drenched in sweat, the straps of his backpack cinched tight. But he did feel better.

"Let's go," he said, already walking.

They marched north, the river to their right, its roar now a constant reminder.

CHAPTER ELEVEN

The Bridge's Skeleton

I
ALEXANDRA

Tonight, she would reveal herself to them.

They deserved to know; more importantly, it would be the last piece of the puzzle to ensure their commitment to her. Their devotion. Their worship. After all the secret meetings, after all the planning and scheming, after all the exchanges of promises and riches, they were already tied to her like the lashings of a ship. After tonight, the lashings would turn to iron chains, never to be removed.

They met in the usual spot, an abandoned basement beneath a fallen warehouse, left to decay by its owners before any of them had been born. How it hadn't collapsed into that basement was a wonder, as was the very maze-like route through the rubble to get to its entrance. *Maze-like.* She'd had the thought without any irony.

Her friend with the horns, who'd refused to reveal his name until a week ago—Mannus, which he must've thought sounded very masculine, indeed—sat to her right around the makeshift table they'd scrounged from the ruins. Six others were there; three women, three men, all dressed in the yellow robes of the Maze. Besides Mannus the heretic, they were all devout followers of the faith, devout to a fault. For them, anyway. They were exactly what *she* needed. And after what they were about to hear—and see—they'd be groveling at her feet. Quite literally.

"Let's begin," she said.

Mannus folded his arms and placed them on the table, leering at the others one by one. His horns rose comically from his head, and Alexandra knew the night wouldn't end before he reminded her once again of her promise—to have those stupid things removed by a professional, someone who wouldn't crack his skull in the process.

"We've got it all set up for Sunday," Mannus pronounced. "Right at noon, when most of our friends in the faith will be gathering at the doors to the Maze for mass."

One of the women—no horns on this lady—spoke up. "I would just like to reiterate what I've said from the beginning. We shouldn't play this out at such a holy time. It's not right."

The man next to her—this guy also was hornless, but every known name of the Gladers of old had been tattooed on various spots of his face—he agreed, apparently. "Yes, I second the motion."

Mannus slammed his hand on the tabletop then refolded his arms. Then he was shouting. "We're planning to kill a member of our own Godhead and then steal the most holy relic in the history of holy relics and you're worried about doing it during the Maze Mass? Did I choose the wrong pilgrims?"

"Calm yourself, Mannus," Alexandra chided. "Or I'll do it for you."

"You've promised us proof that he's fallen from the faith," another woman piped up. Alexandra had decided weeks ago not to bother learning their names. "We see this mission as a manifestation of our devotion, not a blasphemy of it."

"Okay, fine," Mannus grumbled. "Your objections are noted in the record. Notice there isn't any damn record. But I'll remember it. Anyway, Sunday. Noon. We'll meet where the pilgrims are gathered, then sneak away as they really get into their stuff. The House of God is maybe half a mile from there. And we all know the plan once we arrive."

The man with the tattoos spoke next. "If we know the plan so well, why did we meet tonight? Where's the proof you promised?"

Mannus didn't respond, just looked over at Alexandra. It was time.

She stood up. To the gasps of almost everyone in the room, she slipped out of her robe, letting it fall to the floor. Underneath, she wore the finest of clothes, dyed the finest and brightest of colors, interlaced with threads of gold and silver. Then she reached up and pulled the grimy wig off her head, tossed it on top of the discarded robe. Next, she pulled out the pins holding her hair in a bun, letting it fall to her shoulders as she brushed it out with dirty fingers, the thickest, darkest, richest hair they'd ever seen, cascading in waves upon her upper body.

That was all it took.

These people knew who she was. These people had absolutely no doubt who she was. How many times had they lined the streets to watch her pass? How many times had they fallen to their knees and beaten themselves in her holy presence to show their devotion? They knew a member of the Godhead when they saw one. Well, when a member of the Godhead didn't wear a disguise, anyway.

There was shock at first. No one moved, no one spoke, no one breathed. Then the six of them did all three things at once. The next few minutes proved as predictable as gravity, and she allowed it to happen.

The pilgrims tumbled out of their chairs, fell to the floor, bowed their heads to avert their eyes in humility, all of them shouting words and phrases, most of them indecipherable. But Alexandra heard various renditions of, "Praise the Maze," and "Glory to the Gladers," and "Damn the Grievers to hell," and "Touch me, God, please touch me." But mostly she heard wailing and moaning mixed with hysterical cries of joy. Mannus had remained in his seat, but he stared at her in disbelief.

The others crawled toward her—not on hands and knees like a toddler, but flat on their stomachs, in deference to their God, pulling themselves forward with their arms, looking like nothing so much as worms or lizards or some other slithering creature.

Soon they surrounded her, prostrate, but having shown enough humility to now look at her with pleading eyes. They'd stopped making their noises, now only hoping to be shown some grace by one of the Three to whom they'd devoted their lives.

It sickened her.

It did. But she'd committed to a path from which she could *not* turn. When all of this was over, when she alone stood as their God, Goddess, whatever, then things would change. With the Coffin in her possession, things could finally begin to change. But first, she had to be rid of Nicholas. Mikhail, too, perhaps. But Nicholas first because he was the toughest.

"Do you know who I am?" she asked quietly.

This set off another burst of excitement and she had to let *that* go on for a minute or so. Then she raised her hands to silence them.

"I am your Goddess, and you see me for who I am. You have been in my presence and as you search your hearts, you know what you have felt. I am the Evolution. You are my children and one day soon you will Evolve as I have Evolved. Do you believe my words?"

Yes, yes, they did. They made that perfectly clear before she had to silence them again.

"Your Goddess is pleased. What Mannus has directed is what I have directed. The God named Nicholas has broken the seal before its time, a blasphemy. It has been revealed that he must be punished and that I must rise in his place. Behold your new God."

Back in her apartments, she'd spent hours writing this stuff up. Now she found it hard to believe they'd yet to laugh in her face, roll on the floor, holding their bellies while they shook with uncontrollable mirth. But this was the way of the Godhead, wasn't it? Still, faith and devotion could only be relied on to a point. Now, a step up.

"You asked for proof," she said. "I don't blame you. It pleases me that you wouldn't rise up against the Godhead without absolute knowledge that it was the right thing to do. I've decided to give you that proof." She paused for a very long time, trying even her own patience. Finally, one of them couldn't stand it, anymore. One of the men.

"What is it, Goddess?"

No pilgrim in Alexandra's lifetime had been allowed what she was about to grant.

"I'm going to take you inside the Maze. I'm going to let you see for yourselves."

Hysteria.

2
MINHO

People.

He saw people.

He looked over at Roxy, lying next to him on the crest of a hill. "Tell me I haven't lost my mind. Those are people over there, right? Humans?"

"Yes, Minho. I believe those are humans."

They'd been driving for only a few hours that day when they'd come upon the wide river, its current gushing along at a pretty good clip. A bridge arced across the water, but it was in terrible shape, warped and broken. The skeleton of it, however, seemed intact. They could walk across if they wanted, but they couldn't risk the truck.

They'd taken a break, eaten some food—the supplies were dwindling faster than he dared admit to himself—and then heard what they thought was a laugh. Thinking it had to be a bird, but, just in case, the two of them had crawled up this small hill and peeked over the edge.

People.

He saw people.

Four of them.

They were on the other side of the river, which was why the laugh had been so faint. It must've caught just the right spit of wind for them to hear it at all. The strangers hadn't been there when he and Roxy had first arrived, and now he was glad they'd parked the truck in a secluded spot for just this purpose. No matter how long you went without seeing another soul, you always had to act like maybe, just maybe, you *might* see another soul.

"What do we do?" Roxy asked. "Invite them for tea?"

The Orphan smiled, but he didn't feel it. As hard as he tried, he couldn't suppress the dark, dark feeling that rose up in him. His entire life, he'd been trained what to do in exactly this situation. He needed to kill them. He needed to kill them before they got close enough to spread whatever disease might rack their bodies. But telling Roxy that seemed like a bad idea. So he stayed quiet and she returned her attention to the other side of the river.

There were two men and two women from what he could tell. One of the men was huge in both height and strength. The others all seemed rather similar to each other. Each had an overstuffed pack on their shoulders, and the way they were walking, slumped and haggard, showed they'd been at it a long time. They stopped, dropping those heavy packs carelessly to the ground, near the foot of the bridge, perhaps seeing it much like the Orphan and Roxy had seen it—an excuse to stop and rest. In fact, daylight was melting into twilight; they were probably going to camp over there.

"Do they seem like murderers?" Roxy asked.

The Orphan eased backward down the slope until confident of being unseen, then stood up and walked back to the truck. Roxy followed right on his heels.

"Well?" she pushed. "Do they look like bad guys or good guys? I think they seem perfectly harmless."

But he couldn't give her an answer, yet—he wished she'd stayed on the hill. Placing both hands on the hood of the vehicle, his back to her, he closed his eyes and forced himself to take five long, deep breaths.

Minho, he thought. *My name is Minho.* He held on to that, tried to push away the instinct that had come over him. The instinct to kill and ask questions later. But no sooner had he gone that mental route before he doubted himself. *Those people could be infected. Those people might have the same instincts as me.*

"We need to leave," he said. "It doesn't matter if they hear us—we'll be long gone by the time they do. We can just drive farther north, follow the river until we find another bridge—this one is too frail to hold us, anyway."

She didn't respond, not even a grunt of disagreement or an "Mm-hm" of acknowledgment. He sighed, wishing that he could be alone to deal with this. He wasn't in the mood to argue. Releasing another sigh, exaggerated with frustration, he turned around and leaned backward against the truck.

She was gone. Vanished.

He sprinted back up the hill, hoping she'd kept her senses. He reached the top.

No . . . she hadn't vanished at all.

Down below, she'd just stepped onto the rickety frame of the bridge.

3
JACKIE

Her days went through cycles, and after so many days of going through those cycles—usually in the same order as the day before and then again the day after—it all became a routine. A routine dug deep, all the way to bedrock. Jackie gave up on breaking it, even if she had wanted to.

First came the morning wake-up, usually to the brightly beaming face of Dominic, the human rooster who apparently didn't need sleep anymore. Next came the groggy blah of "getting up and at 'em," as her dad used to say. The stretching, the yawning, the meager breakfast, the chit-chat, the breaking of camp, the dread of following Isaac and Sadina's trail for yet another day lost within yet another week. Always close, never far, never there. It was like watching one snail chase another—the first scoots an inch, the second guy follows. No progress whatsoever.

But on they went, and on they'd go.

For Sadina. For Isaac.

Walk all day, make camp, sleep, start again the next morning, Dominic's face like the rising sun. She'd lost track of how many times the daily cycle had begun and ended, but the current one seemed much like the others.

Except for the river. The river brought change, and the change brought hope, even though there wasn't much of a reason for it. She happily accepted it all the same.

They'd been hiking for hours along the west bank of the wide, swift river they'd come across the night before, keeping close to its edge. The water was deep and the current imposing, the roar of its constant cascade a pleasant chorus that brought her peace. Enough rocks jutted from the surface to break the flow with white splashes and spray and foam, eddies and ripples and sideways flumes—the whole riot of movement had the bewildering effect of seeming frozen to her. Nothing changed even as the river did nothing but, the immeasurable immensity of the water passing by in a blur, each drop of it never to be seen again.

Such was her attention on this wonder of nature that she forgot the simple task of watching where she was going. A small depression in the ground caught her foot and two seconds later she had smacked her face on the ground. Spitting out dirt, she looked up and, to her mortification, every single person in the group had stopped to stare at her.

"You okay?" Miyoko asked, trying to hold in a laugh.

Jackie wiped her face and stood up, refusing to show any signs of the pain in her knees, skinned hands, and bruised face. "I'm glad my klutzy butt could entertain you all."

"You're welcome," Dominic said.

This got everyone to take their eyes off of her and on to him—though they should've been used to his comments that almost, but didn't, make sense. Oddly, as the others looked away, her own eyes focused on a spot far downriver, almost to the horizon. She didn't know if the others had noticed it yet, but she sure hadn't.

"Is that a bridge?" she asked, pointing.

Everyone turned to see what she was talking about. Almost like the shadow image of a crescent moon, a large structure definitely stretched across the expanse of the waterway. There was nothing else it could be.

Old Man Frypan was the one to answer. "I'm damn near ninety years old and got the vision of a one-eyed bat. Am I really the only one who noticed that a half hour ago?"

Nobody responded to that, probably feeling like Jackie—a little bit of awe mixed with a strange shifting of time, like the ground beneath them had suddenly turned into sand. She couldn't put her finger on it, but there was just something foreboding about that bridge. And maybe a drifting of mist or cloud had dissipated, because it seemed a lot clearer now. Maybe a mile away.

Dominic asked a very reasonable question. "Are we sure we want to walk near that thing? My mom used to tell me a story about trolls that live under a bridge. Scared the crap out of me."

"Are you saying you think a troll might live under *that* bridge?" Trish shot back, always loving an opportunity to rib one of her oldest friends. "I honestly don't think trolls are real. In fact, I'm ninety-nine percent certain."

"But Cranks are," he responded. "Bridges seem like places a Crank might live. Or hang themselves from. I bet there's a few Cranks hanging from that bridge."

"Did you eat some wild mushrooms?" Miyoko asked. "Maybe don't do that anymore."

The more they spoke, the more their words slowly faded to a weird, muffled buzz drowned out by the rushing waters of the river. Because she thought she saw something, despite the distance. She was almost sure of it.

"Guys," she said, but not loud enough to make them shut up. "Guys!" This time she damn near shouted it. When they finally gave her their full attention, she pointed exactly as she had done a couple of minutes earlier.

"I doubt they're Cranks," she said, her voice shaky, either from excitement or fear, she truly did not know. "But something is moving on that bridge."

They all turned their heads at once. And her doubts dissolved.

Almost in a whisper to herself, she said, "Maybe it's them."

4
ISAAC

"There's a woman over there."

Letti said it, standing at the entrance to the dilapidated bridge, a thing that had seemed a quaint relic of the past until she said those words. He and Sadina were sitting on a rock in the bridge's shadow, enjoying the respite from the sun.

It had been a simple statement. A simple observation. But an oily dread slicked the back of Isaac's throat.

Timon had been rummaging through their meager belongings, starting the process of setting up camp, but stiffened and dropped everything, ran to where Letti stood. After Isaac and Sadina exchanged a worried look, they did the same. Soon the four of them were lined up, facing the long length of the bridge, which looked like it had melted and twisted in the sun, rusted in the rain, half of its former parts long fallen into the rushing waters below. The structure seemed one stiff wind from completely collapsing.

But it held. It held for now, enough of it still put together for someone to walk across.

And someone was. A lady.

Carefully picking her way along the treacherous steel skeleton, she was heading toward them, maybe a third of the way across. She waved an arm in greeting, and for a split second Isaac thought she'd lose her balance and tumble from the precarious perch. But far too cheerfully, she continued her approach.

Timon then said something that Isaac truly hoped the lady didn't hear.

"Should we kill her?"

Letti's response was even worse.

"Yes."

They're just kidding, Isaac thought. No, they'd killed Kletter. Images of his family flashed across his mind, of Kletter, of water and blood and death. Waving his arms, he yelled at the lady to go back, to run away.

Timon snorted a laugh.

The lady kept coming.

5
MINHO

"Roxy!"

He had sprinted to the edge of the bridge's entrance, feeling as if his feet had barely made contact with the ground beneath. Not quite ready to bound across the sketchy, rusted remains of what had once been a mighty structure, he stopped and yelled her name again. She turned her head to look back at him, and he expected a glare of annoyance—the feeling would've been mutual. But instead she had a genuine expression of excitement, of a childlike glee, her eyes wide and a smile stretched across her face. It made her look twenty years younger.

"Come on!" she yelled to him. "It's totally solid and safe!"

The four strangers spotted earlier stood on the far side of the bridge, lined up like young Orphans waiting to be handed instructions for their next trial. They didn't seem especially menacing, but they didn't exactly scream friendliness, either.

"Roxy, we have no idea who those people are! Get back over here!"

She was a sweet woman, an innocent woman, a trusting woman—the biggest evidence of which had been how quickly she'd warmed up to the Orphan himself when he'd straggled up to her house weeks ago, haggard and hungry. Not once had she shown the slightest suspicion toward him. He couldn't let her make that mistake again.

"Please, Roxy! Just come back and we'll figure this out."

At least she stopped. At least she thought about it. Beneath her, the river raged, its watery roar permeating the air along with the mist that rose like smoke from its churning surface. He didn't want her to fall. He didn't want her to keep crossing the bridge. She just stood there, and the seconds stretched out like taffy.

The strangers hadn't moved a muscle. They appeared to be talking —maybe even saying things to Roxy—but the Orphan couldn't make out a single word. And still she didn't move. Maybe a sudden fear had paralyzed her, a sudden realization of the rash decision she'd made.

"Roxy?" He still had to shout to be heard over the river, but he tried to make it as gentle as possible. "Roxy, just come back to this side!"

She might as well have been dipped in plaster and left to dry.

A lady from the other group moved, walking forward onto the bridge, just a few feet. A metallic shriek twisted in the air when she stepped on a weak spot in the structure. It fazed her enough to stop.

Roxy, still a statue. That decided it.

The Orphan, being careful with each step, picked his way onto the rickety wreck and headed for his friend. Creaks and groans and cracks sounded with every footfall, but the tortured metal gave without breaking. The woman on the far side reached into a pocket.

She has a weapon, he thought, not a doubt in his mind. He ran forward, forgetting any sense of caution. He had to save Roxy. *Had* to. Just like Kit.

The Orphan remembered his lifetime of training.

The Orphan was ready to kill to protect his friend.

The Orphan tripped, hit his head, and fell through a gaping hole in the bridge floor.

Roxy probably heard the splash.

6
JACKIE

She saw her friends. There was no doubt.

Isaac and Sadina.

Jackie and the others were running now. All of them, even Old Man Frypan—though he was lagging behind; he yelled at Jackie to keep going when she turned around to wait for him. Miyoko was beside her, Dominic, too, Lacey right on their heels. Ms. Cowan was just ahead, shockingly fast. The other council members kept up for the most part; Carson's long legs almost spirited him to the front of the pack. But not quite. Trish led the sprint, her speed like a four-legged animal, her movement almost a blur.

The river splashed and roared to the right. A cloud went in front of the sun, which was almost to the horizon, casting an eerie pall over the hilly land. The bridge ahead grew bigger with each step, yet still seemed impossibly far away. Too far away.

Isaac and Sadina stood at the west entrance to the twisted structure, two others nearby. A woman was on the bridge, maybe a third of the way coming from the east. And something had just fallen into the river, barely making a splash—it was probably a piece of steel that had jarred loose.

Jackie knew they'd be noticed soon, despite the sounds of the river and the wind, the distractions of the open land and the twilight sky. She didn't know what they were going to do once they got there, although they outnumbered the people who'd taken their friends.

She ran. The others ran.

Up ahead, the man next to Sadina turned and looked at them.

7
ISAAC

He had to do something. He knew he had to do something.

Things were happening so fast. A guy had just tripped and fallen through a thin gap in the bridge, falling twenty or thirty feet into the rushing waters below. The woman on the bridge had screamed but still hadn't moved, as if she'd frozen in fear. And there was Letti, who'd taken a few steps onto the bridge then stopped, reaching into her pocket for who knew what.

A man was at risk of drowning but no one on their side had acted yet.

"We have to save that guy!" Sadina yelled. She started to move but Timon grabbed her by the wrist. "Let go of me." She said it so coolly that Timon actually released her.

"I'll go," the man said. "You stay here."

"And watch Letti slice that woman's throat like she did Kletter?" She nodded toward the potential victim. "What is wrong with you people?"

Isaac wanted to know the answer to that question, feeling as frozen as the terrified stranger on the bridge. Letti was acting weird. She moved back from the bridge, but instead of scanning the river for the man who'd fallen, she kept gazing at the sky, as if wondering how much rain they might get before the sun set.

Timon turned to head for the riverbank, glancing casually back in the direction from which they'd traveled to get there. He stopped, his eyes widening. Isaac quickly spun around to see what he had spotted.

A few hundred yards away, a group of people, maybe ten or so, were running along the banks of the river toward the bridge. They were spread out, some running faster than others, one person clearly in the lead. And he didn't need to see much detail to know who she was.

He had to stop himself from shouting, even though it was obvious Timon had seen the same thing. Isaac elbowed Sadina, gestured at their new visitors. She wasn't able to hold back.

"Trish!" she screamed, already moving toward her approaching girlfriend. Timon grabbed her for the second time in the last minute.

"No, you don't," he said, his voice grinding, threatening against the backdrop of the river's roar. "And you better tell them to stop where they are or the lady on the bridge is gonna be the least of your worries. Tell them!"

Isaac did it for her, holding his hands up, pushing his arms away from his body several times, urging them to halt, to stay away. Not a single one of them obeyed. Trish was only a hundred meters from them, now, the rest lumbering along behind her. He could see, way in the back, Old Man Frypan trotting as if any step might be his last.

"I warned you," Timon said. But instead of doing anything, he looked at Letti, maybe assuming that she'd pull out the knife that had killed Kletter. But Letti was still looking up at the clouds, not the slightest sign of concern on her face.

"Please don't hurt them," Sadina said. "I swear on this Godhead that you won't shut up about that if you hurt a single one of them, I won't care about myself anymore. If it takes my last breath to get it done, you're dead."

Isaac had never heard her say anything like it in the entire time he'd known her.

Trish was almost upon them, just seconds away, shouting Sadina's name.

Letti, seemingly for the first time, noticed the oncoming rush of people. She didn't reach for a knife or anything else. With an exaggerated sigh, she sat down on the line where the steel of the bridge met the decaying surface of the road.

"Timon, calm yourself and take a seat," the woman said as the other three looked down at her with shocked expressions. "And whatever you do, don't try to hurt anybody. This is exactly what we wanted. What we came here for."

Timon's eyes met Isaac's. Isaac shrugged, baffled as to what Letti meant. Timon sat down.

Sadina ran for Trish.

8
MINHO

So many sensations, all at once.

Piercing, biting cold. Clothes and hair soaked and heavy. The rush and gurgle of water from all directions. Liquid in his nose and mouth, trying to force itself down his throat. The raw, rough ache of coughing and spitting it back out. Disorientation as he spun and twisted in the river. The pain, as seemingly every part of his body smacked against the rocks.

It all reminded him of something, in an odd place of his mind that thought about such things even as he was being whisked away from the bridge and Roxy, maybe to his death. It reminded him of the time he and Orange had stolen a couple of artillery suits and tried them without a single hour of training. The medium had been air and gravity back then, but the nausea and pain had been just as stark.

His head burst above the water. He spit then sucked in a quick breath before dropping below the surface again. His back hit a rock; he spun from feet first to head first. Once again his face found the open air. He'd been grasping and clawing for anything to hold on to since he'd fallen, but now he saw an actual beacon of hope.

A fallen tree on the western bank, its branches extending at least two dozen meters across the river. The Orphan grabbed one of the branches, felt his body jerk to a halt and his legs swing around to point downriver. Suddenly the force of the current was like a hundred hands pulling on his clothes, his feet, his arms, a gale of water beating against his face as he held on tightly. The slightest mistake, the slightest slip, and he'd be shot off.

But he was an Orphan, trained from birth to defeat human and beast, nature and pain. Although he had to admit to himself they'd never said a word about being dragged down a raging river.

He solidified the grip of his right hand, squeezing his fingers against the wet bark until it hurt. Then he released his left hand, held it against the torrent of pressure wanting to throw it downstream. He crossed over his right arm and grabbed the branch a half meter closer to the bank. He tightened that grip and released the other hand. Reached toward the bank, grabbed slimy wood again. He did this, over and over, until he brushed against the actual trunk of the felled tree, which served to deflect some of the pressure.

From there, it was easy. Branch by branch, he pulled himself along the trunk, climbing the tree in reverse toward the western side of the river. Soon he reached dry land and pulled himself onto the steep shore, collapsing on his back; he stared at the sky, the clouds thickening, dusk almost upon them, as he coughed and sputtered to get his breath.

A few seconds passed. Then everything came back to his wearied mind.

He scrambled to his feet, using the massive roots of the tree for purchase. He climbed the bank until he reached a flat spot of grassy earth. And he looked.

He'd floated at least a kilometer from the bridge, maybe more, now on the opposite side of where they'd parked the truck. The grayness of the twilight air made it impossible to know the distance for sure. And no matter how hard he squinted he couldn't see whether Roxy was still standing on the bridge or what was happening with the strangers they'd encountered, now on the same side as he was.

There was nothing he could do but run to find out. First, he snapped a long length of thick branch off of the tree that had saved him. He held it up in both hands, weighing it, judging it. With no other choice, it would do.

He then left the tree behind, sprinting toward the bridge. Toward Roxy.

My name is Minho, he thought. It gave him strength.

9
JACKIE

Trish and Sadina had yet to let go of each other, kissing and hugging then kissing and hugging in a loop that might last another day or two. Old Man Frypan had been the last to arrive at the bridge, breathing so hard that Jackie had to look away, terrified he was going to collapse with a heart attack. Maybe if she didn't watch, he'd be okay.

Instead, she focused on the woman and strange man sitting at the foot of the bridge, the people who'd taken Isaac and Sadina. At least she assumed that's what had happened. The strangers didn't say a word and Isaac was too busy greeting all the friends he'd probably thought he'd never see again. Or maybe that wasn't the case at all. This hardly seemed like a rescue and she was very confused.

Dominic had given Isaac a good old-fashioned bear hug, lifting his friend off the ground and swinging him around three times until both of them were probably nauseous. Now Dominic came up to her, and then Miyoko joined them as well. The three of them watched the ongoing reunions as Sadina finally realized that her own mom was waiting to get a hug herself.

"A half hour ago it seemed like the world was ending," Jackie said. "Now it's like we're back on the island about to have the midsummer festival. Our lives are not normal."

"I don't get it," Miyoko replied. "I mean, who *are* those people?" She gave a stiff nod at the strangers who looked on with faces devoid of expression. The big man was not pleasant to look upon.

"Why don't we ask them?" Dominic didn't wait for a response before walking toward the spot where the man and woman sat. Jackie and Miyoko had no choice but to follow him. "Who are you guys?" It wasn't the best of greetings but certainly got to the point.

The man, one of the largest people Jackie had ever seen, was the one to respond.

"I'm Timon, this is Letti. You want answers, ask her."

"Okay," Dominic replied. "Lady, can you give us some answers?"

The woman didn't respond, just looked up at the sky as if she were bored.

Jackie decided that a little tact might rescue the situation. "My name's Jackie, this is Miyoko, and this is Dominic. You can obviously see that we're friends of Isaac and Sadina's. Did you . . . were you the ones who took them? Did you kill Kletter?" Tact be damned. Remembering the sight of Kletter's bloody throat washed tact into the river.

Before anyone could answer, Dominic made a strange gasping noise and pointed toward the middle of the bridge. "Um, who is that?"

Jackie had almost forgotten about the woman she'd noticed earlier, standing there as if frozen, stuck closer to the other bank. She must've overcome her apparent fears because she was now picking her way across the treacherous skeleton of the bridge, well over halfway.

"That doesn't look safe," Miyoko whispered. "Should we go out and help her?"

The woman named Letti stood up and brushed off her pants. "I'll do it."

"Wait," Jackie said. "I think she's going to be fine."

The stranger had regained a lot of her strength and confidence, almost bouncing from foot to foot as she picked up speed. They all stayed silent and watched as she got closer and closer. The woman was probably around fifty years old, but judging by the lines on her face and the weariness in her eyes, life had put up a hard battle.

Finally, she made it. Leaning down to catch her breath, she sputtered out some words. "That was *not* easy, folks. Not easy at all!"

"What's your name?" Letti asked. She was reaching into a small pack that had a strap slung over her shoulder. "Go on, catch your breath, that's okay. Tell us your name, when you can."

The woman stood up, puffed her chest out a little—she probably didn't appreciate the condescending tone she'd been greeted with. "My *name* is Roxy, thanks for asking. My friend fell off that gosh-darn bridge and I'd appreciate your help trying to find him. He's a tough young fella so my guess is he's fine, but . . ." She glanced around in uncertainty, perhaps wondering whether she had just walked into a pack of marauding murderers.

"I'll help you," Jackie said. "All of us will. Come on."

But she'd barely moved one step when Letti pulled a gun from her knapsack and pointed it in the air. An actual gun. She pulled the trigger and the boom of it seemed to shatter Jackie's eardrums and anything else that might be inside her skull. She stumbled away, her hands on her ears, cowering as if the shot might shatter a glass ceiling above them.

"What the hell was that for?" Miyoko yelled.

Jackie had never seen a gun before coming across the sea. She hoped to never see one again.

Ms. Cowan, Wilhelm, Alvarez, Old Man Frypan—everybody had

been slowly making their way over to the bridge. Sadina and Trish stood the farthest away, but now they came marching in. Something told Jackie that Sadina had already had quite enough of this crazy lady and wasn't scared of her anymore.

"Everybody just calm yourselves," Letti said. She slowly lowered her arm and pointed the gun directly at their newest friend, Roxy, who had the bravery to keep standing tall. "Just stay where you are, exactly where you are, and I'll explain what's going on. Sadina, Isaac, don't get brave on me—I've noticed you two these last few days. I know you think it's time to mutiny, take over the bad lady and her giant friend. I have to say, you should be embarrassed you didn't try it earlier."

Isaac was standing a few feet from Jackie, having stayed quiet through all the new developments. But he bristled at this. "Whatever, Letti. We knew our friends were right on our tails and we're not stupid. Now it looks like you're the stupid one. What're you going to do, shoot us one by one until we overpower you? And you choose some lady we don't even know to be the first one down?"

"That's not very nice," Roxy said out of the side of her mouth, her eyes fixed on the end of the gun. "I'm probably the nicest one here, just ask Minho. I think one of you should probably die first, actually. Should we vote?"

Jackie liked this woman. Sense of humor till the very end.

Letti lowered her gun, then dropped it onto the ground with a clatter. "I'm not killing anyone. Relax. I just wanted to get everyone's attention. I only had one mission in all of this, and Timon doesn't even know what it was. Let's just say . . . Well, I'll use a very old phrase I've read about in the history books. Mission accomplished. My job is done."

"What's that supposed to mean?" the man named Timon asked. "What're you talking about, Letti?"

Jackie really wanted to hear the answer to that, but she noticed something creep over the railing of the bridge, right above the bank that sloped up to that spot. It was a man, dripping wet, a giant tree branch clutched in one hand. *What the . . .*

She'd scarcely noticed him before the man became a blur of dark movement. He flashed across the two meters or so between the railing and where Letti stood, who noticed him at the very last second. Too late.

With a savage brutality, and strangely without making the slightest sound, not even so much as a grunt of effort, the man swung the club of wood and smashed it against the side of Letti's head. The wet thunk of it was a sound Jackie wished she hadn't heard. Several people in the group let out a sharp scream at the sudden attack.

Letti collapsed to the ground in a heap, her bloodied head coming to rest just inches from where Timon looked on in complete shock. Everyone stood still, frozen by the abrupt, violent turn of events. The man who'd bashed Letti's head was breathing heavily, and he threw away the thick branch he'd used as a weapon. The clatter of it against the railing of the bridge was like a bell, tolling.

He looked up at them. He was soaking wet, dark hair plastered to his head, a mishmash of clothes sticking to his very fit body. He had dark eyes that somehow still shone with an intense light.

"My name is Minho," he said, quietly, almost speaking to himself.

10
ISAAC

He'd been through some crazy chunks of minutes in his life—especially in the last several months—but Isaac thought that maybe the last few minutes had topped them all. He'd been so overwhelmed by the events as they took place that he'd stood in one spot, looking from person to person as their part in the play came onstage. And now some crazy man had jumped over the railing of the bridge like a monkey and bashed Letti's head in with a giant stick.

And then he'd said his name was . . .

"Minho?" Dominic repeated. "You're named after *the* Minho?"

Isaac looked at his friend. "*That's* the first question you have?"

As for Minho, himself, he ignored them all and went to Roxy, pulling her into a hug as strong and genuine as the one Trish had given Sadina. Enough to squeeze every last drop of air from her lungs. *As a son would hug his mom*, Isaac thought with a tweak of pain.

Timon the Gentle Giant seemed as lost in the last few moments as the rest of them. He'd crawled over to the very spot from which their newest visitor had leaped onto the bridge, leaned his back against it, and was staring with lifeless eyes at his partner, slack on the ground. Her chest moved up and down, still alive, but her bloody head sure didn't look too good.

Someone needed to take charge of all this madness and figure things out, but Isaac didn't feel like he was that person. He stepped over to where Sadina was whispering something to her mom.

Poking her on the shoulder until he had her attention, he said, simply, "Will you do something? Please?"

"What do you want me to do?"

Isaac shrugged in frustration. "I don't know, but something isn't right. Letti said that she'd done her job, that this is exactly what was supposed to happen. What did she mean?"

Instead of answering, Sadina turned to her mom. "You've been a boss for years. Time to earn your money." She smiled as she said it, and Isaac realized she didn't care what was going on. She'd been reunited with Trish and her mom in one fell swoop and the lady who'd tormented her was lying on the ground with a dented head.

Ms. Cowan was ready, taking on the mantle.

She walked over to where the man named Minho and his—mom? grandma?—were standing side by side, several feet onto the bridge. On the way over, Ms. Cowan leaned over and picked up the gun that Letti had dropped. She shoved it in her back pocket as if she knew exactly what she was doing. Isaac knew the woman had never shot a gun—or even held one—in her long life.

"You said your name's Minho?" she asked the man, whose expression was caught somewhere between dark brooding and relief. "And you're Roxy?"

Roxy was the one to answer. "That's who we are and we've been traveling for weeks to find a better place. Looks like we took a wrong turn. Mind telling us who all these people are? Why that nasty woman pulled a weapon on me? It's a good thing Minho showed up because not a one of you lifted a damn finger!"

"She had a gun," Ms. Cowan replied, calm soothing her voice. As if that were answer enough, she then walked over to Timon, squatting and shrunk against the railing. It was the first time Isaac had ever seen him look small. "And you? I hear your name is Timon? You chose the wrong daughter from the wrong mother to kidnap. What the hell is going on? Why'd you take them? Why'd you kill Kletter?"

Surprising everyone watching, she then kicked Timon in the leg, though it barely budged in response.

"Explain yourself!" she yelled, then kicked him again. The trace of calm from seconds earlier had vanished in the smoke of rage.

Timon wearily gazed up at her. "Lady, I'm as confused as you are. I didn't kill your friend, for one thing. And another, I came on this mission to bring your daughter back to people . . . People who need her to do good things. Not bad things. Good things. Other than that, I have no idea what's going on. Letti was hiding something, that's for sure."

Ms. Cowan didn't respond, but she also didn't take her eyes off the man. She was almost shaking with anger. Isaac wondered if maybe someone else should've taken charge, after all. As if in response to the thought, Old Man Frypan appeared from the back of the group. He was a moving statue of wisdom and experience, and they all knew the things he'd been through long before a single one of them had been born.

Although he was visibly wearied from the weeks of marching and the day of running, his voice came out steady and strong as he addressed Timon.

"From what I've heard so far, young man, one thing sticks out to me like fire in a cornfield. Something that sounds all too familiar and makes my hackles rise to the moon. What the hell you want our Sadina for? What do you mean they need her to . . . to *do good things*? Speak, boy, and don't lie to a man who's on the wrong side of ninety. Got no time for it."

Timon finally seemed cowed by someone. "The Godhead. They

sent me. I came all the way from Alaska—they knew what was going on down in California. They knew about Sadina, about her ties to . . . back then. The Godhead know everything. Why do you think they call them the Godhead?"

"Don't get smart with me," Frypan shot back, making Isaac want to pump his fist. "What's this fool nonsense you're spouting? What Godhead? How in the real God's name could they possibly know about Sadina?"

Timon appeared genuinely miserable, perhaps wishing that he'd been the one conked over the head. "Listen. We know about Kletter, the place they call the Villa, the voyage to the island. The Godhead probably had something to do with it! They don't tell me stuff. But if you don't realize there was something bigger behind that trip to the Munie island then you're as big a fool as I am. The Godhead *need* her for the next stage of Evolution."

Old Man Frypan grew visibly frustrated. "Anybody else want a turn at kickin' this big fella? The more words that come out of his mouth the less he makes sense." Isaac almost volunteered—although he didn't altogether hate the man. Letti had channeled most of his hate in her direction.

"I know exactly what he's talking about."

All heads turned to the one named Minho. Isaac swore the young man had grown a few inches taller and miraculously dried off from his unfortunate spill into the river.

"Yeah?" Frypan replied. "Then I'd love to hear it."

Minho looked so serious, so dangerous, in that moment, that Isaac took a step back.

"I came from a place called the Remnant Nation. We know all about this Godhead, stationed up in Alaska. You could say they're our . . . our sworn enemies. I've been taught from the first memory to my last that we should hate them. They represent the Flare and everything that comes with it—they want to accept it, embrace it, manipulate it, make it work for us and not against us. My people only see the evil in the Flare, devoted to eradicating every last speck of virus from the world. You're talking about two religions here, both in a race to the end. And one won't rest until the other's gone."

Dominic sighed and whispered under his breath, "I was really hoping for a happier story than that."

Old Man Frypan pointed down at Timon. "So you two are mortal enemies? Is that what you're telling me? After all the crap that's hit this world?"

Minho shook his head. "I didn't say that, sir. I didn't say anything like that. I happen to think for myself and I have reasons for being out here. Those reasons are my own and not to share."

"Trust me," Roxy added, patting Minho on the arm as if proud of him. "He's as good as they come, and if you gotta choose a side, I'd choose his. Not that . . ."—she waved at Letti on the ground, gave her a disgusted look, then waved at Timon—"not the ones with guns who run around threatening people."

Isaac couldn't have agreed more.

Old Man Frypan was about to respond but then stopped, his mouth halfway open, the words frozen on his lips. He looked around him as if a fly had buzzed in and was driving him crazy.

"What's that noise?" he asked.

As if a lever had been pulled, Isaac now heard it, too.

A thrumming sound. Deep, vibrating the air, coming from all directions at once and growing in volume. It was like the land beneath their feet had turned into a giant piece of metal and someone had struck it like a gong. Isaac could feel the trembling in his feet, in his ears, in his bones. He and the others were like children looking for a lost pet, slowly spinning to look in all directions for the source, stumbling into each other, asking the same questions.

What the hell was that noise?

In a matter of seconds, without any one individual pointing it out, they all naturally turned toward the east, from where it had become obvious the noise was coming. Shadows blotched the dusky, overcast sky, but these were no clouds. At least a dozen dark shapes hovered above the horizon as if by magic, flying toward the bridge from the distant mountains. Although they appeared small at first, almost unmoving, they were growing in size and obviously flying in low.

Isaac knew it wasn't magic. He'd been taught his history. He knew of such things, machines defying gravity—balloons, planes, helicopters, bergs, spacecraft. But never would he have guessed as a child that someday he might see one, himself. Or a dozen, as he saw now, of varying sizes. Most were wide, round, metallic, maybe the size of two or three yurts back home smashed together. A couple of them were much larger than the others.

"Minho?" Old Man Frypan asked. "Timon? Either one of you know anything about this?"

The cacophonous noise had grown, gradually until it seemed like it had been there all along, the roar of the river times a thousand. The machines were almost on them, impossible slabs of metal shooting through the sky. Isaac, in a sudden and inexplicable fit of bravery, ran up to the man named Minho and grabbed him by the shoulder, forced him to turn and face him.

"What are they?' Isaac yelled. "What's happening?"

Minho met his eyes, stunned, lost. He didn't answer the question but he did respond, saying the same thing twice, barely loud enough to be heard.

"They knew all along. They knew all along."

CHAPTER TWELVE

Machines of the Earth

I
ALEXANDRA

They hadn't seen the real sun even though it had risen hours ago—and the fake one barely gave any light at the moment. She sat on a chair and her pilgrims sat on the ground, their heads bowed. Above them, the great stone ceiling of the cavern hung like heavy clouds—but never moving, always thick and dark, always reminding you that a single crack of nature and the world might come tumbling down and crush you.

"Have you seen enough?" she asked, her voice sharply echoing amongst the remnants of the Maze despite how quietly she'd spoken. All around them, monoliths of broken rock and pillars of shattered cement lay scattered like the building blocks of a huge child. Her newest servants—as devout as the Evolutionary Guard—had barely been able to keep their eyes inside their sockets with all the gaping they'd done during the walk to the Glade of old.

Whispers of "Yes, Goddess" and "Yes, oh Holy One" skittered

through the air like the ragged footsteps of mice. Even Mannus, her horned friend who was so vital to the upcoming days' plans, tried to act the part, although he tossed a quick roll of the eyes when possible.

Before them, directly at her back, lay the wide-open Box, its rusted metal doors slid into the recessions hidden under the stone floor. The revealed hole was dark and deep, not showing the slightest hint of what lay below. It didn't matter. Every person on the ground at her feet knew that it was the greatest of blasphemies to open the Box. They had been taught their entire lives that it was to be sealed forever.

"Do you believe me?" she asked, even quieter this time.

The same whispers of affirmation cut across the vastness of the cavern.

She had them. Simply allowing the pilgrims to see the ruins of the Maze would've been enough to buy their eternal loyalty, to take her every word as scripture, her every command as law. They would do anything she asked, without exception. And one day, although they didn't know it, she was committed to rewarding them with the closest thing to life eternal that mere mortals would ever know again.

"What do you think you're doing?"

She almost jerked her body, almost gasped. Almost. But she didn't.

It was Nicholas, First of the Three, Second to None. Or, as she liked to think of him, the Ugliest and Dumbest of Them All. She wondered if he knew that he had less than three days to live?

He had surprised her—but that didn't mean she wasn't prepared. She was *always* prepared.

She turned her body in the chair, saw him standing on the other side of the dark chasm of the Box. "Thank you for joining us," she said.

"Joining you?" he barked. "What . . . Who are these people? What's going on?" He could only show so much anger, only reveal so much truth with actual pilgrims in his presence. She knew that deep down he was already planning a brutal confrontation once they were both in private.

"You've made your decisions," she said calmly, counting through the digits in her mind even as she spoke. "You've made your exceptions to the things we've preached for decades. I accept those, as I ask you to accept mine. Do you agree?"

She hoped the odd, slightly awkward line of questioning would throw him off. She could see the effort he made to maintain his composure, relying on the Flaring discipline as much as she.

"Just . . . explain," he said.

She was happy to. "I've decided to bring several pilgrims under my direct control, to show them things that no one else can see. They'll be able to testify, to preach, to quell the rising curiosity of the other followers in the city. Since you opened the Box, I need to have them, to help me move in the direction you're planning for."

There it is, she thought. If he didn't deny it, openly, right now, the pilgrims would know for certain that Nicholas had been responsible. He'd given her a bonus. His annoyance might as well have been written on his face with charcoal.

But he did his best to recover. With hands clasped behind him, he walked along the edge of the Box until he'd reached her, where she still sat, now facing her new devotees. She didn't rise to greet him, nor did she bow her head, and this upset him—to do such a thing with pilgrims present. But now those pilgrims would see that in her own mind, and therefore in their own, collectively, she was already their new God.

Nicholas addressed them. "I'm . . . humbled that all of you would be here, to see the magnificence of the Maze, where all things began. Although I wish Alexandra had given me warning, I accept your pilgrimage. Your God is pleased. Before you decide to spread the word, I ask for time. The Godhead must discuss these things and come up with the best plan. Do you understand?"

He directed this last question at Alexandra, who merely looked at him and nodded.

Nicholas then did what he used to do all the time, once upon an age. He stepped through the small crowd of followers and touched them, lightly, once on the forehead, once on the nose, once on the chin. He told each pilgrim in turn that he loved them, and that someday soon the Evolution would accept them all into its graces.

Then he left, not meeting Alexandra's eyes even once since she'd nodded.

I've got you, she thought. *After thirty years, I've finally got you.* Maybe she'd have them cut off an ear or two and turn them into holy relics. Hell, maybe she wouldn't stop there.

Alexandra was having too much fun. But she knew, somewhere on the periphery of her consciousness, that all of this was to hide a pain that had been trying to break through, break out, crack the surface for a long time. A pain she hadn't thought of for many years. Why, now, did it come to her? For the thousand thousandth time in her life, she pushed it back into the darkness.

Then she stood up and spread her arms to the sides.

"Pilgrims, arise."

2
ISAAC

The airships hovered above them, at least a dozen of the things, the hum of their engines vibrating Isaac's skull, the blue flames that kept them afloat unlike any fire he'd ever seen. Air swirled in great pockets, blowing his hair and clothes one way and then blowing them another. He still stood next to Minho, who merely looked up at the flying machines with something like dread. Isaac figured this wasn't a good place to be, but that to run at this point would be as fruitless as using a towel while still in the ocean.

Nearby, his friends huddled in small groups—Trish, Sadina, and her mom; Dominic, Miyoko, and Jackie; Alvarez and Wilhelm; Carson and Lacey. Old Man Frypan stood apart and alone, his face unreadable as he peered up at their heavenly visitors.

Several minutes passed after the flying machines arrived, no further action, no sounds other than the overwhelming roar of their engines. A couple of the airships were indeed far larger than the others, cumbersome and clunky, their hulls almost like giant, dented globes—where the others were relatively flat, more streamlined for movement. Isaac waited along with the others, wondering what could possibly be in store.

"They're called Bergs." Minho had stepped close enough to say it directly into Isaac's ear.

"I've heard of those."

"I knew my people had such things, but . . . not this many."

"How do you know it's them?"

Minho pointed at a spot on the bottom edge of the airship—the Berg—that was directly above them. A simple depiction of a person had been painted there, neither man nor woman, raising their right arm, elbow bent at a right angle. A wide circle of red encircled the hand, which was open with fingers splayed as wide as possible. Jagged points rose above the circle like spears, maybe a dozen in all, making it look like the wall of an ancient fortress, or perhaps a crown.

"It's definitely them," Minho shouted, having pulled his head back. "It's them and I think they let me go, followed me here. I'm . . . sorry. I don't really understand."

Isaac pointed at Letti, still prone on the ground. "Did it have something to do with her? Have you ever seen her before? Or him?" Now he pointed at Timon, gawking at the ship-spotted sky just as much as anyone else.

"Never."

They might have talked more, but things changed as soon as the word came out of Minho's mouth. The Bergs began to move, shifting their positions in a coordinated effort. The two spherical behemoths floated to the center of the group, the flatter, smaller ones creating a perimeter around them. The roaring sounds of the blue flames and the mechanical clanking of machine workings that Isaac didn't understand—the noise of it all slammed into the tiny holes of his ears and pierced his brain. He thought of all the good times he'd had in the Forge, making such things as nails and hammers and plows. How outrageously primitive it all seemed now.

A crack of light appeared along the bottoms of the two globe-ships, then expanded as doors slowly, really slowly, began to spread open. At the same time, three of the escort Bergs on the outside of the group dropped toward the ground, stopping several dozen meters above the whipping grass. Cracks of light appeared in these, too, but of a different sort. Half of their bottom surfaces lowered away from the ship like a ramp, angling down until their edge thumped to a stop, hovering open in mid-air.

Things appeared in the light from within, shadows moving upon shadows, all of them human-shaped. And then . . . and then they were tumbling out of the ships, from all three of them. Bodies, chained together, clothing in tatters, flopping like discarded trash on top of each other when they hit the soft, grassy earth. It happened in three spots, together forming a rough semicircle on their side of the bridge, trapping Isaac and his friends. The bodies were moving, pushing and pulling on each other, struggling to stand up. They were human enough, for certain—except the eyes. The eyes had almost no life in them at all.

That voice, which had grown quiet in recent days, once again screamed inside Isaac's head.

CRANKS!

Could it be? Could it really be possible?

"The bridge!" Old Man Frypan shouted. "Everyone head across the damn bridge!"

But then he noticed what Isaac was just now seeing. A fourth Berg had dropped a pack of bodies on the other side, and they were already stumbling onto the rickety skeleton of steel. Isaac looked back at the other groups. Somehow they'd stood up, stopped fighting each other, and seemed to be coordinating without words. They spread out, chains linking their hands and feet together, forming a fence that soon stretched in one continuous arc around Isaac's friends, bank to bank in a half circle, the bridge entrance at its core.

Trapped. They were really trapped.

By Cranks. By the boogeymen of every scary story he'd ever been told.

He grabbed Minho by the shirt. "What can we do? What . . . what do we do?" He was shouting, throwing all the fear he'd ever felt in his life into the words.

Minho shook his head, his expression pained, but empty of fear. The guy wasn't scared.

"Tell your friends!" he shouted. "Tell them not to fight or they'll be killed!"

Isaac was ashamed to admit it, but he'd never once considered fighting. Not against an army of Cranks and a sky full of flying machines, shooting blue flame like the power of a thousand forges. After everything, he'd never felt so completely hopeless as he did in that single moment.

He looked up at the hovering globes of metal, their doors now completely open.

From within their hulls, lowering to the ground like ancient gods, giant machines descended—all steel and glass and wires and hoses and four attachments that extended downward like legs but looked like giant wheels with spikes protruding in all directions. They descended to the sound of grinding, angry, screaming metal, until they landed with a rumbling boom of thunder that seemed to shake the entire earth.

All the while, unconsciously, Isaac and the others had slowly stepped backward to make room for the inexplicable vessels, to avoid being crushed. There was nowhere to run and there was nowhere to hide.

He looked at Sadina. At Trish. At Dominic. At Jackie. At Miyoko. At Old Man Frypan, Carson, Lacey. He looked at all of his friends, even Timon, even Letti, even Minho and Roxy. He looked at all of them and wondered, simply and with surprising peace, if it was all over. If, like for many of his ancestors, the world had come to an end.

The machines made a horrible screeching sound, the wheels and spikes moving in a coordinated, horrifying dance, then headed toward them.

PART FOUR

Old World, New World

I'm in a truck. On a road. A road scattered with the remnants of a world.

My life is over.

But I don't feel sad. I feel worry and hope for Keisha and her kids. It's enough to push the sorrow aside. I'm so glad I met them before the end. I feel loss for Thomas, Minho, for all of them. But I worry and hope that they'll succeed, that they'll win. That they will survive and be happy. It's enough to push the sorrow aside.

What does it matter? The madness is knocking. The madness is creeping in, under the door.

They say that some things are worse than death. That might be true. Probably is.

But life and death are the beginning and end of beauty. You can't have one without the other.

I feel like maybe I'm rambling.

—*The Book of Newt*

CHAPTER THIRTEEN

Belly of the Beast

I
JACKIE

"Are you okay? Are you okay?"

Miyoko had her arms wrapped around Jackie, speaking those lines repeatedly into her ear. She nodded each time in response, but it must not have been convincing. Jackie herself wasn't convinced. In fact, she knew it not to be true.

She wasn't okay. Not at all.

She and a few others were locked up, stuffed into a tiny compartment within one of the flying machines they called Bergs, one of only a million things in the last day that were so foreign to her. Things she'd heard from old people and read in books and imagined in her head as a child. Vehicles that defied gravity, fire burning from holes like dragon breath. Machines the size of mountains that walked on spiked wheels. Guns. Bridges. People in strange clothing that certainly hadn't been made by a little old lady and her loom.

And those freaks. The ones in chains, their eyes full of death and madness, moving in sync as if they were all part of a single organism. *Cranks.* The word itself conjured nightmarish stories told around a fire and morbid jokes amongst friends on the island. Cranks. They'd been Cranks, though not quite like any description she'd ever heard.

Ms. Cowan squeezed her knee, bringing her back to the current nightmare. She sat directly in front of her, pressed so close they had to interlock legs. With a forced effort that made her want to cry, she smiled. Dominic was there, also, to her left, next to Old Man Frypan. The other two men from the east coast of the island—to whom she'd never said more than three words—were crammed on both sides of Ms. Cowan. Miyoko was to Jackie's right, arms wrapped around her because she must've appeared the most distraught after what had happened.

Taken. They'd been taken. Stolen.

She could barely recall the details without shaking, without her mind pushing it away before shutting down again. But images flashed across her vision, even with eyes open.

The Cranks, stepping closer and closer, as one, tightening the noose of their trap.

The two walking machines—dropped from the globe-shaped Bergs like birthed animals—whirled and clanked, moving in ways she couldn't comprehend, the wheels and spikes churning in constant motion. There were strangers running around, dressed in black clothing that glinted like quartz in the sun. Then something hard and cold had extended from the bottom of the machine like an arm and wrapped around her torso, gripping her tightly, ripping her from the ground and into . . . inside the monster itself, into its belly of steel and darkness. Soon Miyoko was dropped in, then Dominic and Ms. Cowan, then the three old men. So far there'd been no sign of their other friends.

Dead, she thought. *Please don't be dead.*

That was all. There was nothing else. Nothing to think, nothing to say. She didn't understand what was happening to them, and she'd never felt anything like the terror that shivered inside her. She could only hate herself for ever getting on that damn boat.

The machine purred and clanked and roared as it rolled to destinations unknown.

Like that machine, she trembled.

2
MINHO

After they'd been captured, literally lifted by the claws of the Grief Walker, he'd been placed in a cell, all by himself, enraged to be separated from Roxy. He was as confused as he was angry. Nothing made much sense to him. Well, except for one thing. He was a naive, gullible, reactionary fool. To think he could outwit the Grief Bearers, the priests and priestesses, the entire Remnant Nation. How could he have believed that one young man, raised and trained by a people that killed strangers on sight, by a people that had established a brutal, survivalist regime that devoted their lives and civilization to preserving their own and destroying the Godhead . . . How could one man fight against that?

What had he been thinking? That question was all he could . . . *think* about.

A door opened with a metal shriek. A man stepped inside. The door closed with a metal shriek. The man wore a mask, an oval of hard metal with slits for eyes and mouth.

"Orphan, bow your head," he commanded. Nice fellow. "I'm Griever Barrus. From this moment on, you have no room for error. One more mistake, no matter how small, and you're going to Hell." He smiled at the double meaning.

Minho knew that phrase was used as an insult in the very old days. But this man, this man with the mask, he meant it in a very literal way. Hell—the floor below the lowest floor at the fortress. So near to the place where he'd saved the boy, where he'd saved Kit's life.

He was brave enough to speak. "Griever Barrus, am I allowed to ask questions and be honest? I can still help with whatever it is you're trying to accomplish. What I did isn't what it seems. If you'll let me explain . . . present my case." He despised having to grovel and beg like this, though he was no stranger to it. "Please, just hear me out."

The man, slightly stooped, wearing the mask and rough robe that showed his humility, took a seat on the other side of the small room, crossed his legs, then stared straight at the Orphan.

"You were never this talkative back home in the fortress." The man's voice came to him muffled and distorted, an electric charge oddly buzzing and sparking against certain sounds and consonants. Almost . . . robotic, though Minho had rarely seen such marvels of science. "I'm certain I heard you say more words just now than in your entire previous life."

Minho leaned forward, against the restraints clasped around his hands and ankles. He closed his eyes and forced a few deep, penetrating breaths, holding them inside of his heart and lungs for a spell then blowing it all out again.

He decided to get right to the point. "My goal was to infiltrate the Godhead. Any way possible. No matter what. I knew that mission would never be approved by the Great Master in the Golden Room, and so . . . I took a risk. I'm sorry for the deceit. But it was working. Those people you captured can get us into the Godhead city."

The Grief Bearer coughed. "You do realize that we've been aware of your location since the second we left you to wander the wilderness? That we were in league with the woman named Letti? That this was all a plan for us to get these people?"

Minho nodded. "Yes, sir. I know it'll be hard to believe, but I suspected it. I had no choice but to continue on the mission, knowing our goals were aligned." *I'm talking too much, and not very naturally*, he chided himself. Every lie was only making the one before it more obvious.

"Is that so?" The man chuckled; his laugh sounded like the buzz of a cracked lightbulb, his mask bouncing along with the forced mirth. "Enough of this. I honestly don't care what you intend or don't intend. Say nothing else of our order, of our nation, but we are certainly the most pragmatic of pragmatists. Do you understand? All that matters is accomplishing what lies ahead. Are you willing to help us, or not?"

Minho had truly become the Orphan again. For now. He simply nodded, and resolved to ditch the hastily concocted plan of talking his way out of things.

"Wise choice, son. The only choice, really. Now, are you ready to listen?"

The Orphan nodded once more.

The man shifted in his seat, changing which leg was crossed over the other. The movement looked like large snakes rustling beneath his robe. "In the last hour, I would hope that you've asked yourself some questions. For one, why did we let you go on the wilderness-wandering in the first place, and why did we feel the need to have you involved?"

The Orphan opened his mouth to respond on instinct but quickly shut it.

"Also, why bring our entire armada of Bergs and Grief Walkers, just to capture you and a dozen other people? It's taken a full three decades of effort to bring those Bergs back to working condition, to find the resources to make it happen. It's taken the most recent decade to design and build just two functional Grief Walkers. We only have two, Orphan. And yet we brought both to that river, that bridge. Doesn't that make you wonder? Doesn't that make you question?"

The Orphan nodded. He was doing a lot of that.

"It's called a trial run, boy. Make sure things work in a real-world setting before the true test comes. And what about the infected? You may have known about the machinery and the Bergs, but certainly not the infected. It seems blasphemous to our teachings and our ways, does it not?"

The Orphan didn't nod. It seemed a question that had no good answer.

"In the fight against evil, you must sometimes use the evil against them. I want you to ponder these things, boy. The more you realize on your own, the more valuable you'll be in the coming days. Locked up in here, you can't see the outside world as we fly. Think about that as well. We've sent all but two of our Bergs ahead to scout and make preparations."

A few seconds passed, neither of them saying a word. The Orphan felt a trickle of sweat slither down his cheek, leaving an icy trail.

The Grief Bearer stood up. "I'll give you a hint, lad. We're not going home, not for a very long time. So settle in and we'll talk more soon."

The door opened with a metal shriek. Griever Barrus, the man in the mask, stepped outside. The door closed with a metal shriek.

Belatedly, the Orphan nodded.

3
ISAAC

He was lying down, on a thin mattress—a bit narrow and a little bumpy. His hands and feet were chained to the railings of the bed, maybe to protect him in case he had a bad case of the sleepwalks. Or, another idea might be that he'd been captured by a giant dinosaur of a machine with wheels and spikes and claws—someone had called it a Grief Walker—and was now imprisoned in a Berg with a bulbous belly and modified containment cells.

Sadina had a cot of her own, right next to Isaac, only a few centimeters of a gap in between. She lay on her side, watching Isaac, not taking her eyes off him even if he closed his own for a while. Trish was on the other side of her, pressed close, arms wrapped around her stomach. It was a sweet sight within the rattling, clanking, jostling, impossibly loud hellhole of unsweetness that was this Berg. No one else was in the room.

All of it, all of it, made for a very unpleasant day. With every twitching muscle in his body he wanted to be back home, back on the island, squirreling his way through the streets and down to the beach, to the Forge, where he could singe his hair and soak his skin with sweat and beat the living daylights out of red-hot, very large things.

"What are you doing, Isaac?" Sadina asked him in a slightly irritated but mostly kind voice.

He'd drifted off a bit, or maybe he'd been hoping she'd think him asleep, but it hadn't worked either way. He opened his eyes and saw that she glared at him as if they were having a staring contest, a nice remnant of the old days in primary school.

"Answer her question." This was Trish, peeking over the edge of Sadina's right shoulder. "Be sure it's a good enough answer to shut her up or we'll be seeing dawn or death before she finally does."

"Oh, what a sweet pumpkin," Sadina responded with all the sincerity of a half-starved rat.

Isaac figured he better start talking before the mushy stuff really got into full swing.

"You guys don't need to worry about me," he said, shifting his body to get more comfortable, yanking on the restraints to conquer a little more freedom. "I'm just spacing, trying not to think, trying not to worry about why we've been kidnapped by complete strangers twice in the last month. Kinda three times if you count Kletter and the boat."

"Seems like you're trying to *not* do a lot of things." Sadina gave him a condescending frown. "I can tell the truth when it comes to you, Isaac. I don't care if your eyes are closed, open, rolled up or peeking down, crying or stung from something caught in your eyeball—none of that matters. I can read you, I've always been able to read you, and I'll be reading you to the day you have your last gasp and die. Now talk to me."

Isaac found just enough of a bright spot inside to let a little laugh escape. "You got me, kid, you got me. Let's see . . . what devious things am I thinking right now? Hmmmmm. What could it be? Let's see . . ."

"Cut the horse crap, Isaac," Trish said tersely. "Just tell us what's on your mind about all this and we'll do the same. We've gotta use our brains to get out of this nightmare."

Isaac knew it was time to get serious, to stop deflecting with the usual avoidance mechanisms. He'd coped with the loss of his family; he could cope with this new, terrifying situation. He sat up, leaned his back against the metal frame of the headboard, pulling the chains attached to his feet to the very lengths of their restraint.

"Okay, let's talk through this, step by step, and make a list of what we do know, what we definitely don't know, and then things we may know, things we're not certain about, guesses, whatever."

"Alright," Sadina said. "So . . . three columns . . . Know; Don't Know; Might Know. How's that? If only I had a pad and pencil."

"You forgot your pad and pencil?" Isaac asked. "Shame on you. Look, let's just talk through it one time, see if we're all on the same page. Pun not intended."

"And we better hurry," Trish added, still peeking like a spooked child from behind Sadina's upper shoulder. "No telling when we'll be yanked out to go somewhere else."

Isaac took a big breath. "Okay. Kletter arrives on our island, convinces us she's legit, that they need Sadina, maybe her mom, maybe some others of us, as many as they can get. She feeds us all that stuff about science and studies and still having a chance to eradicate the Flare forever."

Sadina had been nodding the entire time he spoke. "Yeah, and maybe we were idiots to go, naive enough to think we'd come back to the island soon, whatever. But we went. That's that."

"Right. We get to the continent, safe and sound. Even Old Man Frypan has somehow *not* died and gone to join the Great Gladers in the sky. All is pretty well and we've seemed to gain a liking to Kletter. She tells us about the Villa, lots of scientists and doctors, interested in the bloodlines that descend from the original Gladers—especially Sadina through Sonya. Sound about right?"

Sadina nodded. Trish nodded.

"So I'll go next," Trish says. "We're feeling good, heading toward the Villa that Kletter told us about. Then you two knuckleheads decide to go follow a creepy man into a damned haunted house just for kicks and giggles. And you meet Timon and Letti."

Sadina picked up. "Letti kills Kletter, like there was nothing to it. Or like she'd planned to do it all along. Then they take Isaac and me away, mainly keeping us in line with threats. We left clues for you guys, and I'm pretty sure they knew we were doing that the whole time and didn't do a single thing to stop us. That's why all of you stayed right on our tail, always close."

Isaac's turn. "Which lines up with what Letti said before getting bashed in the head. Do we even know if she's still alive? Anyway, she said this had always been the plan, to get everyone together in one spot —including, I assume, that Minho guy and Roxy. And then, I swear, Letti kept looking up at the sky, scanning it from horizon to horizon, searching for something without even trying to hide what she was doing. It was weird then, obvious now. She knew those Bergs were coming. No doubt. She's in on it, and I have to guess that Timon the Gentle Giant is, too—although he seems a little more braun than brains if you know what I mean."

"Okay," Trish said. "So then these people show up with a dozen Bergs and those weird-ass monster things with spiked leg-wheels and claws and snapped us up."

Sadina rubbed her face and let out a small groan. "Don't forget the whole line of Cranks—yes, Cranks, something I never thought I'd see—tossed out of a Berg like garbage. Chained together, moving around as if they were some kind of sophisticated toy. Then they were a human fence, pressing in, making sure we had nowhere to go."

"Snatched up and here we are," Isaac said. "Why are we here? Why did they need not only giant flying ships and those Grief Walkers or whatever . . . I mean, that wasn't enough, they needed an army-chain of Cranks, too? To capture a dozen people with no fighting skills, no weapons, no sense of direction, no plan whatsoever. The whole thing is bonkers and yes, that's the best word I can think of in the heat of the moment. It's bonkers."

"Don't worry, it's a solid choice," Sadina proclaimed.

Trish thirded the motion.

Isaac leaped to the next logical questions.

"So. Okay. First, what does that all mean? Second, what do we do now?"

A moment passed, each of them avoiding eye contact, looking down as they put some thought into it. Isaac tried hard, letting the succinct pile of details they'd just gone through swim around in a small space within his mind. Back and forth and up and down, one by one, passing his internal reference of vision as he tried to put the pieces together.

"Here's all I know," Sadina said. "We've been flying through the air for at least a few hours, now. I can't quite tell which direction we're going or how fast, but it's not a short trip. That much is obvious. Wherever they're taking us, I don't think it can be good. Simple as that."

"Simple as that," Trish agreed.

"Simple . . . enough, I guess," Isaac whispered, not sure it was simple at all. "So . . . what's your point?"

Trish and Sadina looked at each other, then both turned their gaze to Isaac.

Sadina spoke. "We've gotta get off this fancy ship, Isaac, before someone on this fancy ship kills us or worse."

Simple as that.

With a heavy heart, Isaac realized that after all that talking, they'd gotten absolutely nowhere.

4
JACKIE

Hours in that little cell, crammed in with those bodies, breathing each other's breath, smelling their odor and sweat and feet and all manner of unpleasant things, listening to their whimpers and cries and silent prayers—it had all added up for Jackie. Hours. Barely able to find air to suck into her lungs.

There had been a lot of movement after being captured. Enough to make her stomach jump into her throat, especially one particular shudder and jolt that made her think the machines had been pulled back into the Bergs, and the Bergs had once again taken flight. Flight. Flying. It was beyond her capacity to envision and yet she was doing it. Flying above the earth.

She'd finally detached herself. Closed her eyes, thought of better places, refused to respond to any physical stimuli or noise or voice. She pretended, absolutely, that she simply wasn't present and accounted for. Hours.

A door opened.

Cool, swirling air whooshed into the room, so clean and full of oxygen that Jackie teared up as she sucked in breath after breath, pulling them deep, deep into her chest, holding it there, sighing it out in a gush, ready to start over again. She instantly felt better. But the insurmountable, crushing weight of her worries remained, all the same.

A man dressed in a robe of coarse material darkened the small space revealed by the door, silently watching for far too long to seem normal. Bright light shone behind him, and the whirs and beeps and hums of heavily running machinery grew much louder. The robed man had an odd mask on his face—an oval of hard plastic or metal, slits for eyes to see and a mouth to speak and breathe. Creepy as hell, this guy.

"Who speaks for this group?" the man asked. "I need a representative."

What an unfeeling thing to say, Jackie thought. Knowing the uncertainty and terror they must all feel, but not a word of compassion or empathy. It was something to grasp, something to hold on to. She could hate this man, and yank herself from the swamp in which she'd sunk. Everyone but Miyoko was asleep, knocked out from exhaustion and fear.

"I'll do it," she said, weakly, but raising her hand to make it clear she'd volunteered.

Miyoko gaped at her, maybe the only person more surprised than she was, herself.

"What're you doing?" she asked, probably wondering what had come over this deflated person she'd been comforting for hours. "Ms. Cowan or one of the council members should do it. Or make Dominic go. He's the biggest."

This bugged Jackie but solidified her decision. "I don't think we need older or bigger right now. I think we need smarter."

Miyoko smiled at that, then reacted in the best way possible. She nodded, firmly.

"Come on, then," the masked creep said. "I'm not asking for a human sacrifice for Flare's sake. Just someone to talk for the rest of you. Come on. Please."

Jackie couldn't read the man. Maybe he was just an errand boy. Regardless, she stood up, shook away the fear that had tried so hard to drown her in the last few hours, and followed him out of the cell.

5
MINHO

A young woman was brought in, dark of skin and hair, eyes that burned with emotion, though he couldn't quite tell what that emotion was. Something between childlike fear and murderous rage. She had a long, thick braid of hair draped over one shoulder. Griever Barrus saw to it that she sat in a chair across the table from the Orphan, then quietly slipped out.

The Orphan had been told what to do. But the deepest workings of his inner machinery clanked against his heart, dismayed that Roxy wasn't the one sitting in front of him.

"What's your name?" he asked.

"Jackie. What's yours?"

He had one of those life-defining moments, then, a moment that lasted less than a second. He considered several options at once. He chose.

"I think you already know. Um . . . Minho." He paused, half-expecting her to show amazement that he'd committed such a blasphemy as to name himself openly. And he knew . . . *they* were probably watching, listening, so it had been an incredibly risky calculation. But that's what it was, exactly. A calculation. Show too much resignation and they couldn't possibly believe that he'd repented of his subordination.

"Yes, Minho, that's right," she replied with a forced smile. "I like it.

Your parents must've really thought you'd turn out pretty great. Looks like maybe you didn't though." She gestured at the walls of the small room, obviously meaning much more.

"I don't have parents."

She showed no pity at that—he had to remind himself that she assumed he was one of the bad guys. Worse, she was right. Which only made him all the more resolved on what he must do.

"They want you to tell us about the group you came with. Especially the one named Sadina."

"Came with?" She repeated. "The group I came with? I think you meant to say the group that *your* people captured with a giant, horrible claw of metal. What is this, anyway? You're barely older than I am. Why're you in charge?"

"I'm not." Frustration stretched his nerves so thin he worried they'd snap. "They must've thought you'd feel more comfortable around someone your own age. Look, that doesn't matter. We have about three hours before we get to where we're going. That's three hours they've given us to talk. You don't have to tell me anything right away. But . . ."

He sighed, ashamed of the sweat that had broken out on his forehead. He wanted information from her, and yet not for the reasons that Griever Barrus requested it. Minho wanted to know who these people were and where they'd come from. He *needed* to know. Information might prove to be the only real weapon he could wield in the new plans slowly formulating in his mind. For Roxy, for him, for everyone.

"I don't really care how we do this," he said. "I'm just an underling and I'm doing what I was asked to do. Telling us things can only help you. You're not the enemy to them. And they shouldn't be the enemy to you. It's—"

She interrupted him. "The enemy of my enemy is my friend. Something like that?"

He nodded. "Yeah."

"So who's the enemy? Who's your enemy? And mine, apparently?"

Minho had to tread carefully. "The Godhead. Heard of them?"

Jackie showed a crack in her shell for the first time.

"So you have," he said. "Listen, that's what this is all about. The

Godhead. You talk to me, and I'll talk to you. It can only help the both of us."

She didn't answer at first, eyeing him long and hard. Finally, she appeared to come to a decision, although he wasn't so sure it was a decision that either he or those watching would like very much.

"What would you like to know?" she asked, her smile now genuine.

It was that smile that worried him.

6
ISAAC

At least a half hour had passed since Sadina or Trish said a word. It was as if they'd come to the same realization as he—talk all you want, but when you're chained to bed railings there's not a lot of good it'll do you. He lay with his shackles, staring at the low, gray ceiling, trying to ignore the very real fear that slowly gripped his stomach in an ever-tightening vise.

What was the Evolution that Letti had told him and Sadina about, keeping most of the details a secret. Who was the Godhead? *Were* the Godhead? He couldn't even ask the question correctly in his own mind.

A door opened and two young people came into the room, one boy and one girl. Both of them were dressed exactly the same, in the oddest set of clothing Isaac had ever seen. Black from top to bottom, with a sparkle to it that almost made it seem wet, one-piece suits clung tightly to their skin, broken up by bulges of pockets along their arms and legs, chest and stomach. These pockets were stuffed tightly with something unknown, as if they had to carry their every last possession wherever they went. It looked neither natural nor comfortable, and Isaac wanted desperately to ask them about it.

"We're here to unlock your restraints," the male said. He was a skinny kid, cursed through genetics with a very unfortunate nose, bent to the side like he'd slept with all of his weight on the poor thing every night of his life. "You'll be free to use the attached bathroom, and they're going to serve a meal soon. Just don't do anything weird or stupid and we won't lock you up again. They told us to tell you that we're all on the same side, here."

"Wow," Sadina replied. "Yeah, sure feels like that's the case."

Trish elbowed her. Isaac agreed with the sentiment. Get unchained first, *then* be a smart aleck. He'd learned a few things during the last month of being someone's captive, enough to know that anyone can be manipulated through subtlety and patience. On both sides.

The two guards—that's the word that popped into Isaac's mind to describe them, dressed as they were, with keys to their chains—came over to the small beds, now looking three feet taller as they stood there. Both of them had short hair, or hair slicked underneath the black caps that they wore, it was hard to tell. The girl had a stern look on her face, as if she *really* hated her job, and when she tilted her head one way, Isaac could see that her hair was actually bright orange. Now that was something he'd never seen before.

The boy, stern enough but a downright gentleman compared to his partner, bent over and quickly set about unlocking the shackles with a long metal key. Clicks and clacks replaced the silence as he worked at it, his awkwardly crooked nose not always moving in the same direction as the rest of his body.

"You guys have names?" Trish asked.

"No," the girl snapped. But then the boy answered in a sad, reserved manner. "No, we don't have names. Not yet, anyway. We're Orphans, and we're all one and the same." He had finished Trish and Sadina, and now moved to work on Isaac's restraints.

To his surprise, the girl's entire demeanor changed in an instant, sporting a devious smile and an excitement in her eyes. "You can call me Orange. That's what your friend, the Orphan, calls me. And he calls this guy Skinny because calling him Nose would've really hurt his feelings."

"That's just mean," the boy known as Skinny muttered. "You guys will find that Orange is a very interesting, adventurous, humorous person, and that I'm pretty much the most boring human being ever born." With a satisfied sigh he unclasped the last lock on Isaac and stood up. "But we call your Orphan friend Happy behind his back because he's the exact opposite of that. When he has a bad day he likes to beat his fists against a stone wall until the knuckles bleed. But he's not all that bad. Sometimes he shares his food."

"Wait," Sadina said, rubbing her eyes, now sitting on the end of her bed, almost touching the one named Orange with her knees. "Wait . . . just wait. Lots of questions, here, but who is this Orphan friend you keep talking about? We don't have an Orphan friend, unless you're talking about Isaac." She reached back and squeezed his hand. "But you say the word like it's some kind of title, and the same as you. I promise we don't have any friends who walk around bragging that they don't have names or parents."

"But he was with you when our Bergs arrived," Skinny said.

"You mean that Minho guy?" Trish asked. "The crazy dude that climbed out of the river with a log and bashed Letti over the head? The guy who showed up with his grandma?"

The questions were enough to make both Skinny and Orange look perplexed.

"His grandma?" Skinny repeated, as if that might be the strangest word uttered in the entire conversation.

"Let's get on with it," Orange said. "We only have a couple of hours before we get to Alaska, so we better get a move on."

"Alaska?" Isaac, Trish, and Sadina said all at once.

"No more questions," Orange commanded. "It's not our place. Get cleaned up, use the bathroom, we'll be waiting at the door. You have fifteen minutes."

Isaac and his friends stood up, stretched, made annoying moans and grunts as they did so.

Sadina pointed at the black, sparkling material wrapped around Orange's body like a second skin. "What's with the . . . the weird pajamas? You guys ever take those off?"

Orange frowned but Skinny seemed willing enough to share. "They're called artillery suits. Not many Orphans are trained on how to wear them and use them, but we are. Maybe someday you three can be as cool as us. They're a lot of fun, in practice anyway. Probably not so much if we'd ever have to use them . . ." He didn't finish and appeared to regret opening his mouth in the first place.

"It takes a lot of skill," Orange added, as if implying that none of them had such skills.

"What are the pockets stuffed with?" Isaac asked. They bulged like elongated tumors on their arms, legs, and down the front of their torsos.

Orange replied with a condescending glare. "What do you think? It's called an artillery suit."

"Not a lot of artillery where we come from," Trish replied. "Not many Bergs or giant machines with spiked wheels, either."

Isaac found himself completely mystified by the artillery suits, himself. Why would you walk around with pockets stuffed to bursting with explosives? Seemed slightly dangerous, call him crazy.

"Artillery." Sadina sounded out the word in contemplation. "So . . . are you guys, like, living bombs? Do they shoot you out of a cannon?"

Skinny started to say something but Orange cut him off. "Enough of this. No more talking. You have ten minutes so I would hurry if I were you."

"I thought you said fifteen?" Isaac asked.

"You just wasted five of them. Now get on with it. We'll be right outside. And don't worry. We're . . . we're friends. It's going to be okay."

She and the skinny boy with the unfortunate nose left the room and closed the door.

7
JACKIE

The Orphan—that's what he insisted on being called because *Minho* would get him into trouble—had asked her plenty of questions so far, none of them very memorable. About the island, about the boat and Kletter, about each person who'd come from the island. Jackie gave him all the details he wanted because none of them seemed to matter all that much. And when it came to Sadina—about whom he was particularly interested—she could be honest and say she didn't know much. Because she didn't.

But there had been something odd in his questioning. He didn't put much sincerity into the effort, as if he didn't care one whit about the answers. And he kept widening and squinting his eyes, tilting his head in subtle ways, fidgeting with his hands. She guessed that he was trying to send subtle clues, but the only thing she got out of it was that this guy either had a serious neurological problem or that maybe, just maybe, he wasn't in league with the people who'd taken them. An attempt to show that he was on her side.

But she had her own goals. Learn what she could. If she had to be buddies with this Orphan fellow, then so be it.

He opened his mouth to ask away again but she held up a hand to stop him.

"No. If you want me to keep going, then I want answers to some of *my* questions."

He didn't seem to like that, his eyes flickering to the door as if his bosses might barge in at her audacity. But nothing happened.

"Okay," the Orphan said. "Go for it. Um, some things I might not be able to talk about. Just letting you know."

She dove in. "Where are you from? And these people you work with?"

"We're from the Remnant Nation," he said after a pause. "Our whole civilization exists to fight the Flare and all its variants. And to fight the Godhead, who want to *use* the Flare to turn humans into an entirely different species. It's a battle that's been going on for decades. Not a literal battle, but a . . . philosophical one, I guess."

"Seems to me that maybe that's changing." Jackie raised her eyebrows.

The Orphan looked so uncomfortable that she felt sorry for him. "Yeah. Looks that way."

"Tell me more about the Godhead. I mean . . . are they supposed to be actual gods? And how has the Flare changed since it first broke out? How many variants are there? Are they all bad?"

The Orphan started coughing. He kept at it, covering his mouth, not stopping. Jackie thought it was an act, and a poor one at that. He stood up.

"Sorry, I need a break. Need to use the bathroom. Do you?"

For the first time, all the weird things he did with his eyes, trying to say something without saying it, clicked for her. He had a message to give, and it was killing him that he couldn't come out and spill it.

"Yeah, I do, actually. Gotta pee real bad."

"Come on. It's close."

He opened the door and waited for her. They stepped into a narrow hallway and she followed him ten feet or so to another door. He was just about to open it when he leaned toward her, close, his nose almost brushing her ear.

"We can't let them get all the way to Alaska. It'll be too late if we make it that far."

She pulled him into a hug, hoping that anyone who watched might think they'd made a connection during the interrogation. She'd heard of that before in school—something called the Stockholm Syndrome, where the captive gains a closeness to the captor. She banked on it, now.

Whispering back to him, she said. "You're going to get us off this ship?"

"Yes."

"Me and all my friends?"

"I'll try. *We'll* try. I'm gonna need your help. But we have to do it in the next hour. In the next hour or never."

"Okay," she said, unsure of exactly what she was committing to, trusting this weird guy who called himself the Orphan. "So . . . how?"

"Two of my friends are on the other Berg. I didn't know they were coming, but they came. And that changed everything. Gave us a chance. Roxy is over there, too. Just be ready." He quickly pulled back from her hug and looked down the hallway at a man approaching.

Much more loudly, and a little too formally, he said, "We appreciate your willingness to help. Would you like to go first?"

It took her a second to realize he meant the bathroom. She nodded, thanked him, and opened the door, stepped inside. She really *did* have to pee, anyway.

8
ISAAC

He didn't know how he felt about this Skinny and Orange, the two guards with the funny names, but they moved several notches up the rankings when they put a plate of steaming hot food in front of him. There was meat. There were beans. There was something that looked like a blue potato. It could've been worms for all he cared. As famished as he'd ever been, he tore into the meal and greedily drank from the metal cup of water he'd been given.

It was a reunion meal, of sorts. Some of the others had joined him, Sadina, and Trish in the room with the table and chairs—Timon the Gentle Giant, whose face was covered in bruises, and Letti, who had a bandage wrapped around her head. Neither of them so much as met Isaac's eyes, not even once. Also there was Carson and Lacey, their friends from the west side of the island. And, oddly enough, the lady who'd stood frozen on the bridge for so long. Roxy was her name.

But no Jackie. No Dominic. No Miyoko. No Ms. Cowan or Old Man Frypan. No Wilhelm or Alvarez.

"Where are the others?" Sadina asked, even as Isaac tried to swallow an enormous mouthful of charred beef without choking. They'd been expecting everyone to join them but that hope had been quashed when Skinny closed the door. "Where's my mom?"

Orange replied in a voice without the slightest hint of emotion. "They're on the other Berg, flying next to us. The other ships have gone on, well ahead of us. Mommy's okay, so chill your bones."

Isaac reached under the table and squeezed Sadina's leg before she could explode. "I'm sure they're okay, just like us. Eat. It's really good."

That earned him a death-stare but even Sadina couldn't ignore her hunger for long. She and everyone else at the table dug into their food, manners forgotten. Carson and Timon looked big enough and hungry enough to eat everyone's dinner between them. Maybe they could've been friends in another life. As for Lacey, Isaac didn't know her very well, and she'd always been quiet, but she looked so sad as she ate that it broke his heart.

"Why're you guys here?" Sadina asked, pointing her fork at Letti. "Wasn't this all a setup by you? Shouldn't you be in a suite, having your feet rubbed while you eat grapes?"

Letti's eyes were bloodshot and she winced with every move, even the workings of her jaw as she spoke. "It never pays to be a traitor. A lesson people always learn too late. Including me. Looks like our friends that, um, I'm sorry, but the ones that helped us take you from that house . . . Well, it appears they weren't friends after all."

Timon grumbled and darted a hard look at Sadina, then at Isaac, but soon returned to stuffing his mouth with meat and beans.

"Does anyone know what happened to Minho?" the woman named Roxy asked. She seemed a sweet, matronly lady, and the concern in her eyes also hurt Isaac's heart. He set a goal to stop looking at people altogether. "Anyone? I haven't seen him or heard a thing about him."

Orange stepped up to her, put a hand on the woman's shoulder. "He's fine, ma'am. On the other ship and totally fine. I bet you see him soon." Her eyes found Isaac as she said that, staring at him with intensity. Trying to say something but he didn't know what. "But if I were you I wouldn't call him Minho while the bosses are around. They don't like that sort of thing. You know, names and such."

The other guard, Skinny, stood by the door, fidgeting and rocking back and forth on his feet. The bulky, sparkling, tight-wound suit that he wore creaked with all of his movements. *Artillery suit*, Isaac thought. *What in the world does that mean?*

"Why would you do this to us?" Trish asked Letti. "Why would you kill Kletter, take my friends away, lead us to all this?" She gestured at whatever it was that ensnared them within its belly. "How could you do that to such innocent people? I wish you'd died when that guy whacked you over the head. I hope you still die, and I'm glad you were betrayed by your so-called friends."

"Hey!" Timon shouted, spitting out a tiny bit of food. "Easy for you to talk like that, growing up on your safe little island. Things aren't so easy in the real world. We'll see how you get along, kid. We'll see what you do when it comes down to it. You or them. It's not a hard choice. So shut your mouth until you've lived a real life."

Sadina wasn't having any of that. She stood up, threw her plate at Timon's head. He ducked, picked it off the floor, threw it back. Trish knocked it aside right before it struck Sadina's face. Then there was a lot of yelling and Isaac didn't hear a word of it.

He stared at a spot on the far wall, lost in thought. Something was going on. Something to do with Orange and Skinny, and that guy who either was or wasn't named Minho, depending on who you talked to. Something was about to happen.

As if she'd read his mind, Orange was suddenly kneeling right next to him. He met her eyes, and she smiled, along with a barely perceptible nod. She squeezed his arm.

"What . . ." he began without finishing. He didn't know what to ask her.

"Just be ready," she whispered. "And when the time comes, find something to hold on to."

His heart rate leaped so hard he could feel it in his throat. "What . . . how will I know?"

She stood back up, softly speaking as her head passed his.

"Oh, you'll know."

CHAPTER FOURTEEN

According to Plan

I
ALEXANDRA

It was happening today at noon. Finally. After a solid month of meticulous planning.

Mannus sat in a chair, just a few feet in front of her. No one else was in the room, and only Flint still remained in the residence, waiting in the front hall. The amount of deceit, the amount of stealth and secrecy, the amount of sheer guts—all that had been expended and risked in the last month was almost beyond her Flare-enhanced comprehension. It truly surprised her that she hadn't been caught, that her head wasn't on a pole somewhere, like in medieval times, glaring with rotted eyes at the people as a warning.

Medieval times. That gave her a whimsical thought.

"Mannus, you know what? In ancient days, I hear that kings would often say, bring me their heads. Do you think that's true?"

He looked at her like she'd lost her mind. *MADNESS!* She imagined him thinking it. The word was like a wounded animal inside her head, screaming in pain, pulsing with its own heartbeat. Madness. The greatest fear she'd ever known.

"Just answer the question, Mannus."

He shrugged. "Yeah, seems like I read that somewhere. What the hell? Shouldn't we be finalizing things? Not doing history lessons?"

She bristled at that. This man had been given a lot of leeway—she needed him far more than he could even guess—but it still bothered her greatly. Once this was all over . . .

"Careful, Mannus. My point is this—that's what I want. I want you to bring me back his head. It's the only way I can know for sure. The only way."

His eyes found the floor, and she assumed he was trying to hide his frustration. "The Coffin won't be enough to prove it? That he's dead?"

"No. It won't. And I may need something like a head for proof to *others*. I'm starting to think they knew what they were doing way back then."

When he looked up at her again, he'd composed himself. "Okay, Goddess. We'll bring back both things. Can we put the head *into* the Coffin? Make it easier to carry?"

He was joking. She knew he was joking. And he knew she knew. But it was still the most dangerous thing he'd ever uttered in her presence.

"Mannus, I'll know if you, if any of you, open that Coffin. You can't imagine the punishments that will define the rest of your life if you allow such a thing to happen."

"I understand. I'm sorry."

She allowed her anger to show, allowed her face to flush, allowed her eyes to rage. She could've hidden it with the Flaring discipline, with a quick recitation of the digits, but she wanted it to be seen.

"I can't say it too many times. There is pain and suffering that you can't begin to fathom, Mannus. The Coffin is *not* to be opened. If it is, there's not one spot on earth in which you could find a hiding spot. Is that clear?"

She'd shaken him. A rarity. He nodded and bowed his head low.

"Good. We've gone over the plan. All the people are in place.

Mikhail will not be in the picture today, nowhere near Nicholas. You have the codes, the weapons, the passwords, the muscle. Is there anything we've left out or not considered?"

He hesitated, still shaken.

"Speak freely, Mannus."

"It's all there, Goddess Romanov. We've been through every single detail a thousand times. It will go exactly according to plan. I swear it."

Things rarely did, but she thought that this time it just might. The Evolution had never brought her so much certainty and comfort. And it was the Evolution that she served.

"Well, then that's that," she said. "You can go."

He left quietly, the mission begun. In a few hours, she'd have two very precious gifts that would change the world forever. Two simple things, really. In fact, the head would probably be the hardest part.

She released her mind into the Flaring before the impatience could creep its way in. She closed her eyes.

2
ISAAC

"Go back into your room," Skinny said, very firmly. They stood outside the door to where they'd been earlier, lying in beds like a cruise vacation on Old Man Frypan's rickety homemade yacht. "Orange will come in and lock you back up. For safety."

"Now wait a damn minute," Sadina almost shouted. "I thought we were all on the same team now? Something like that? Prove it by not chaining us up."

"Please," Trish added.

Isaac was running completely on hunches, now. On guesses. But a lot of small things over the last hour had built up inside him. Each one, left alone, would mean absolutely nothing. But put together, he had an overwhelming feeling that something special was about to happen. Maybe scary, maybe terrifying, maybe deadly. But something that was good. That was for them.

Trish and Sadina had sulked their way into the room and sat on their beds, resigned to the shackles. Isaac hurried to sit next to them. Feigning a hug, he pulled them close enough to whisper into their ears.

"We need to be locked up. Buckled in. It'll be for our own good."

"What're you talking about?" Trish asked.

"Yeah," added Sadina. "You're acting weird, Isaac."

"Trust me for once, guys. Listen to me. I think that Minho and a couple of his friends have a plan to get us out of these stupid Bergs. I was told to hold on really tight when it happened, and to . . . be ready."

He probably deserved their looks of doubt, but he didn't know what else to say.

"Let's just see what happens," he muttered. "Hope for the best. Just humor me and hold on tight to the restraints, okay? Promise me?"

That earned him smiles this time, and then Trish and Sadina leaned in from both sides and gave him a good wet kiss on each cheek. Because of course they did.

Orange had the duty of locking up the shackles and it all went smoothly. Clinks and clanks, rattles of metal links, the click of engaged locks. Soon the three of them were as comfortable on the small beds as you can be while strapped down with chains.

Orange held her hand out as if she wanted to shake Isaac's hand. He obliged, although a little embarrassed at the awkward way he had to do it, the chain pinching his arm as he pulled to loosen some of the kinks. They finally grasped hands in a firm grip, and Isaac felt the cold press of metal against his palm. Orange let go, giving the object one last push with her index finger to make sure Isaac got it and knew he was *supposed* to get it.

"Try to steal a nap, guys," she said as she walked toward the exit. "Life's gonna be crazy pretty soon. Until then, don't move." She left and closed the door behind her.

Isaac looked down at what lay in his hand.

A very large key.

3
MINHO

The Orphan stood in a hallway near the back of the Berg, squeezed in a narrow spot between the bulbous back of the Grief Walker and the wall. He hoped he was isolated enough to inspect the bag of stuff he'd stolen from the commissary. Things weren't as bad as he feared—the Grief Bearers, priestesses, and whoever else was on the ship had their hands full just trying to keep the Berg flying and functioning. It wasn't like any of them had done something on this scale before. He also knew they'd taken it for granted that the prisoners had no choice but to wait in their chains until they arrived in Alaska.

My name is Minho, he thought. *Yes. From this point on, my name is Minho and always will be. No more going back. For Roxy and Kit.*

He pulled the awkward, bulky artillery suit from the bag, held it to his chest to size it up. It looked small but the things were supposed to fit tightly. The material was heavy with the two dozen inserts of explosives and guidance devices. *What kind of person voluntarily wears something like this?* he thought. *Orphans do. Orphans and former Orphans named Minho.*

It took a while, with lots of yanking the crystal-flecked material and wiggling his every body part. But finally he was set, fully wrapped in the most dangerous suit in the world. He reached into the bag and pulled out a smaller bag—this one full of tiny capsules of explosive, each of them rigged with a simple, mechanical timing device.

He took a breath. A deep one. Then another. Then another.

He thought of the note left in his quarters by Orange and Skinny, explaining the plan and that Roxy was safe. It was a good plan. They had at least a fifty-fifty chance of surviving it.

He reached for one of the explosive capsules and jammed it into a crevice at the bottom of the wall. He set the timer. It was on, it was really on.

He stood up and headed for the confinement cell.

4
JACKIE

Once again, they were all crammed into the tiny room like chopped wood in a stove. Just waiting for someone to throw in a match to ignite the whole bunch. They were all there as she had left them—Old Man Frypan, Ms. Cowan, Miyoko, Dominic, the two council members. They, of course, battered her with questions once she'd returned from the meeting with Minho, aka the Orphan.

"Why didn't you wake me up?" Ms. Cowan had asked, but not with much strength. Sadina's mom was weak and tired, despite the food they had brought while Jackie was gone. Wilhelm and Alvarez stayed silent, probably ashamed that a young person had gone in their place.

"I'm glad you're safe," Frypan had uttered several times. "I was worried sick." Such a kindness from a man she'd barely known until the boat voyage.

"Tell us what happened," Miyoko said, finishing off a chunk of hard cheese. Each of them had been given a sack of dried meat, cheese, and bread.

Dominic pestered her with an annoying ritual of saying one or two words between bites of food. "Who did . . . you . . . talk to?" Then, "What . . . did they . . . say?"

Jackie had mostly been ignoring them, stuffing herself with the nourishment. She'd thought she had found strength in volunteering to be the representative, but now the food tripled it. Despite her own doubts and weakness from before, she felt strong enough to take on the world. And that chance might be coming, though Minho had given no details.

"Jackie," Miyoko intoned with annoyance. "What the hell happened out there? If you take one more bite I swear on Old Man Frypan I will punch you in the face."

"I will, too," the man added with a chuckle. "But it won't hurt much."

"Okay, okay," Jackie replied. Most of her food was gone, anyway.

"They took me to a room and I sat at a table with the guy named Minho. The one who climbed out of the river and smacked the lady . . . um, Letti . . . in the head. Somehow he's involved with these people that captured us, but he seems to be rebelling for all I can tell. He said he and a couple others are going to—"

An abrupt and terrifying thought closed her throat. What if they were listening? They probably *were* listening.

"Jackie?" Dominic touched her shoulder. "What's wrong?"

She tried to recover. "I didn't really understand much of what he said. Mostly he wanted to ask *me* questions, about you guys, about where we're from, stuff like that." She widened her eyes in a look of warning, then tapped her ear. She wanted to scream at herself. *Idiot, you should've kept your mouth shut.*

Someone rapped on the door, a quick series of metallic knocks that made her heart ball up into a fist. *Like clockwork*, she thought. *I said too much and now they're here to take me away, throw me out of a flying machine.*

But when the door opened, Minho stuck his face in. He gave her a quick and reassuring nod that filled her with so much relief she almost fainted from the rush.

"Jackie," he said. "It's a go, soon. Have everyone hold on to something. Tight."

He didn't wait for a response. He closed the door and was gone.

5
ISAAC

He hadn't taken his eyes off the key since Orange had passed it over with a handshake. Some part of him worried the sliver of cut metal would magically disappear if he glanced away.

"When are we supposed to unlock ourselves?" Trish asked. "What's supposed to happen?"

"Isaac?" Sadina added when he didn't respond, gawking at his new talisman.

"I . . . I don't really know. Orange just told me to be ready and that we'd know."

"Know what?" Trish asked.

"I don't know." This made him laugh, though it sounded slightly hysterical to his ears. "But they must be planning on a bumpy ride because she wants us to stay locked up until . . . Until whatever."

"Well put it in your pocket," Sadina said, pointing at his raggedy pants as if he didn't know what a pocket was. "We don't wanna lose it."

"Ya think?" he responded.

"More than you do, usually." She sighed then, a weighty one that he'd heard from her before, usually before she was about to say something serious. "I love you, Isaac. I hope you know that. Trish and I both do. Somehow we're gonna get through this and we're going to do it together."

He found the strength to say, "I love you guys, too. Cheesy, aren't we?"

"Cheesy is the only way to go," Trish said.

Isaac finally slipped the key into his front pocket. The thing was a large solid piece of metal, like something from an old castle. "It's hard to believe what we were up to just a couple of months ago. I mean, did we ever really live on an island and not worry who was gonna kill us or hurt us every hour of every day?"

"It was kinda boring if you think about it," Sadina said.

Trish scoffed. "I miss being bored."

"Yeah, me—"

The world around them jolted, a hard bounce that threw Isaac to the limit of his chains—his head bounced off the wall. Sadina shrieked; Trish yelled something that was drowned out by another jolt and bounce, accompanied by a terribly grating sound of metal scraping across metal. Isaac reached for the railing of the bed, dazed in the sudden movement and noise. His fingers had just brushed the cool steel when the room tilted, jumped, tilted some more. He was thrown against the resistance of the chains again, pain biting into his arms and legs.

And then the ship was falling, his body floating up from the bed as if gravity had disappeared from the earth.

"Hold on!" Sadina screamed.

6
MINHO

Noise. Spinning. Nothing else.

Minho had just left the containment cell, had just told Jackie and her friends to hold on and get ready, had just gathered his courage to ignite another explosive and charge the cockpit of the Berg—when he found himself flying through the hallway as if left and right had become up and down. He slammed into a wall that moments before had been in front of him, not beneath him. He crumpled his legs and rolled as he'd been trained, then grabbed onto a railing and made his arms rigid, waiting to see if the ship righted itself.

But it didn't. The ship was in a fast tumble, rotating three full times before he lost track and fought back the nausea surging up his throat. There were so many sounds of groaning steel and breaking glass and people screaming that it all became an unbearable noise, made him wish he could let go and cover his ears. But his body flopped around with the changes in direction and gravity and holding on became the only thing left to do.

What had happened? What had gone wrong?

The ship righted itself for a moment then fell into a steady dive, the roar of the engines now overpowering all the other sounds. His feet settled against the floor of the hallway, now tilted at roughly a forty-five-degree angle. The Berg shook violently, surely ready to rip apart at any second. The turbulence became too much and he lost his grip on the railing, sliding down the floor until he hit a door, which opened on impact.

He fell into a room filled with complete chaos; he grabbed the edges of the doorframe before he became a part of it. Wind rushed and roared, seemingly from all directions at once. Debris and boxes and scraps and ruins of all manner of things churned through the air, swirling in circles as if caught in a tornado. A gaping hole had been torn in the side of the Berg and with horror he saw the world outside, the slanted line of the horizon, objects and birds whipping by as the ship plummeted, moving ever closer to the ground.

The edges of the hole were jagged and sharp, the torn petals of steel bent inward as if a cannonball had been shot through the skin and frame of the craft. From the outside. Something had torn through solid metal *from the outside.*

Minho shot his gaze to the other side of the room, opposite the circular gash in the ship.

A badly mangled person was pressed against the wall, crumpled halfway into it as if the materials of the wall had been molded around the body. This person was wearing an artillery suit, just like the one he wore. The head was smashed, the arms and legs twisted at weird angles, blood everywhere. Several of the explosive packets within the suit had exploded, tiny scraps of cloth flapping in the wind along with the tiny wires of the obviously failed guidance devices.

Almost nothing of the victim was intact enough to be identified with ease. But the face, as mangled as it was, had a very familiar nose. And the body, even padded by the artillery suit, had belonged to a very thin human being.

Minho, his hands hurting from how tightly he gripped the doorframe, his leg muscles shaky from the effort of planting his feet against an angled floor, could only stare.

Is that . . .

It was. It definitely was.

It was his friend, Skinny.

7
JACKIE

Her island had an earthquake when she was a little girl. She'd been in the closet, playing with the action heroes her grandpa had carved out of wood. She liked hiding in the small closet because no one could bug her, or make fun of the adventure stories she made up on the spot, every figurine playing its own part. When the earthquake hit, she'd been flung about, the wooden heroes scattering and clunking off each other and her head. It had seemed to her endless, and as if the tiny room in which she'd been playing had been lifted by a god and tossed across the ocean.

That was exactly how she felt, now, and the childhood memory flashed across her mind as she and Miyoko and Dominic jostled and jounced, their bodies banging into one another just as her wooden figures had done. The others fared no better.

If it hadn't been for Minho's warning, they might all be dead. Eyehole rivets, handles, railings—there were enough small things to hold on to that prevented the group from truly bouncing from one end of the room to the other, cracking skulls and breaking limbs. But even as each of them gripped whatever had been closest, they still flopped this way and that as the Berg rolled completely upside down then right again, three or four times. Jackie's legs and torso slammed into Dominic's and Miyoko's in turn, feet flying up to the ceiling then slumping back to the floor. It took every last slice of her energy to maintain that grip on the railing of metal she'd found near her head.

Screams and shouts filled the room. The piercing shriek and groans of crumpling, twisting metal, the roar and sputter of engines. The thumps of their bodies hitting this and hitting that. The lights had gone out almost immediately, so Jackie could barely see, adding to the terror. She squeezed her fingers around her lifeline of steel, prayed they'd survive. Somehow.

Get me through this, she called out to the universe. *Get me through this and I'll get us back home.*

The ship jolted hard. Someone slammed into her then locked their arms around her legs. She made out just enough of his silhouette to know it was Old Man Frypan.

"You okay?" she yelled.

"Hell, no!"

"Well don't let go!"

He squeezed harder, pinching her legs together, and she felt it as a comfort.

The Berg stopped spinning, but now it was in a definite and steady dive, tilted at least forty-five degrees toward the ground below. The growl of air resistance—and engines trying to fight that resistance—drowned out everything else. Jackie and the others settled into awkward positions, still holding on but helped by being pressed against each other, adding support. The ship shook as it descended, rocked by a bounce every few seconds, just strong enough to make Jackie's stomach swirl with butterflies.

"We can make it!" Frypan yelled up to her, his words almost lost in the avalanche rumble of it all. "These bastards are tough! As long as we don't—"

Thump. Every person in the room vaulted three feet into the air and back down again as they hit a rough pocket of air. The floor tilted a few more degrees; Jackie winced—someone had fallen hard into her side with an elbow or knee. She groaned; it felt like half her organs had ruptured.

"What did you say?" she asked Frypan, shouting through the pain.

"Who the hell knows!" he yelled back. Jackie really liked this man.

She let out a scream of frustration, aching, trying to release her desperation and will to survive into the ether, into the air, into existence.

The Berg hit something with a violent crunch of metal against wood, the world now filled with the sounds of breaking tree trunks and limbs, their shattered parts scraping against the outside hull of the ship. Jackie and the others bucked and jiggled and screamed and held on. Their speed slowed even as the ferocity of the Berg's rampage through the trees increased—it had to be trees, each one snapping like a small stick. Jackie felt as if her every tooth had come loose, all of them rattling against each other. Her brain seemed pulverized into mush from the savage turbulence of the crash.

Slower. Slower. Shaking and rattling and crunching.

The ship slammed into one final obstacle; Jackie lost her grip and flew across the small room and crashed into the opposite wall, then slid to the floor, landing on someone else. They'd come to a complete stop and the apocalyptic sounds had ceased along with it. Jackie groaned from the aches of her body, but she rolled to get off the person she'd slumped upon. A panel on the ceiling had jarred completely loose and a beam of sunlight shone from above. The room looked like a dumping ground for unwanted bodies, but the bodies she saw were squirming with movement.

"Thank you."

It was a pathetic-sounding voice, coming from right below Jackie. She looked down to see Dominic, flat on the floor, staring up at her.

"Your butt was on my face," he whispered, wincing from some unspoken pain of his own.

And then, somehow, amongst all that insanity, the two of them laughed.

8
ISAAC

The world had grown still. Miraculously, impossibly still.

Isaac lay curled into a ball, his body squeezed tightly against the corner where his bed met the conjoining walls. His every muscle ached from holding that position during the crash, the chains on his ankles having come loose somewhere along the way. His wrists remained shackled, the metal digging into the tendons that pressed taut against the skin. He tried to unwind his stiff torso and limbs but they wouldn't move, stuck in place with trauma, as if he'd died and entered rigor mortis.

"Isaac," someone whispered. "Isaac." He couldn't tell if it was Trish or Sadina, his back to them, cinched up like a fetus as he was.

"Hey, Isaac." It was Trish. "How about that key, huh?"

The fact that he hadn't heard Sadina yet released a new wave of adrenaline, like an injection of oil through his system that loosened up the joints. He uncurled himself and turned to look at his friends.

Both alive. Both with eyes open. Well, Sadina had only one eye open—her other was closed up from swelling.

"You okay?" he asked, the relief at seeing them alive far greater than the worry about their injuries. "That is one nasty looking . . ."

"Yeah, bashed my face against the bed railing. It hurt."

"I can't believe we're not dead," he whispered. It sounded silly but it was his prevailing thought. He'd spent the last five or ten minutes thinking that his life was certainly over and done with, extinguished, gone. No grand reunion on the island. No more trips to the Forge for him. No more bragging about how he'd built his own yurt and once sailed across the ocean.

"I can't, either," Trish agreed. "Let's get that key of yours and unlock ourselves."

"Yeah. Yeah." Though every movement brought an ache or a jolt of pain, and his muscles groaned from stiffness, he retrieved the key from his pocket and set about unlocking himself, then Sadina, then Trish. The ship was at a slight angle, but not enough to prevent them from getting their balance when they stood up. Isaac put the key firmly back into his pocket then rubbed his wrists, feeling elated at the freedom from the shackles. And the freedom from death.

"Come on," Trish said. "Let's find the others."

They moved like old people at first, but soon enough their blood started to flow and their muscles relaxed. The door to their room had bent and twisted enough to break free from its hinges. Trish gave it a hard shove and they entered the hallway. Smoke filled the air, with halos flaring constantly as sparks buzzed all over the place.

Isaac coughed, the smoke too thick to breathe. "How do we find anyone in this mess?"

Someone grabbed his arm from behind.

With an embarrassing yelp he spun around to see the guard with the orange hair. She was battered, bloodied, her suit ripped in a couple of places. It seemed as if she'd been thrown down a mountain and dragged through a river of rocks.

"Skinny screwed up," she said. "He screwed up bad."

"What happened?" Sadina asked.

Orange shook her head. "No time—we gotta get out of this trash heap. We're all gonna die from the fumes if the thing doesn't blow up and kill us a lot faster."

"What about the others?" Trish asked. "Our friends?"

She shook her head again. "I'm sorry. I'm really sorry. I'm not sure they made it. Come on!" She yanked Isaac so hard that he almost fell down. He righted himself, nodding his head to let her know he was coming.

"My mom!" Sadina yelled from behind. "What about my mom!"

Orange stopped and screamed back at her. "Just shut up! A lot of them were on the other Berg so I don't know. Maybe they're okay. But we *have* to get off this stupid ship or it won't matter, will it?"

Sadina, shaken and pale, muttered assent.

They followed Orange through the wreckage.

9
MINHO

Roxy. Where was Roxy? He had to find Roxy.

He looked through the gashed wound in the hull. He was shocked to see that one of the other Bergs had crashed as well, only two hundred meters or so away, the trees between them completely flattened and splintered. Skinny, now a mangled corpse, had been on that ship, but now lay enmeshed against the wall behind him, like a grisly decoration.

What could possibly have happened to cause both ships to fail? Minho knew the answer before he completed the thought. *Ugh.* His idiot friend had completely botched the use of his artillery suit, probably underestimating its power and the subtlety of the guidance mechanisms. Minho tried to picture it in his head—Skinny's body exploding like a missile, catapulting through the hulls of two separate Bergs, causing them to fail. The suit must've ejected other explosives during that short and fatal trip to cause so much damage, or maybe the ships had collided in mid-air.

"Minho!"

He turned around, saw Jackie standing in the doorway to which he'd been clinging for his life mere minutes earlier. She looked distraught, breathing heavily, several of her friends standing behind her.

"When I told you to hold on," he said, "this is *not* what I meant. We're lucky to be alive, any of us."

"Not everyone made it," she whispered, almost talking to herself.

He nodded, feeling a little ashamed that he'd only thought of Roxy. "I know. How many of your friends made it? Any signs from the other ship?"

Jackie stepped into the room, followed by an ancient man with dark skin and white hair, a middle-aged woman, and then two younger people. He knew their names from the interview he'd had with Jackie —Frypan, Ms. Cowan, Miyoko, and Dominic. Roxy was on the other Berg and he was trying so hard not to think about it yet. He wilted, terrified to find out if she'd survived.

"Are you hurt?" Jackie asked, running to his side.

"No, no. I'm okay. But we need to get to the other Berg—we both have friends over there and I can see the ship. It looks like it's in worse shape than ours, but hopefully they have survivors, too. Come on."

They picked their way down a couple of hallways and then found a much larger gash in the Berg that allowed them to crawl out, where the shattered plain of flattened trees greeted them. The smell of smoke and burnt fuel hung heavy in the air. Minho had barely stepped from the wreckage when he saw a man buried beneath a large chunk of the Berg that had fallen off. It was a Grief Bearer, a mask covering his face.

Maybe it was Barrus. The chest didn't move at all, and there was blood in all kinds of bad places. Dead, then. Minho felt no pity.

Then, for the second time since the crash, someone yelled his name.

"Minho!"

He looked up, and coming toward him, carefully stepping over a stack of logs, was Roxy, somehow smiling despite ripped clothes, several cuts, and dirt covering her every inch. The sickening weight in his gut vanished. He had never known the love of a mother, but he felt it then so powerfully that he fell to his knees and, for the first time in his life, wept like a child.

Through his tears, he saw the others.

CHAPTER FIFTEEN

The Cranks of Change

I
ISAAC

"Wait."

Isaac stopped at Orange's command. They stood a few feet from a large crack in the Berg, light spilling into the ship, casting its interior with a gloomy malaise. Orange was peeking around the edge, looking outside, her right hand held up to stop them from coming any closer. She finally turned back to them and pressed against the wall, her eyes wide with concern.

"What's wrong?" Sadina asked.

"There's . . ." For the first time, the guard in the intimidating artillery suit looked like a scared little girl. "Cranks. Cranks are out there. Right behind that lady named Roxy. They're all slowly making their way over the broken trees to the other Berg." Although she gave them the details patiently, her words had a shaky, shrill ring to them. "This ship must've been carrying them. No one told me that. No one told me that! I didn't even know we had those things!"

She was losing it, definitely losing it.

Trish grabbed her by the shoulders. "Calm down. You know better what to do than any of us."

Sadina walked past them and took a look for herself. Isaac felt like his feet had been stapled to the warped floor of the hallway.

Sadina stepped back and faced them, her poor black eye even puffier than before. "They're all chained together—just like at the bridge. Probably fifty or sixty of them! Half are walking, climbing, stumbling, the other half are being dragged along."

"And Roxy's out there?" Isaac asked.

"Yeah, but she's got a good lead on them. I don't even know if she's noticed them yet but she's going as fast as she can."

Isaac turned his attention to Orange, who had her eyes closed, taking deep breaths.

"Okay, guys, I'm sorry," she said. "I just had myself a little panic attack is all. We can do this. We have to hope people survived over there, and we need to get to them. They might be hurt or there might be Cranks in their ship, too. Although it has a Grief Walker so I don't think it had room."

"Alright," Sadina said. "Let's do it. My mom's over there, right?" Somehow she managed to keep her own voice under control, despite the terrifying possibility that her mom was dead. Or . . . worse.

"We obviously have the advantage," Isaac added. "If they're all chained together and stumbling over each other, then let's run around them." He had a hard time believing he was standing there, speaking those words, living in this world. It was like he floated above them, watching strangers.

"Then let's go." Orange patted some of the stuffed pockets of her suit. "They better not mess with us."

She darted out of the ship, and once again, Isaac and his friends followed.

2
JACKIE

"They're back," Old Man Frypan said. "Those bastards are back, straight out of my younger days."

Jackie was standing with him, arm in arm, supporting his weight—the crash, not to mention the last few weeks of his life, had taken a heavy toll on the man. The scene before them, as they stood right on the threshold of the ripped opening of the Berg, was a nightmare in the making. Roxy—Minho's mom, grandma, whoever she was—had almost made it across the gap between ships, and Minho had run to greet her, half-carrying her as they stumbled their way across the remaining clatter of fallen trees.

But behind them. Behind them was the nightmare.

Cranks, the same ones at the bridge by the looks of it. Chained together like slaves of ancient Rome, walking, straggling, dragging their way closer. Cranks. How often had she been told stories late at night about these mythical monsters of old? The only thing stalling her fear was how slowly they approached, hampered by the chains, having to move as one entity.

Minho and Roxy made it back. Ms. Cowan was on the woman immediately, asking about her daughter as Miyoko and Dominic stood right behind her, demanding answers. Where was Sadina? Where was Trish? Where was Isaac?

"I don't know, I'm sorry," Roxy answered. "They were on my ship but I didn't see them after the crash. I'm so sorry. I had to run from . . ." She looked back over her shoulder, trembling even as Minho still held her in his clutches. "From them."

"We have to get over there, now!" Ms. Cowan yelled, her composure cracked.

"Wait a second," Jackie said. An idea had come to her from nowhere, but she acted on it. After making sure Frypan was okay, she scanned the crashed Berg and saw a path to the top. With more speed and agility than she would've guessed she possessed, she scrambled up the side of the vessel, finding plenty of hand- and footholds to help along the way. When she got to the top, twenty or thirty meters above the wrecked forest floor, she steadied herself and examined the view.

"I see them!" she yelled down to the others. "Four of them!"

The group of Cranks stretched out in a haggard line, maybe fifty meters long, the chains slowing them considerably. Much quicker were the four people leaping between tree trunks, skipping over them like rocks on a pond, skirting the long line of Cranks.

Isaac. Sadina. Trish. Someone with orange hair.

"They're okay!" Jackie yelled. "Going around!" She pointed at the creepy mob, barely resembling humans.

But then she caught another sight. Seven or eight people were approaching the line of Cranks from the opposite side of where Isaac and the others had appeared. They'd come out of an open hatch in the other Berg. Jackie had never seen the new arrivals before, and they looked incredibly strange, despite the distance. Her eyesight had always been good, and now it gave her a very ill feeling.

They were strong, tall, dressed in the similar, worn, haphazard clothing of the Cranks in the field of trees, except for a major difference. No tatters, no rips, no grime, no blood. They walked steadily and soberly, almost mechanical in their carefully laid steps. Heads shaved, faces devoid of expression, their gazes set on the struggling line of Cranks, the strangers each held something in their hands, although it was impossible to discern, from where Jackie stood, exactly *what.*

She was at a little bit of a loss for words, mesmerized by these new arrivals.

"What's going on?" Ms. Cowan yelled from below.

Jackie swung her attention to the left, where Sadina, Isaac, Trish, and the fourth person were making excellent progress. They'd already cleared a wide berth around the outermost edge of the Cranks.

She pointed. "There! See them?"

Ms. Cowan did. Others, too. Several ran in that direction to help, to hug, to reunite.

Jackie took a breath, was relieved and surprised to feel how cleanly and fully the air filled her lungs. Her heart had slowed. The pressure on her chest had eased. They could outrun these Cranks and the more stable newcomers. They had a chance, now, especially bright compared to what she'd felt when first captured by that awful machine—the machine that now lay curled up and silent within the ship she stood upon. She was about to climb down when she noticed a shift in movement and purpose by the newcomers from the other Berg.

Their actions became more deliberate and less rote. There were eight of them—she could see that clearly, now—and they split up, walking to different sections of the Crank line, deftly leaping over broken tree trunks and branches. The first of these strange people came to the far-right end of the line as the others made their way toward the left, spacing apart. Jackie crouched down, throwing all her effort into focusing on what that first strange person was doing.

It reached the chaotic tussle of Cranks without showing any fear. They stilled at its presence, deferentially kneeling or bowing. In unison they raised their shackled hands as if offering some kind of religious sacrament, these ragged, barely human animals who'd seconds earlier seemed completely without sense or reason in their movements. The stranger reached toward the first of them, making use of whatever he, she, or it had been carrying.

Keys, apparently.

The encouragement Jackie had felt vanished, and the air she'd so easily breathed seemed suddenly toxic. She stood up and shouted at anyone who would listen.

"They're unlocking the chains! They're unlocking the Cranks' chains!"

Without the slightest caution, she started climbing down the side of the broken Berg.

3
MINHO

It had seemed an impossible thing, to shift so quickly from one emotion to another. Seeing Roxy had filled him with a relief and joy like he'd never experienced, not once in his life, and it was as if his body had filled with sunlight and sugar and music, almost unbearable. And then he'd seen the Cranks, right behind her.

All those emotions, all that feeling, had vanished, like the life of a crushed beetle.

And in its place, flooding in like the greatest of waterfalls, came the training of his existence.

He was the Orphan. The Orphan named Minho.

The world around him a noisy blur, he had sprinted across the field of crushed logs, his feet barely tapping them before leaping into the air again. He'd reached Roxy, saw the supernatural way she was able to smile despite a horde of infected lunatics at her back, and that smile completed the circuit of his purpose. He would not, could not rest until she was safe.

Not wasting time on words, he leaned a shoulder into her stomach, wrapped his arms around her, then lifted her as easily as a sandbag—a task he'd performed often in training, and so recently with the boy named Kit. She made a sound that was awfully close to a giggle, a thing he might've expected her to do in the face of so much chaos and destruction and madness. He spared a glance for the line of Cranks, half of them strewn about the logs, dragged by the others. What a pitiful sight it was—these bloodied and half-naked, raving things who'd once been sane. Minho wanted to kiss those greasy chains that slowed the group to a splinter-filled crawl.

He headed back toward the Berg and away from the writhing monsters that represented the very worst of what the Remnant Nation fought against. *The Flare, someday to be eradicated by the godlike Cure, blessed be Her name*, he thought with a heavy roll of his eyes. As he leaped from one huge chunk of wood to another, he allowed himself for once to see the good in his nation's intentions. Who *wouldn't* want to rid the world of those things crawling and hobbling along behind him? But which was the enemy—the virus or those trying to destroy the world to be rid of it?

Did it even matter? He'd chosen his path and there was no going back.

"Here, let me help." The one known as Frypan helped him gently lower Roxy to the ground once he'd made it back to the Berg. She seemed well enough, and gave Minho the biggest hug ever known to humankind. He returned it, but quickly pulled away.

"We need to get inside," he said to Roxy and the old man. "We can barricade ourselves in the Grief Walker for now. It probably doesn't work well, if at all, but I know it's intact."

Frypan nodded, leaning on Roxy for support. "Best plan I've heard all day. Those Cranks are gettin' too close for my liking and I'm done running. My legs feel like rotten carrots."

Minho noticed Jackie, climbing down the side of the Berg—she jumped the last several feet, stumbled, then ran straight to him.

"They're unlocking them," she panted. "There's people out there, unlocking the Cranks!"

Before he had time to process this, several other survivors suddenly appeared all at once, as if they'd just returned from a picnic. He didn't know them all by name, but Jackie had told him enough details to see these were her friends, a few of them from the other crashed Berg. And then he saw Orange, looking battered but whole. She gave him a sad smile and a stiff nod, showing that she already knew about Skinny—the boy never had a chance of surviving whatever malfunction or miscalculation that had catapulted him through the walls of two different Bergs.

"We need to *go*," Jackie said, breaking up the brief moment of reflection. "Half the Cranks have already been let loose. They're coming." The calmness of her voice was something Minho knew he'd never forget.

Eleven people stood there, each with a strange expression that somehow mixed relief with sheer terror. And they were all staring at *him*.

Frypan, exuding the natural wisdom and presence of his grand old age, put a hand on Minho's shoulder and turned to the others.

"This young fella has a plan."

4
ISAAC

"We can trust him," Ms. Cowan whispered to Sadina and the others standing next to her. "Jackie does, and he gave us a warning before the ship crashed."

Orange must've overheard this because she stepped up and agreed. "I'd trust that handsome sack of muscle with my life. Do what he says."

Isaac didn't know the first or last thing about this Minho guy, but he hoped he lived up to the legend of his name. He was about the same age as Isaac, maybe a little older, and definitely bigger and stronger. Adding credence to what Orange had said, he wore the same bulky suit of weaponry as she. They were obviously friends, and on their side in all this, as much as Isaac could discern the sides.

"Follow me," Minho said.

He ran to a spot on the crashed ship where a large gash had split it open, and one by one the group disappeared into the darkness of the interior. Sparks still popped from one section of the gash, a few meters above the ground. This Berg was different from the one in which Isaac, Trish, and Sadina had flown. This one was at least twice as big, with a globular structure jutting from its middle, obviously the storage tank for the monstrous machine with spiked wheels that had dropped on them at the bridge. Isaac had no idea how or why some of them had ended up in the smaller ship on the other side of the oncoming Cranks. It had all been a blur, flashes of terror.

Isaac was in the back of the line, Dominic right in front of him. Ms. Cowan entered the Berg ahead, right after Trish and Sadina, nursing her wounded eye.

Dominic placed a hand on the metal of the hull and looked back over his shoulder. Isaac looked as well. Most of the Cranks had been freed from their shackles, and although they still had major difficulties maneuvering over the dozens of flattened trees, they were getting close. Maybe thirty meters away, now.

"I sure hope this guy knows what he's doing," Dominic said.

"Those people look hungry and I think they might like the taste of islanders."

"We don't have much choice, do we," Isaac muttered.

Dominic slipped through the gap, then Isaac.

5
JACKIE

The Berg seemed huge from the outside, far larger than any single building she'd ever seen back home on their island. Larger by a long shot. And yet its insides felt cramped and tiny, narrow corridor leading to even narrower corridors, small rooms and storage centers to the left and right, appearing just as small as the tiny cell into which they'd been crammed during the flight. She'd thought at the time that stuffing them in there had been an act of cruelty, but now she realized the whole ship was like that. Like the dollhouse her mom had built for her eons ago.

She and the rest of them picked their way along, around corners and around more corners. The ship was dark, lit only by a few sparks here and there and glowing red emergency lights, half of which were broken. Old Man Frypan was directly in front of her, a little bit of a spring back in his step. Miyoko was behind her, patting her on the shoulder every once in a while for comfort.

She knows, Jackie thought. *She knows what I'm feeling*.

Carson and Lacey were dead. Dead. Jackie didn't know who'd confirmed it, but Ms. Cowan had told her outside that they'd been lost. Wilhelm and Alvarez, too. The chaos, the Cranks, the danger—all of it allowed no time to mourn their friends, and certainly nobody wanted to talk about it. But the pain ached in Jackie's chest, ached so badly she found it hard to breathe.

Carson. Lacey. Dead.

Her mom once told her that the oldest cliche in the book was that you had to take life one step at a time. Her mom also said that no cliche had ever spoken more truth.

Jackie took another step.

"It's here!" Minho yelled from up ahead, his voice bouncing along the small hallway in echoes. "And it's intact!"

Jackie had no idea what he was talking about, but he seemed pleased enough.

She took another step.

6
MINHO

The Grief Walker, as big as Roxy's house, appeared solid and unspoiled, which didn't really surprise him. The Berg itself was always meant as a cushion for the invaluable machine cocooned within it. Although he didn't know much about the machines, there was no doubt what an important project it had been for the Grief Bearers and all of the Remnant Nation, a project that had gone on for decades.

The round hatch before him was solid steel, a mechanical latch-lever thing that kept it closed. Minho grabbed the lever with both hands, then Orange joined him. They pulled in tandem, groaning with the effort. Minho finally lifted his feet off the ground, hanging every pound of his Orphan-trained body on the handle. It gave with a squeak, gave a little more with a squeal, then collapsed downward and the hatch popped open. It happened so suddenly that he let go and sprawled across the floor. Instead of helping him up, Orange darted through the hole and into the Grief Walker.

Roxy was on him instantly, threading her arms beneath his armpits, hampering more than helping as he got back to his feet.

"Thanks," he whispered. It was kinda cool having a mom.

They followed Orange into the machine, their other friends crowding up behind them. Orange had stopped at the railing of the walkway that circled the entire circumference of the Walker—the control center was recessed into the rounded bottom of the vessel with dozens of windows to view the ground below while it was in motion.

Minho stepped forward beside Orange and saw why she had stopped.

A Grief Bearer and an acolyte were seated at the controls, having just begun the maneuvers to start up the machine. Two Orphans, Orphans he didn't know, dressed in the rough vines and cloth of a wilderness-wandering, stood nearby, both of them holding the rifles that Minho knew all too well. And each gun was aimed—one at Orange, one at Minho.

Damn it, he thought. He'd really hoped they'd all died in the crash.

7
ISAAC

He and several of the others were crammed together in a small opening outside the hatch of the Grief Walker, the hatch small enough that they could only enter one at a time. About half of them were inside, and Ms. Cowan was just leaning through the hole when she abruptly pulled back and turned around.

"People are in there!" she said in a biting whisper. Although that much was obvious, Isaac knew what she meant. *The* people. The ones who flew the ships, the ones who'd taken them into the sky. She faced the hatch again, gave a worried look back at them, then entered the large machine anyway. Trish and Sadina did, too. Then Miyoko.

Dominic stood in front of the hatch. Jackie was right next to him, peeking over his shoulder.

She turned and spoke to Isaac, about as defeated as someone could sound. "They have guns, I guess. Ordering us to come inside."

Isaac felt as if he'd just shrunk two inches and lost thirty pounds. Dominic climbed through the hatch and then Jackie moved to follow. Out of the frying pan and into—

A noise rattled behind Isaac. He was just beginning to twist around when a hand slammed atop his shoulder, then another hand stuffed a wadded rag of cloth into his mouth. Footsteps pounded up the small hallway, something pushed him to the side, a figure ran past him. That person attacked Jackie, threw her to the floor and stuffed her mouth with cloth as well, then grabbed her by the ankles. Isaac was barely registering this when he was yanked backward, lifted off his feet and pulled away from the hatch.

Then he was being dragged down the hall, fear like an expanding balloon in his throat, watching helplessly as Jackie met the same fate.

8
MINHO

He heard whispers from behind, but he could only focus on one problem at a time. Two Orphans, rifles raised, their barrels aimed at Orange and him. A priestess of the Cure, working switches and controls as if she hadn't noticed them enter. And then there was Glane, his Grief Bearer and master for many a year, having now stood from his own chair to face his pupil, the one in whom he'd been so proud. Minho had not known until that very moment that the man had accompanied the others on this trip.

"Orphan," Glane said. "It looks as if you've strayed from the wilderness. I believe your forty days ended without your triumphant return to the Remnant Nation. But all's well, as they say. Griever Barrus made it clear that we could still use you. He gave you the pragmatist speech, I believe. True?"

"I didn't know you came with him," Minho said.

"I did."

He said nothing else, letting the absurdity of his response linger in the stale air.

"I'm . . . glad."

"Are you? Are you on our side, Orphan? I want to believe it, despite every single action you take saying otherwise."

Orange stood right next to Minho, and yet Glane hadn't so much as looked at her. Roxy and the others crowded in behind him, still and silent, no more whispers. Orange moved her foot against Minho's, then pressed against it with the lightest of touches. Message received.

"Speak, Orphan." Glane's voice reminded Minho of why he'd kept walking west, even on the brink of starvation, sick and weak. Roxy had saved him, body and mind. And now, to save her, his left hand needed only to move two inches.

"Now," Minho finally said, probably not the response his master had been expecting.

His finger made it one inch before a shot rang out, from the Orphan on the left. The second inch was accomplished before the echo of that shot had even begun. The bullet pinged against the railing, just as his finger triggered the burst packet on his waist. Orange triggered the burst packet on *her* waist. In sync, with the sounds of twin explosions, their bodies lifted from the landing and curved into the space of the globe, then flipped as they continued to manipulate the dynamics of the packet's guidance device. Feet first, with the precision that had come from years of relentless training, they slammed into the faces of both armed Orphans with the force of booted cannons.

Minho and Orange ignited a rebound repression just as they made contact, preventing them from slamming against the wall of the Grief Walker. Minho fell on to his back, the breath knocked from his chest. As he struggled to recover, struggled to get breath into his shocked lungs, the priestess leaped from her command chair and came at him, a long curved blade having appeared in her hand. Weak from the effort just expended, he raised an arm, a useless attempt to block her as she dove, weapon first.

But then a long object swung in from the left of his vision, slamming directly into the face of the priestess. The woman screamed, blood spurted, she dropped the knife, collapsed, and went still. Minho, finally pulling in a pathetic attempt at a breath, looked up, tried to see what had happened.

Roxy stood there, brandishing the rifle dropped by the Orphan whose face Minho had ruined with the flying missile of his feet. The butt of the rifle, a little blood dripping from its tip, was actually dented from Roxy's assault on the priestess. Minho didn't have enough air to utter a single word, but their eyes met with all the power of a lightning strike.

"No one hurts my son," she said. "An Orphan no more."

9
JACKIE

Her head thumped twice against the floor as the bald-headed freak dragged her down the hallway and around a corner. Then he dropped her next to Isaac, who lay on his back with a look of the purest terror gripping his features. In the devil-glow of the red emergency lights, Jackie stared at the people who'd pulled them like sacks of garbage away from their friends.

They were two of the mysterious strangers she'd spotted from the top of the Berg, the ones who'd unlocked the chains of the Crank horde. Standing over her and Isaac, they looked down at them with wide, haunted eyes—eyes lacking some crucial element that would've made them closer to human. Jackie didn't know what it was. They were both bald, dressed in drabby gray clothing, androgynous. One of them yanked the rags out of their mouths.

"Who are you?" Isaac asked.

Jackie was relieved that he'd recovered his wits enough to speak.

"What do you want?" she added.

The one on the left spoke, revealing teeth that had rotted considerably. Its voice was surprisingly normal, neither deep nor high. Not even that creepy.

"We're the in-between, kid. We want no trouble. We only want the girl. Give us the girl and we won't hurt any of you. That's a promise, sworn on the Flare. And *she* won't be hurt either. The girl will be safe."

"Why does everyone want Sadina so bad?" Jackie whispered,

mainly to herself. *How could one person be so important to all these people?*

"Are you Cranks?" Isaac asked. "I didn't think Cranks could talk."

This time the one on the right answered, its voice a little deeper. "Don't use that word, boy. It's not nice. We come from a different variant, anyway. But I hear all of you are immune. What a sad thing for you. What a sad, sad thing."

"Will you give us the girl?" the one on the left asked.

Jackie couldn't take it anymore. She simply couldn't.

"Isaac," she said, not caring that their captors heard because it wouldn't matter. "We have to do this together."

"I know," he replied, an answer that was somehow both resigned and brave at once.

Jackie balled her right hand into a fist and swung it upward, smacking the face that hung over her like a cloud. She'd never punched anyone in her life but surprise was on her side—the creature's head jerked to the left so hard that it hit the wall. She grabbed its shirt and yanked, pulled it to the ground while it was stunned, then rolled on top of its torso. Holding both of her hands together in one tight ball, she smashed it into the thing's nose, lifted her arms and did it again. It screamed, a wet sound of agony. She hit it again, ignited by enough rage that she knew she had another dozen or so in her.

To her left, Isaac was being strangled.

10
ISAAC

He knew there'd been other times when he felt as if he couldn't breathe. They just weren't coming to him as the bald-headed half-Crank squeezed his neck with both hands. Jackie was winning her battle, beating the ever-living hell out of the one she'd chosen to attack, all of which Isaac could see rather well since his eyes were half-bulged from their sockets.

He beat at his attacker's arms, beat at its chest, kicked with his legs, tried to squirm his body left and then right. None of it was working. He flailed, feeling for anything, any object nearby that might help. The life was squeezing out of him, leaking out, and the ugly expression of the one doing it, that face just a small distance away from his own, made Isaac desperate not to let it happen.

His pocket. He remembered his pocket.

He reached for it, brushed across its fabric, felt the hard solid length of what nestled inside. Choking, dying, making no sound because there was no air to do it, he fumbled with his fingers, reached into the front pocket of his pants, found the object, gripped it tightly in his hand. It was the key, the big, metal key, the one Orange had given him to unlock their shackles.

His vision was muddled, full of sparkling diamonds of light that obscured everything in sight. He could only make out the bare outline of his attacker's head. The pain, the pain in Isaac's throat was a great and sharp and terrible thing. His lungs begged for air, his eyes were on the verge of absolute detonation from the pressure.

Somehow, he found the strength. He reared his arm to the right, then swung it with every last speck of his remaining power toward the creature's neck. The key, as solid as any key ever made at the Forge by Captain Sparks, found the perfect spot, sliding into the soft tissue and releasing a beautiful fountain of blood. The half-Crank let go of Isaac's neck and clutched its own, but it was over for the pitiful creature. Even as Isaac sucked in the most glorious breaths of his life, the attacker toppled to the side and bled out.

Isaac rolled over, looked at Jackie, straddling the one she'd fought. Her fists were bloodied and her face glistened with sweat.

"I can't believe we just did that," she said through several gasps. "I can't . . ."

Isaac heard all kinds of noises, now. Creaking, moaning, footsteps, screams, incoherent babbling.

Cranks! The familiar word flashed inside his mind.

He was weak, his adrenaline spent. But he saw shadows moving down the hallway. Human-shaped shadows that were growing in size, along with an increase in volume of their terrible sounds.

"Come on," Jackie said. "Come on."

Helping each other, leaning on each other, holding on for dear life to each other, they stood up, shuffled their way back in the direction from which they'd been dragged down the hall. They found the hatch. It was open, and Dominic was just stepping out of it.

"Oh, there you guys are. Hurry up, would you?"

They entered the belly of the beast and shut the heavy door.

II
MINHO

Cranks swarmed outside the Grief Walker, especially energetic after being freed from their shackles. Minho heard them banging on the hull. He saw them through the viewports on the bottom of the rounded control center. Scratches of fingernails against metal sounded from above. All of it was enough to encourage Griever Glane to assist Minho in getting the giant machine up and running. Of course, the man didn't have much choice now that Roxy and Miyoko possessed the discarded rifles. But Glane actually knew very little—the real expert, the priestess, was on the floor, knocked out cold from Roxy's devastating blow.

Jackie and Isaac had just appeared, looking like Cranks, themselves. Sweaty, dirty, bloody, traumatized—evidently they'd been dragged away, forced to fight their way out of it. Minho was ashamed to admit that he didn't even know they'd been missing. Other matters had taken precedence.

Initially, his hope had been to barricade themselves, utilize the food supplies, maybe get enough power to use whatever weapons were available. But the Grief Walker was intact, and the Grief Walker was functional. Based on the scattered knowledge he had of the machines, they could very well break through the wreckage of the Berg and escape the invading Cranks.

As he frantically worked with the petulant Glane to figure things out, Jackie came up to him.

"What happened?" he asked her. She must have been in horrified awe of his capacity to remain detached, to repress emotion—one of the many skills he'd learned as an Orphan of the Remnant Nation. Roxy was the only weakness in the armor he'd felt in a long time.

"Minho, it's not just Cranks we have to worry about," she said, her voice surprisingly steady. "There's . . . others, people who look like them but aren't as . . . I don't know. They were smarter, talked to us, almost killed us. Maybe they're just early on in the disease."

Isaac had joined them, looking even worse than Jackie. "They said something about being in-between. They were just as creepy as those guys." He pointed down at the closest viewport, where a Crank was bashing its head against the glass. *Thump, thump, thump.* A small crack had actually formed.

"Did you kill them?" Minho asked.

It took a moment for Jackie to answer. "Yes, Minho, we killed them."

"Good."

Engines hummed and growled; gears cranked and scraped; grinding echoes of machine parts rubbing against other machine parts made the entire vessel tremble and rumble. The controls were mechanical and straightforward, even labeled in most cases.

"Minho!" Jackie shouted.

He jerked his attention away for a moment and looked at her—she was pissed at him for no reason he could think of.

"What?"

"You look like you're having a grand old time with this thing but I'm telling you there was something strange about those people who tried to drag us away."

He nodded, wishing she'd leave him alone. "The Flare has a lot of variants, Jackie. I don't know as much as you think I do. We all have a lot to learn. We *will*. But for now, we have to crunch our way out of this Berg and get the hell out of here."

"You really think we can do it?" Isaac asked. "In time?" The sounds of dozens of Cranks—and worse, the sight of them at the viewports—trying to get inside the machine obviously had him and everyone else on edge.

"Yep," Minho replied. "It has to."

He turned back to the controls, certain he had it figured out. He smiled, thinking of how much Roxy had loved driving her truck, how terrible of a driver she was, and how she had refused to let him take a turn. This would be the ultimate revenge. He met her light-filled eyes and wondered if she was thinking the same silly thing.

"Everyone grab on to something!" he yelled.

They moved with a hard jolt, then another, then another. There were crunches and creaks and groans and the scream of engines, the crumpling of metal. Outside the hull, Cranks fell and Cranks were crushed. All around Minho, people held on to anything they could find as the machine's giant spiked wheels and appendages of terror obliterated the Berg shell that encased them.

The Grief Walker rose from the earth like a resurrected demon.

CHAPTER SIXTEEN

The Future of the Future

ISAAC

Safe.

As much as anyone could be in such a scary part of the world, Isaac and his friends were safe. For now, anyway. And that was a much better situation than they'd had in a long time.

After escaping the scene of the Berg crashes, the Grief Walker had spiked and rolled and steamed its way through forests, across a river, over giant boulders and all manner of terrain, finally settling down in a remote area nestled between two wooded mountains. They had food stores, a stream of fresh water nearby, weapons to hunt if needed. And, most importantly, Minho had no qualms threatening the man named Glane and the odd, headachy priestess, telling them that if the other Bergs showed up, they'd be shot. That was how the thing called a transmitter had been discovered, and promptly disabled.

The sun had set, though the nights were shorter this far north. Isaac and the best friends of his life sat around a campfire, as if they had somehow been transported back to the island they called home.

The wood of the fire crackled and spit out sparks, warming them in the cool, windless air, the smoke rising straight up, toward the crescent of the moon. Watching the flames, smelling the charred wood, Isaac thought of the Forge and ached with memories.

"Hell of a week, eh?" Dominic said. After a pause, he repeated the phrase. "Hell of a week."

Isaac could tell he'd been on the cusp of making a joke but then faltered, remembering that lives had been lost. Carson. Lacey. Wilhelm. Alvarez. There'd been no sign of Letti or Timon so they were probably dead, too. Six friends, probably dead. But maybe not. Maybe not.

With a little shame, Isaac was grateful for the ones who'd survived for certain, that they were the ones he'd cared about the most, those who sat there with him. Black-eyed Sadina and Trish. Miyoko and Dominic and Jackie the Crank-Slayer. Ms. Cowan and Old Man Frypan. Isaac had lost his family in a freak storm, lost them in the terrible waves. But all these crazy people sitting in a circle had made that loss a little more bearable. Even Minho, Roxy, and Orange were well on their way to worming themselves into the fold.

"So what's next for us?" Sadina asked, cozied up with Trish. "Kletter was the whole reason we came here and she's not around to tell us what to do."

Miyoko was poking the logs with a stick. "I think we should go back to Los Angeles and find that Villa she kept harping about. We were almost there."

"No way," Dominic said. "We should go back home. Forget the old world. This place sucks."

"It definitely sucks," Jackie agreed. "I'd love to go home. Maybe we can find us a nice Berg and avoid that whole boat thing." Isaac remembered her throwing up on the voyage. A lot.

"What do you think, Ms. Cowan?" Trish asked.

The woman who'd once been the leader of the island's Congress just shrugged her shoulders. "I don't know, you guys. I can't pretend to have the slightest idea. But I'm glad we're together."

Isaac didn't have much of an opinion—at least not yet—but he knew someone who did.

"Unless we want to walk back to the ocean," he said, "we'll do whatever Minho says. He's pretty much the captain of our big machine over there. And he says we're going to the Godhead city. At least that's where *he's* going."

Old Man Frypan spoke up for the first time that evening. "Isn't that where all the other Bergs from his damn country went? To set up for an attack or some such nonsense?"

"I think so, yeah," Isaac replied.

The man sighed, looking wistfully at the fire. "You've all heard my stories a million times. I won't bore you with any, now. But let's just say I've had my fill of battles in Alaska. I think I'll just stay right here and eat plants and rabbits until my heart calls it quits."

"Yeah, right," Jackie said. "You're gonna outlive us all, old man."

As he often did, Frypan gave that a hoot and a holler. "Don't I wish. First thing I do every morning is check my pulse and see if I'm dead yet."

Jackie gave him a hoot and a holler right back, as did most of the others. Isaac smiled, but he wasn't quite ready for laughs, yet. He couldn't get his mind off the Forge and its fires and its red-hot metals and its steam and its smells of sweat, leather, and things burnt. It was ironic, in a way. He'd worked his tail off at the Forge in the year after he'd lost his family to help him forget about the tragedy of it all, at least for pockets of time. But now, remembering that place, his favorite place, made him think of his mom, his dad, his sister. And that horrible day.

Frypan cleared his throat and leaned closer to the fire. "Ah, to hell with it. Ya'll want a story? We don't have to make any decisions tonight."

His question was met with a resounding *yes* and he was happy to oblige, using names that all of them knew very well. "Sweet little Chuck was always up to no good, and there was this one night when he got Thomas in on the act. Well, Gally was doing his thing on the toilet, you see . . ."

As Old Man Frypan told his story, Isaac listened and watched the campfire and all the memories that came with it. The smoke rose in a ghostly pillar, the flames flickered and danced with bright heat, and the night didn't seem all that dark.

EPILOGUE

Two Boxes

ALEXANDRA

She sat in the library of her residence, her prized possessions resting on the table before her. Mannus and her pilgrims had delivered in every way she had hoped. Initially, she thought it unwise to be here, where she'd lived for years, having what she now owned. But then she remembered that there was nothing to fear. Nothing at all. Not even Mikhail would dare move against her, now.

She slid the first box closer to her, lifted its lid. To get a better view, she stood up, looked down into the open container from directly above. The eyes of Nicholas stared back at her, his eyelids removed so that they could never close again. She smiled at him, half-expecting what was left of the dead man to return the kind gesture. He did not.

After closing the lid, she slid the box away from her and replaced it with the other one, pulling it close as she sat down again. Although called the Coffin, it looked more like a briefcase, small enough that she could easily hide the thing wherever she wished. It was made of hard red leather with white stitching, six metal latches keeping it closed and secure. Each latch had a mechanical dial of numbers with its own code, six codes in all. Only three people in the world knew those codes. Well, two did, now.

With an emotion approaching the hysteria she'd seen in her pilgrims when she'd taken them to the Maze ruins, she meticulously, almost reverently, turned the dials one by one until all the codes were set. Then she flipped the latches open, relishing the six successive clicks of metal on leather.

She lifted the lid with care, settling it as far back as it could go on its hinges.

Most of the interior was taken up by a gray spongy substance, its purpose to cushion the precious, priceless contents. Five small, round holes had been evenly spaced in the protective material, where five metallic vials—sealed with a technology that Alexandra didn't yet understand—had been placed. Five vials that could Evolve the Evolution itself, change the world forever, as trite as that sounded.

She pulled one of the vials—about the length of her hand—from its slot and examined its smooth, unbroken surface, perfectly rounded on both ends. There were no seams, no cracks, no labels. Only shiny, unblemished, silvery metal. What filled its cylindrical interior would shape the future of the Flare and its many variants. A course that would be set by her, Alexandra Romanov, Goddess to her people. No, no, that title wouldn't do anymore. *God*, period. She carefully placed the item back in its slot.

She looked upon her possession with indescribable joy.

The vials contained blood samples of a person who'd lived long ago, a name that was known in every corner of the surviving world, spoken often in the seven decades since his tragic death. A name that conjured dread in some, hope in most. For Alexandra, it conjured the sum total of her every reason to exist. For she knew a secret that most did not.

The boy known as Newt had not been immune to the Flare.

No, he hadn't been immune in the slightest, unlike most of his friends in the Maze.

But he *was* the cure.

Yes. That boy. The one named Newt, Subject A4, the Glue, brother to Sonya . . .

The Cure.

THE END OF BOOK ONE

Have you read
The Maze Runner Novella?

Turn the page to experience the first chapters of

CRANK PALACE

the bridge between **The Maze Runner** and **The Maze Cutter** series.

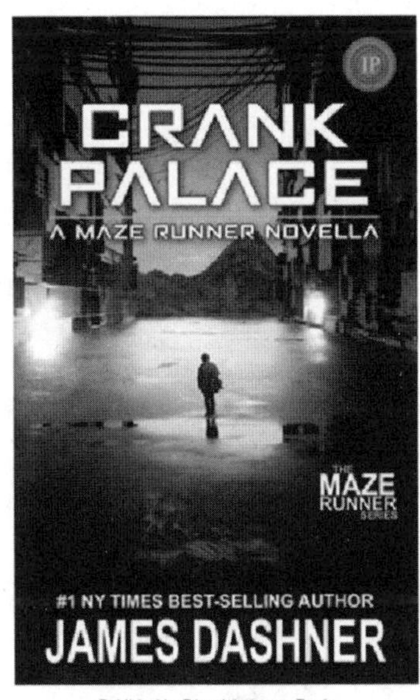

Published by Riverdale Avenue Books

Newt has been to hell and back with his friends.

The Glade. The Maze. The Scorch. The inner halls of WICKED. But now he has a burden that can't be shared with Thomas and the others—the Flare. And Newt can't bear the thought of his friends watching him descend into madness as he succumbs to the virus.

Leaving only a note, Newt departs the Berg before the Gladers return from their mission into Denver, Colorado. From there, he experiences the gritty nightmare of life on the streets, running from the infected and those hunting them, until he ends up in the Crank Palace, the last dumping ground of those without hope. Although Newt thought he was running away from his friends to save them from himself, along the way he meets a young mother named Keisha and her son, Dante, who end up saving Newt in a way he could never have imagined.

Taking place during the latter events of The Death Cure, Crank Palace tells the story of Newt like never before, from inside his own mind, as he searches for meaning in a life gone horribly wrong. He will try to fulfill a new-found destiny before his path leads to its inevitable conclusion—and one last meeting with his best friend.

Published by Quest, an imprint of Riverdale Avenue Books.
ISBN 978-1626015678
Published November 22, 2020

Part One
Welcome to the Neighborhood

Chapter One

There they go.

Newt looked through the grimy glass of the Berg's porthole, watching as his friends walked toward the massive, imposing gate that barred one of the few passages into Denver. A formidable wall of cement and steel surrounded the city's battered-but-not-broken skyscrapers, with only a few checkpoints such as the one Newt's friends were about to use. *Attempt* to use. Looking up at the gray walls and the iron-colored bolts and seams and hinges of the reinforcements on the doors, it would be impossible not to think of the Maze, where the madness had all begun. Quite literally.

His friends.

Thomas.

Minho.

Brenda.

Jorge.

Newt had felt a lot of pain in his life, both inside and out, but he believed that very moment, watching Tommy and the others leave him for the last time, was his new rock bottom. He closed his eyes, the sorrow bearing on his heart like the weight of ten Grievers. Tears leaked out of his squeezed eyelids, ran down his face. His breath came in short, stuttered gasps. His chest hurt with the pain of it. A part of him desperately wanted to change his mind, accept the reckless whims of love and friendship and open the Berg's slanting hatch door, sprint down its rickety frame, join his friends in their quest to find Hans, get their implants removed, and accept whatever came next.

But he'd made up his mind, as fragile as it might be. If ever in his life he could do one thing right, the thing that was unselfish and full of good, this was it. He'd spare the people of Denver his disease, and he'd spare his friends the agony of watching him succumb to it.

His disease.

The Flare.

He hated it. He hated the people trying to find a cure. He hated that he wasn't immune and he hated that his best friends were. All of it conflicted, battled, raged inside him. He knew that he was slowly going insane, a fate rarely escaped when it came to the virus. It had come to a point where he didn't know if he could trust himself, both his thoughts and his feelings. Such an awful circumstance could drive a person mad if they weren't already well on their way to that lonely destination. But while he knew that he still had an ounce of sense, he needed to act. He needed to move, before all those heavy thoughts ended him even sooner than the Flare.

He opened his eyes, wiped his tears.

Tommy and the others had already made it through the checkpoint —they'd entered the testing area, anyway. What happened after that was cut from Newt's view with the closing of a gate, the final puncture in his withering heart. He turned his back to the window, pulled in several deep breaths, trying to dampen the anxiety that threatened him like a 30-meter wave.

I can do this, he thought. *For them.*

He got to his feet, ran to the bunk he'd used on the flight from Alaska. He had almost no possessions in this world, but what little he owned he threw into a backpack, including some water and food and a knife he'd stolen from Thomas to remember him by. Then he grabbed the most important item—a journal and pen he'd found in one of the random cabinets on the Berg. It had been blank when he'd discovered the compact book, though a little tattered and worn, its endless white pages flipping by like the rattled wings of a bird when he thumbed through it. Some former lost soul, flying to who knows where on this bucket of metal, had once thought to write down the story of their life but chickened out. Or died. Newt had decided on the spot to write his *own* story, keep it a secret from everyone else. For himself. Maybe someday for others.

The long blast of a horn sounded from outside the walls of the ship, making Newt flinch and throw himself onto the bed. His heart sputtered out a few rapid beats while he tried to reorient. The Flare made him jumpy, made him quick to anger, made him a sodden mess in every way. And it was only going to get worse—in fact, it seemed like the bloody thing was working overtime on his poor little brain. Stupid virus. He wished it was a person so he could kick its arse.

The noise stopped after a few seconds, followed by a silence still as darkness. Only in that silence did Newt realize that before the horn there'd been the ambient noise of people outside, erratic and… off. Cranks. They must be everywhere outside the walls of the city, those past the Gone, trying to get inside for no other reason than the madness that told them to do it. Desperate for food, like the primal animals they'd become.

What *he* would become.

But he had a plan, didn't he? Several plans, depending on the contingencies. But each plan had the same ending—it was just a matter of how he got there. He would last for as long as he needed to *write* what he needed in that journal. Something about that simple, empty little book, waiting to be filled. It had given him a purpose, a spark, a winding course to ensure the last days of his life had reason and meaning. A mark, left on the world. He would write all the sanity he could muster out of his head before it was taken over by its opposite.

He didn't know what the horn had been or who had blown it or why it was suddenly quiet outside. He didn't want to know. But perhaps a path had been cleared for him. The only item left to settle was how to leave it with Thomas and the others. Maybe give them a little closure. He'd already written one depressing note to Tommy; might as well write another.

Newt decided that his journal would survive if it weighed less by one page. He tore it out and sat down to write a message. Pen was almost to paper when he stalled, as if he'd had the perfect thing to say but it floated out of his mind like vanished smoke. Sighing, he itched with irritation. Anxious to get out of that Berg, walk away—limp or no limp—before something changed, he scribbled down a few lines, the first things that popped in his head.

They got inside somehow. They're taking me to live with the other Cranks.

It's for the best. Thanks for being my friends.

Goodbye.

It wasn't totally true, but he thought about those horns and all that commotion he'd heard outside the Berg and figured it was close. Was it short and curt enough to prevent them from coming after him? To get it through their thick skulls that there was no hope for him and that he'd only get in the way? That he didn't want them to watch him turn into a mad, raving, cannibalistic former human?

Didn't matter. Didn't matter at all. He was going one way or another.

To give his friends the best shot they had at succeeding, with one less obstacle.

One less Newt.

Chapter Two

The streets were chaos, a mass of disorder shaken up like dice and spilled across the land.

But that wasn't the scary part. The scary part was how *normal* everything felt—as if the world had been arcing toward this moment since the day its rocky surface first cooled and the oceans ceased to boil. Remnants of suburbs lay in scattered, trashy ruin; buildings and homes with broken windows and peeled paint; garbage everywhere, strewn about like the tattered pieces of a shattered sky; crumpled, filthy, fire-scorched vehicles of all sorts; vegetation and trees growing in places never meant for them. And worst of all, Cranks ambling about the streets and yards and driveways as if merchants were about to begin a massive winter market: *All items half-price!*

Newt's old injury was acting up, making his limp worse than usual. He stumbled to the corner of a street and sat down heavily, leaned against a fallen pole whose original purpose would forever remain a mystery. In the oddest, most random of occurrences, the words *winter market* had rattled him. He didn't understand fully why. Even though his memory had been wiped long ago, it had always been a strange thing. He and the others recalled countless things about the world that they'd never seen or experienced—airplanes; football; kings and queens; the telly. The Swipe had been more like a tiny machine that burrowed its way through their brains and snipped out the specific memories that made them who they were.

But for some reason, this winter market–this odd thought that had found its way into his musing on the apocalyptic scenes around him–was different. It wasn't a relic of the old world that he knew merely by word association or general knowledge. No. It...

Bloody hell, he thought. It was an actual memory.

He looked around as he tried to process this, saw Cranks of various stages shambling about the streets and parking lots and cluttered yards. He could only assume these people were infected, every one of them, no matter their actions or tendencies—otherwise why would they be out here, out in the open like this? Some had the awareness and normal flow of movement that he still did, early on in that infection, their minds still mostly whole. A family huddled together upon wilting grass, eating scavenged food, the mom holding a shotgun for protection; a woman leaned against a cement wall, her arms folded, crying—her eyes revealed the despair of her circumstances, but not madness, not yet; small clusters of people talked in hushed whispers, observing the chaos around them, probably trying to come up with plans for a life that no longer had plans anyone might desire.

Others in the area were seemingly in-between the first and last stages, acting erratic and angry, uncertain, sad. He watched a man march across an intersection with his young daughter in tow, holding her hand, looking for all the world as if they might be going to a park or to the store for candy. But right in the middle of the street he stopped, dropped the girl's hand, looked at her like a stranger, then wailed and wept like a child himself. Newt saw a woman eating a banana—where had she gotten a buggin' banana?—who stopped midway through, tossed it on the ground, then started stomping it with both feet as if she'd found a rat nibbling at her baby in a knocked-over pram.

And then there were, of course, those who had, without a doubt, traveled well past the Gone, that line in the sand that divided humans from animals, people from beasts. A girl, who couldn't have been older than 15 or 16, lay flat on the ground in the middle of the nearest road, babbling incoherently, chewing on her fingers hard enough that blood dripped back down onto her face. She giggled every time it did so. Not far from her, a man crouched over a chunk of what looked like raw chicken, pale and pink. He didn't eat it, not yet, but his eyes darted left and right and up and down, empty of sanity, ready to attack any fool who dared try to take his meat away. Farther down that same street, a few Cranks were fighting each other like a pack of wolves, biting and clawing and tearing as if they had been dropped in a gladiator's coliseum and only one would be allowed to walk away alive.

Newt lowered his eyes, sank onto the pavement. He slipped the backpack from his shoulders and cradled it in his arms, felt the hard edge of the Launcher he'd stolen from Jorge's weapons stash on the Berg. Newt didn't know how long the energy-dependent, electric-firing projectile device would last, but he figured it couldn't hurt to have it. The knife resided in the pocket of his jeans, folded up, a pretty sturdy one, if it ever came to hand-to-hand battle.

But that was the thing. Like he'd thought earlier, everything he saw around him had become the "new normal" of sorts, and for the life of him he couldn't figure out why he wasn't terrified. He felt no fear, no apprehension, no stress, no innate desire to run, run, run. How many times had he come across Cranks since escaping the Maze? How many times had he almost soiled his pants from sheer terror? Maybe it was the fact that he was now one of them, quickly descending to their level of madness, that stayed his fear. Or maybe it was the madness itself, destroying his most human of instincts.

And what of that whole winter market thing? Was the Flare finally releasing him from the hold of the Swipe he'd been subjected to by WICKED? Could that perhaps be the ticket to his final journey past the Gone? He already felt the most acute and abject despair he'd ever felt in his life, abandoning his friends forever. If memories of his life *before*, of his family, began to invade him without mercy, he didn't know how he could possibly take it.

The rumbling sound of engines finally, mercifully, ripped him from these increasingly depressing thoughts. Three trucks had appeared around the corner of a street that led away from the city, although calling them trucks was like calling a tiger a cat. The things were massive, 40 or 50 feet long and half that in height and width, heavily armored, windows tinted black with steel bars reinforcing them against attacks. The tires alone were taller than Newt himself, and he could only stare, wondering in awe what he might be about to witness firsthand.

A horn sounded from all three vehicles at once, a thunderous noise that made his eardrums rattle in their cages. It was the sound he'd heard earlier from inside the Berg. Some of the surrounding Cranks ran at the sight of the monsters-on-wheels, still smart enough to know that danger had arrived from the horizon. But most of them were oblivious, looking on much as Newt did, as curious as a newborn baby seeing lights and hearing voices for the first time. He had the advantage of distance and plenty of hordes between him and the new arrivals. Feeling safe in the most unsafe of places, Newt watched things unfold—though he did unzip his backpack and place one hand on the cool metal surface of the stolen Launcher.

The trucks came to a stop, the shattering noise of their horns ceasing like a shattered echo. Men and women piled out of the cabins, dressed to the hilt in black and gray, some with red shirts pulled over their torso, chests armored, heads covered with helmets as shiny as dark glass, all of them holding long-shafted weapons that made Newt's Launcher look like a toy gun. At least a dozen of these soldiers began firing indiscriminately, their aim fastened on anyone who moved. Newt didn't know a single thing about the weapons they used, but flashes of light shot from their barrels with a noise that reminded him of Frypan—when he'd bang a heavy stick against a warped piece of metal they'd found somewhere in the nether parts of the Glade. To tell people his latest and greatest meal was ready to be devoured. It made a vibrating *whomp* sound that made his very bones tremble.

They weren't killing the Cranks. Just stunning them, temporarily causing paralysis. Many of them still shouted or wailed after they'd fallen to the ground, and continued to do so as the soldiers dragged them with the least amount of tenderness possible toward the huge doors at the back of the trucks. Someone had opened them while Newt observed the onslaught, and beyond those doors was a cavernous holding cell for the captives. The soldiers must've eaten a lot of meat and drank a lot of milk because they picked up the limp bodies of the Cranks and tossed them inside the darkness as if they were no more than small bales of hay.

"What the hell are you doing?"

A voice, a tight strum of words, came from right behind Newt's ear, and he yelped so loud that he just knew the soldiers would stop everything they were doing and charge after him. He spun around to see a woman crouched next to him, shielded by the fallen pole, a small child in her arms. A boy, maybe three years old.

Newt's heart had jolted at her voice, the first time he'd been startled since coming outside, despite all the horrors developing around him. He couldn't find words to respond.

"You need to run," she said. "They're doing a full sweep of the whole damn place today. You been asleep or what?"

Newt shook his head, wondering why this lady bothered with him if she felt it so important to get out of there. He searched for something to say and found it in the haze that filled his mind lately.

"Where are they taking them? I think I saw a place from the Ber—I mean, I've heard of a place where they keep Cranks. Where Cranks live. Is that it?"

She shouted to be heard over the commotion. "Maybe. Probably. They call it the Crank Palace." The lady had dark hair, dark skin, dark eyes. She looked as rough as Newt felt, but at least those eyes had sanity with a dash of kindness thrown in. The little boy was as scared as any human Newt had ever seen, eyes cinched tight and his arms wrapped around his mum's neck like twisted bars of steel. "Apparently there are people who're immune to the Flare"—Newt bristled at that word, *immune*, bristled hard, but kept silent as she went on—"people who are kind enough or stupid enough or just paid a crap-ton money enough to kinda take care of them at the Palace until they're... you know. Un-take-care-able anymore. Although I heard the place is getting full and they might be giving up on that whole idea. Wouldn't surprise me one damn bit if this roundup ends at the flare pits."

She said the last two words as if it were something anyone with half a brain knew all about, an image that seemed appropriate for their new world.

"Flare pits?" he asked.

"What do you think the constant smoke on the east side of the city is?" Her response said it all, though Newt hadn't noticed such a thing. "Now, are you coming with us or not?"

"I'm coming with you," he said, each word popping from his mouth without any consideration.

"Good. The rest of my family is dead and I could use the help."

Even through the shock of her words, he recognized the self-serving motive in coming to him; otherwise he would've suspected a trap. He started to ask a question—he didn't know exactly what yet, something about who she was and where they were going—but she'd already turned around and sprinted in a direction away from where the soldiers were still tossing lifeless but living bodies into the hold of the trucks. The wails and cries of anguish were like a field of dying children.

Newt threw his backpack onto his shoulders, cinched the straps, felt the dig of the Launcher against his spine, then took off after this new friend of his and the little one clutched to her chest.

Chapter Three

The woman had more energy than a Runner from the Maze, and those guys ran the corridors, blades, and slot canyons of that beast all day long, day-in and day-out. Newt had gotten out of shape at some point, sucking air until it felt like someone had stolen all the oxygen from Denver with a magical net. His buggin' limp didn't help matters. They'd gone at least a mile before he finally found out her name.

"Keisha," she said as they stopped for a breath inside an old wreck of a neighborhood, right under the skeletal, long-dead branches of a maple tree, almost no other person in sight. Newt felt a little better when she doubled over, chest heaving, to put the toddler down so she could rest. Human, after all. "My kid's name is Dante. You might've noticed he doesn't talk a whole lot—well, that's just the way it is. Not a thing I can do about it, is there? And yes we named him that because of the epic poem."

What epic poem? Newt wanted to ask. He had no idea what she was talking about, though he had a sense of memory knocking on his brain from the other side of a hidden door. Maybe he'd known before the Swipe. He tried not to wonder what might be wrong with her kid that he didn't speak. Traumatized? Impaired, somehow? Maybe just shy? He wanted to know their stories but wasn't sure he had the right.

"The poem about the nine circles of Hell?" she prodded, mistaking his internal thoughts and musings. "Didn't read too many books in your neck of the woods growing up, huh? Shame. You missed out big time on that one. It's a doozy."

Newt was certain he'd read books, as certain as he knew he'd eaten food and guzzled water before they'd taken his memory. But he didn't remember any of the stories, and the thought filled him with a heavy sadness.

"Why did you name your kid after Hell?" he asked, really just trying to lighten the mood.

Keisha plopped onto her butt and gave little Dante a kiss. Newt had expected the boy to be a brat, cry his lungs out in a place like this. But so far he hadn't made a peep.

"We didn't name him after Hell, you moron," Keisha responded, somehow saying it kindly. "We named him after the guy who *defined* Hell. Who embraced it and made it his own."

Newt nodded, lips pursed, trying to show he'd been impressed without having to lie and say it out loud.

"Corny, I know," Keisha replied after seeing his expression. "We might've been drunk."

Newt knelt next to them, still trying to take in deep breaths without making it too obvious that he needed it so desperately. "Sounds about right. Drunk and corny's the way to go these days." He reached out and gently pinched Dante's cheek, tried to give the kid a smile. To his astonishment, the boy smiled back, showing a mouthful of tiny teeth that gleamed in the afternoon light.

"Ah, he likes you," Keisha said. "Ain't that the cutest thing. Congrats, you're his new papa."

Newt had been squatting, but that comment made him fall backward onto his rear end.

Keisha laughed, a sound as good as birdsong. "Relax, dumbass. You don't look like dad material and it was just a joke. Doesn't matter. We'll all be *Looney Tunes* crazy in a month anyway."

Newt smiled, hoping it didn't look as forced as it felt. Leaves scattered across the pavement of the street as a breeze picked up, making the branches above them go clackety-clack as they banged against each other. He could hear voices and shouts in the distance, seeming to ride on that breeze, but not close enough to panic. They were safe enough for a few minutes, anyway.

He got up his nerve and asked the question that had been on his mind. "You said your family was dead. What did you mean? Did you lose a lot of people?"

"That I did, my fine-haired friend." Keisha had a unique way of saying light-hearted things very sadly. "My hubby. Two sisters. A brother. My old man. Uncles. Aunts. Cousins. And my other... my other..." Here she lost any pretense that the world was still a place where you called people your *fine-haired friend*. Her face collapsed into despair, head literally dropping toward the ground along with it, and tears dropped from her eyes onto the cracked pavement of the sidewalk. Though silent, her shoulders shook with a hitched sob.

"You don't have to say," Newt said. It was as obvious as the sun being hot and the moon being white. She'd lost one of her children. Poor Dante had not been an only child. "I'm... I'm really sorry I asked." *I'm such a turd*, he chided himself. He'd literally known this woman for all of an hour at most.

She sniffed hard, then brought her head back up to look at him, wiping away the tears that had managed to stick to her cheeks. "No, it's okay. " She said these words in a distant monotone, somehow wistful and haunted at once. "Just do me a favor. Don't ever ask me—never, ever—how I lost them all. No matter how long we survive or if I know you one day or one month. Never ask. Please." Her eyes, glistening wet, finally met his, the saddest eyes he'd seen since Chuck gave him one last look right outside the Maze.

"Yeah, I promise," he said. "I swear. We don't need to talk about that stuff. I shouldn't have started it."

Keisha shook her head. "No, stop being a worry-wart. Just as long as you don't ask me... you know. We'll be good."

Newt nodded, selfishly wishing he could vanish into thin air and end this awkward, horrible conversation. He gazed down at Dante, who was sitting still and quiet, looking at his mom as if he wondered what was wrong with her. Maybe he wasn't old enough to remember all the bad things that had happened to those who shared his blood.

"What's your plan, anyway?" Keisha asked after a minute or so of silence. "You don't have to tell me your story or anything—fair's fair—but what were you doing lying there like a spent popsicle stick, just waiting for those A-holes to come get you?"

"I..." Newt had absolutely no idea what to say. "I found out recently that I've got the bloody Flare and I couldn't stand the thought of my friends seeing me degenerate into a raving lunatic. Or take the chance that I might hurt them. So I left. Didn't even say goodbye. Well I left a note tellin' them I was gonna go live with the infected—that Crank

Palace, I guess, the one you told me about. Oh, and I left another note asking my best friend to kill me if he ever saw me going completely bonkers and—"

He cut off when he realized she was staring at him with giant eyes, no trace of tears left to shine against the fading sunlight.

"Too much?" he asked.

She gave a slow nod. "Too much. I don't even know where to begin. Do I need to be worried, here? You're not gonna try to eat my arm, are you? Or my kid?" She coughed out a fake laugh that made him cringe.

"Sorry. I just... I don't know. I'm not in a good way, I guess."

"Yeah, none of us are. But... what the hell. So many questions. I mean, first off, your friends didn't catch the Flare from you? What, did you escape from inside Denver or something?"

He shook his head. "No, no, it's a long story." He wasn't ready to tell any*one* any*thing* about all the crap he'd been through and that he'd cruelly been thrown in with a bunch of people who were immune to the virus. What would be the point? He and all these people would be dead or past the Gone soon enough.

"Okay," Keisha said slowly, acting now as if she humored the tall tales of a child. She must've had plenty of practice with such a thing. "Then let's fish another fry—"

"Fish another what?"

Her face scowled in rebuke. "You're gonna have to get used to my humor, young man."

He almost protested again—she couldn't be more than 10 years older than him—but he fell silent when her scowl deepened even further.

"Now listen to me and listen to me well. What in *the* hell and what on God's green earth were you going on about when you said you want to go live with the infected, live at the Crank Palace? I know we're heading toward crazy, now, but we don't seem too ready to get off the train just yet. Or at least I thought so, anyway. But if you're gonna sit here and yap about wanting to go to *that* place, then you were crazy long before you got the Flare. Don't come at me again with something so stupid."

She probably would've kept on going but now it was her turn to stutter to a stop when she saw *his* wide eyes.

"What?" she asked. "You don't believe me?"

Newt stumbled through a few words of nonsense before he got out anything coherent. "Mainly I just wanted to leave my friends behind before I went off the rails. But maybe it's the best place to go. Be with the other sorry saps who're infected. For one thing, maybe they have food and shelter, there, everybody's in the same boat." Newt didn't believe a single word coming out of his own mouth. "What else am I gonna do? Go settle on a farm and raise cattle for the jerks in Denver?"

"Raise cattle for the..." Keisha's words trailed into silence as she shook her head in wonder at the apparent stupidity of his full statement. "Look, I'm just gonna have to treat you like my third child, okay? Deal? I don't have time for this nonsense talk. Now, let's get up and go. The sweeps will probably go all night 'till they can't find another soul to toss into those trucks. They don't like dirty rats like us getting too close to their precious city."

She stood up, helped little Dante stand as well, holding him by the hand. Newt got to his feet, neither in the mood nor having any basis to argue with her anyway. Didn't matter. He was away from Tommy and the others and that had been the main goal all along. Who cared what happened to him now.

Keisha pointed in the direction of the sun, now sinking with earnest toward the horizon, which was hidden by houses and trees and distant mountains in the gaps. "From what I hear we just have to make it a few more miles and we can probably find a house to sleep in. Hopefully some food. Most of the crazies end up congregating like ants around the city so we should be safer the farther out we—"

An electronic charging sound cut her off, a sound way too similar to the charge of a Launcher, which filled Newt with instant dread. He spun around to see three red-shirted soldiers standing there, all of them pointing the barrels of those unwieldy weapons at Newt and his new friend. The blue glow of the guns was bright even in the light of day.

"I need those hands up in the air," one of the soldiers said, the voice coming through a speaker in the helmet. A woman by the sound of it. "You look like decent people, but we need to at least test you and see if—"

"Don't bother," Keisha said. "We've got the damn Flare and you know it. Just let us go. Please? I've got a kid for heaven's sake. We promise we'll just keep walking the other direction—won't bother a soul. We'll never come near the city again. Cross my heart, hope to die, stick a needle in my eye."

"You know we can't do that," the woman replied. "You came too close and you should know better. We want these streets empty."

Keisha made some kind of angry noise that Newt had never heard expelled from a human before, not even a Crank. Something from deep within her chest, like a growl. "Didn't you hear what I just said? We're gonna keep walking *away* from the city. You'll never see us again."

"If that's the case then you won't mind us giving you a lift, will you?" The soldier hefted her weapon to make a point, stepped closer, the barrel now aiming squarely at Keisha's head. "Ya know, this thing will knock you out no matter where it strikes, but shots to the head are especially bad. You'll be puking and seeing double for a week. Now come along nice and easy, got it?"

Keisha nodded. "Oh, I got it."

The next two seconds happened so quickly and yet so slowly that Newt felt as if he'd been transplanted to a dream, where nothing made sense. Keisha had pulled out an old-school revolver from seemingly nowhere, as though it had materialized through a magic spell. Even as her arm jerked up, even as it let out the *pop-pop* of two shots, the soldier who'd been talking ignited her weapon, firing that strange flash of lightning along with its *thwack* of thumped air, an almost silent thunderbolt that was felt more than heard. Blue energy arced across Keisha's face and she screamed a bloody shriek of murder and pain. Her body collapsed to the ground, arms and legs shaking with spasms. Little Dante was less than a foot from her, and for the first time since they'd met, he began to wail like the child that he was. The combined sounds of their anguish—mother and son—was enough to ignite a cauldron of rage inside Newt, coursing through his veins like flooded pipes.

He yelled–a primal, animal yell–and ran for the closest soldier, who stood there as if stunned, doing nothing, his weapon pointed at the pavement. The woman who'd shot Keisha was down on both knees, nursing a wound to her stomach. The third soldier lay flat on the ground, a crimson pool of blood widening beneath his or her bullet-shattered helmet. Newt dove at the only one standing, the one who seemed at a complete loss.

Newt's shoulder crashed into the person's chest, even as the man—at least Newt thought he was a man—shouted a muffled cry for help into whatever communication system the soldiers used. Newt's arms wrapped around him, the momentum of his dive catapulting both of them to the ground in a violent tackle, the other man's weight cushioning the fall. On some level, Newt knew he was being reckless, that an irrational rage had consumed him, that he was being... unstable. But that didn't stop him from screaming again, from sitting back on the soldier's stomach, from reaching forward to grab the man's helmet with both hands and lift it, slam it back into the ground. He lifted it again, slammed it again. This time he heard a crack and a whimpering groan of pain that faded like a last breath.

The soldier's entire body went still.

Newt's breaths were pouring into his chest like a bellows, his chest heaving so much that he almost fainted, almost swooned off the man. But then another kick of adrenaline burst through him. He felt invincible. Elated. Hysterically euphoric. While still tethered to reality enough to know that the virus was changing him more and more each day. This would be his life soon. Seeking the thrill and feast of enacted rage.

But then something hit him in the back of the head and his brief stint as a warrior ended with him flopping to the ground like a collapsed balloon. He didn't quite fade from the day around him—could just see Keisha lying on the ground with Dante beside her, panicked and bawling—but a few seconds later Newt vomited all over himself.

Why the bloody hell had he ever left that Berg?

Chapter Four

The next hour was a lifetime of headaches, nausea, and strange movements.

Newt stayed awake for all of it; the hyper-enthusiasm he'd experienced for all of two minutes had completely vanished. Spent. He had no energy whatsoever, in fact, didn't lift a finger to defend himself as reinforcement soldiers did whatever they wanted with him. At least they didn't separate him from Keisha and Dante. He couldn't bear the thought of losing the small connection he had with those two after so short a time.

A truck rumbled up, much smaller than the behemoths they'd seen earlier by the massive walls of Denver. Two people picked him off the ground, with not the least amount of gentility, and threw him into the back of the open bed of the vehicle. He expected to land on a pile of writhing bodies, a dozen Cranks fighting and clawing and trying to get out. Instead he landed on the hard steel of the truck bed and lost his breath for a moment. Keisha came next, still no sign of voluntary movement in her limbs.

But her eyes.

Her eyes were lit with awareness and understanding, the purest panic Newt could imagine. But that eased a bit when Dante was plopped right next to her, offered a little more care than they'd been given. The kid still cried, but it had almost become a constant, a background noise, like the strong flow of a rapid, rocky river nearby. He laid his head down on his mum's shoulder and wrapped his tiny arms around her neck. Tears leaked from Keisha's eyes.

"She's okay," Newt murmured, though he doubted the kid heard or understood. "She's just... she'll be okay soon." Every word he uttered rang in his head like a broken bell.

A soldier jumped into the back of the truck with them, squatted with his back to the window of the cabin. He held something that looked more like a machine gun than an energy weapon, and Newt figured they had less than one chance left for misbehaving. The next time would be rewarded with a few bullets in the brain to end things.

The truck roared its engine, then set off from the quiet neighborhood—probably quiet because the sweep-up of Cranks had already been through that area. Newt had the distant thought that spying eyes might've reported them from within the windows of one of those seemingly innocent homes, frightened eyes that spied from the darkness, from behind torn curtains and broken glass. Surprised at himself, Newt found that he didn't care. Maybe the virus had eaten that part of his brain first—the part that worried and agonized over what lay in his immediate future. It just didn't matter. Madness awaited him at the end of the track, and there was no slowing that train. He couldn't bring himself to care how bumpy the ride might be.

Newt relaxed onto his back and looked up at the sky as they drove. Blue and white, more clouds than not, the kind with no shape or substance, just scratched across the azure heavens by a painter with no discipline. Some people said the sky never had quite the same color once the catastrophic sun flares struck a couple of decades earlier. Newt would never know, could never know. What he saw seemed natural enough, and despite his sudden indifference to the world, it gave him a small squeeze of comfort that saddened him a little. Saddened that he'd never have a chance to live a full and meaningful life under the skies above.

The truck jostled to a stop sometime later, how long Newt didn't really know. Maybe a half hour. They had parked between two platforms of cement, both seeming to hover just a few feet above the lip of the truck bed, bordered by steel railings. Several people stood up there to each side, dressed in bulky, overbearing protective gear that looked like something you'd see at WICKED on a bad day. Newt quickly glanced at Keisha, who had her back to him, her arms wrapped around her son. She might've been asleep—he saw her back rise and fall with even breaths. He sighed in relief.

Glancing skyward at the strangers staring down, he shifted his elbows to prop himself up. He opened his mouth to say something—

ask something—but a firehose appeared at one of the railings, its nozzle pointing in his direction. It was enough to silence him.

Water—he *hoped* it was water—abruptly flushed out of the hose in a torrid stream, wetly smacking into him so hard that he slammed against the truck bed, yelping at the slicing, biting cold of the onslaught. The force of it was painful enough, but the frigidity made it feel acidic, stinging like a million slaps against his skin. He tried to scream against it, but water filled his mouth and set him off to choking and coughing instead. The person above directed the stream at Keisha and Dante, then, just as he thought he might drown. Keisha seemed completely back to normal because she squirmed and kicked and shielded Dante as best she could. The hose set upon Newt again, then back to Keisha, then back to Newt. This torture lasted another minute or two before some angel turned it off. Newt and Keisha were left to sputter and spit and catch their breath, all amidst the backdrop of Dante's high-pitched screams.

"What the hell was that for?" Keisha yelled, sounding like someone who'd just swam 50 feet underwater and finally came up for air.

A mechanized voice responded, filtered by the hazard suit. "That's the best we can do out here to disinfect. Sorry. We don't have a helluva lot of choices anymore. Hope the kid's okay." With that compassion-dripping statement, he gave a wave of the hand. The truck jolted and the engine squawked, and they were off again.

They picked up speed. With their wet clothes, it felt as if the temperature had dropped 30 degrees. Keisha fully grasped her maternal role and pulled Newt close to her, cradling both him and her son. Dante had gone silent, perhaps shivering too violently to cry. Newt had no complaints, snuggling into Keisha's grasp for as much warmth as possible. He had flashes of a woman in his mind, shadows made of light, no features, more a presence than anything. His mind was loosening, he knew that now, the irony of it so thick it seemed possible to chop at it with an axe. He would remember his mom soon, remember her fully, just in time to forget her in the madness of the Flare.

A few minutes later they drove through the opened doors of a gate, providing entrance past a huge wall of wooden planks, a sign on one of the doors that flashed by too quickly for Newt to read the words printed there. Several people stood around, scratches and bruises on their faces, all of them holding Launchers. Not a one looked too thrilled to have visitors. Then there were trees, half of them dead, half of them green and bright and hale. The world was coming back to life, slowly but surely, especially in these higher elevations.

The truck came to a stop again. Barely enough time had passed for Newt's skin to dry, much less his hair or clothes. Both doors of the vehicle opened and closed, and something told Newt their journey was over, that they might never be in another car or truck for the rest of whatever remained of their lives.

"Are you going to kill us?" Keisha asked the empty air above them in a shaky voice, the first time Newt had seen her show genuine fear. "Please don't hurt my children."

Children. Was it her fleeing mind, imagining that Newt was her daughter, come back from the dead? Or did awareness still cling to her strongly enough to hope for more leniency granted a mother and her kids? Before anyone bothered to answer, the three of them sat up, letting go of their temporary cuddle of warmth. Two soldiers stood at the tailgate of the truck, the gate still closed. They were helmeted, their faces nothing but shiny black glass, as soulless as robots. That now-familiar, muffled, slightly mechanized voice came from one of them, a low growl that sounded almost like static.

"You're lucky to be alive," it said. "Especially after killing my friend. So if you complain I'll beat the living hell out of you. I swear it on all your dead relatives."

"Wow," Keisha said. "Harsh. Wake up on the wrong side of the bed this morning?" Newt was amazed that she had the guts to make even the slightest of jokes.

The soldier who'd spoken gripped the upper edge of the tailgate with gloved fists, the leather creaking as he squeezed. "Say another word. Just one more word. You think this would be the first time we've *accidentally* broken an order? Sure would be a shame for that kid if his mama died because she wasn't... cooperative."

To Newt's immeasurable relief, Keisha didn't respond. She looked at Dante, finding all the strength she needed in his eyes, in his life.

"Just get out of the truck," the other soldier piped in. "Now. You're gonna spend the rest of your life in this hellhole so you might as well make yourselves at home." She pulled on a latch and the tailgate flopped down with a heavy metallic crack.

Newt had a sudden and almost overwhelming rush of panic, the uncertainty of his life now, all at once, taking on meaning again. He moved to deflect it, scooted himself forward until he could jump down from the truck bed onto the ground, a mishmash of dirt and weeds. A quick look around showed a lot of trees and dozens of tiny cabins and tents, as haphazard as the early days of the Glade. Newt felt a longing for his friends and old days past, as hard as those old days were.

Keisha handed Dante to Newt, then jumped down and landed right next to him. It was the first time Newt had held the child, maybe the first time he'd *ever* held someone so young. To his surprise, the kid didn't cry, probably too enticed by his new surroundings, probably still feeling a false sense of elation from the absence of a raging firehose. Even Newt felt that. It was fresh on his mind, and oddly made everything in the world seem a little brighter because he didn't have a rushing explosion of ice-cold water battering his face.

One of the soldiers closed the tailgate, secured the latch. Then they headed for the doors of the truck without saying anything, opened them, readied to step up and onto the seats.

"Wait," Newt said, handing Dante back to his mum. "What're we supposed to do?"

The soldier on the passenger side ignored them, got in, slammed the door. The driver paused with a foot on the instep, but didn't turn around to face them when she answered.

"Like we said, just be glad you're alive. Hardly anyone's being sent here anymore. Almost full. Most Cranks are just... you know. Taken care of."

The Crank Palace. A sicker version of Newt would've laughed. He'd ended up here after all, even after Keisha's less-than-subtle declaration that it had been the dumbest idea ever.

"But why?" Keisha asked, gently swaying with Dante in her arms. "If you're offing most of the infected, then why not us? After what we did?" There was no apology in her voice. None at all.

"Are you complaining?" the soldier countered. "I'd be happy to take you to the flare pits if that's what your heart desires. It's what you deserve."

Newt quickly spoke up. "No, no. Thank you. We're fine." He gently grabbed Keisha's arm, tried to pull her away from the truck. He wanted nothing to do with these people ever again. But she resisted, seemed intent on getting them killed or burned in the pits.

"Why?" she asked. "What're you not telling us?"

Even though they couldn't see the soldier's face, every inch of her armored body screamed out what her facial expressions couldn't. Frustration. Annoyance. Anger. But then she relaxed, all of her muscles slackening at once, her foot dropping back to the ground. She turned toward them and spoke with that mechanized voice, void of feeling.

"It's him." She pointed at Newt. "They know who he is and... *she* wants to keep track of him. You and your kid are just lucky you made a new friend. Otherwise you would've been dead long before you made it to the pits. Now goodbye and have a wonderful life. Short and sweet, as they say."

With that, she jumped in the truck and drove off, the back tires spitting up rocks and dirt.

"Who was she talking about?" Keisha asked. "Who is... *she*?"

Newt only shook his head, staring at the truck as it grew smaller with distance. Finally it turned a corner around some trees and was gone. He looked at the ground.

"Later," was the only word that came out.

She.

He couldn't bring himself to say her name.

The #1 New York Times Bestselling Maze Runner Series From

JAMES DASHNER

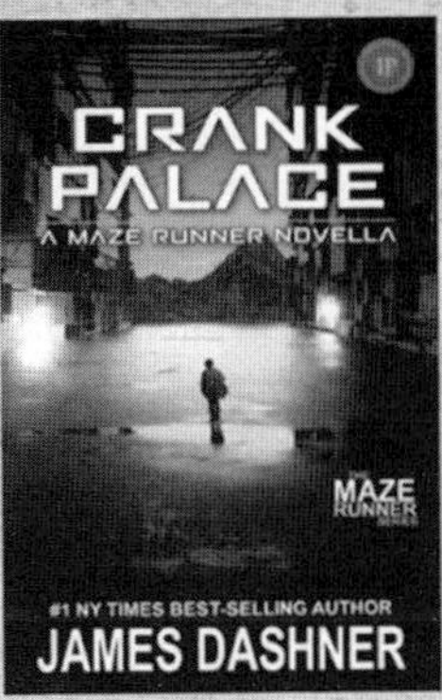

Published by Delacorte Press, an imprint of Random House Children's Books, and by Riverdale Avenue Books.

 **@JamesDashner**

 **@DashnerJames**

JamesDashner.com

ABOUT THE AUTHOR

James Dashner is the author of the #1 New York Times bestselling Maze Runner series (movies by Fox/Disney), including The Maze Runner, The Scorch Trials, The Death Cure, The Kill Order, and The Fever Code, and the bestselling Mortality Doctrine series (The Eye of Minds, The Rule of Thoughts, and The Game of Lives). Dashner was born and raised in Georgia, but now lives and writes in the Rocky Mountains.

Join the #DashnerArmy for exclusive content and giveaways at JamesDashner.com